MORE THAN
MEETS THE EYE

BOOKS BY IRIS JOHANSEN AND ROY JOHANSEN

(in order of publication)

KENDRA MICHAELS SERIES
"With Open Eyes" (short story)
Close Your Eyes
Sight Unseen
The Naked Eye
Night Watch
Look Behind You
Double Blind
Hindsight
Blink of an Eye
Killer View

STANDALONES
Silent Thunder
Storm Cycle
Shadow Zone

For a complete list of books by Iris Johansen and Roy Johansen, as well as previews of upcoming books and information about the authors, visit IrisJohansen.com and RoyJohansen.com.

MORE THAN MEETS THE EYE

IRIS JOHANSEN

ROY JOHANSEN

GRAND
CENTRAL

New York   Boston

Grand Central Publishing
Hachette Book Group
1290 Avenue of the Americas, New York, NY 10104
grandcentralpublishing.com
twitter.com/grandcentralpub

First published in hardcover and ebook in February 2023.
First Mass Market Edition: February 2024

Grand Central Publishing is a division of Hachette Book Group, Inc. The Grand Central Publishing name and logo is a trademark of Hachette Book Group, Inc.

The publisher is not responsible for websites (or their content) that are not owned by the publisher.

The Hachette Speakers Bureau provides a wide range of authors for speaking events. To find out more, go to www.hachettespeakersbureau.com or call (866) 376-6591.

The Library of Congress has cataloged the hardcover as follows:
Names: Johansen, Iris, author. | Johansen, Roy, author.
Title: More than meets the eye / Iris Johansen, Roy Johansen.
Description: First edition. | New York : Grand Central Publishing, 2023. | Series: Kendra Michaels
Identifiers: LCCN 2022042130 | ISBN 9781538726235 (hardcover) | ISBN 9781538741597 (large type) | ISBN 9781538726259 (ebook)
Subjects: LCSH: Women private investigators--Fiction. | United States. Federal Bureau of Investigation--Fiction. |
Murder--Investigation--Fiction. | Serial murderers--Fiction. | LCGFT: Detective and mystery fiction. | Novels.
Classification: LCC PS3560.O275 M67 2023 | DDC 813/.54--dc23/eng/20220909
LC record available at https://lccn.loc.gov/2022042130

ISBNs: 978-1-5387-2624-2 (mass market), 978-1-5387-2625-9 (ebook)

Printed in the United States of America

OPM

10 9 8 7 6 5 4 3 2 1

CHAPTER

1

If it was a good day, she'd soon be looking at a corpse that had been rotting in the ground for over two years.

FBI Special Agent Cynthia Strode shook her head at what now passed for a "good day." The bar was getting lower by the week.

It was a rainy morning in Southern California, and she was part of a twelve-car caravan driving down a remote two-lane road east of the San Diego burb of Pine Valley. The FBI agents, local cops, and two corrections officers were escorting serial killer James Michael Barrett to the body of his first victim, twenty-four-year-old U.S. Foreign Service employee Dayna Voyles. Barrett had just completed the third week of his murder trial when he obviously realized that the witness testimony and forensic evidence were too much for his defense team to overcome. In his quickly negotiated plea deal, Barrett agreed to reveal the location of his victim's body in exchange for having the death penalty taken off the table.

FBI Special Agent Roland Metcalf sat in the passenger seat next to Cynthia. He'd just turned thirty, and the Barrett investigation had been one of his first big cases. They'd worked it together, and she was impressed by his intelligence and instinctive ability to separate the relevant from the irrelevant, the truth from the bullshit. Metcalf had impressed a lot of people at the Bureau, and she was sure he would be impressing many more in the years to come.

Strode knew this was probably one of her last big cases, at least as far as media attention went. Although she was still two years from the Bureau's mandatory retirement age of fifty-seven, she'd been getting none-too-subtle inquiries ever since she passed her qualifying twenty-five years of service a while back. Nothing like a gentle shove out the door just when you think you've found your groove.

Metcalf turned toward her. "Have you ever been on one of these?"

"A perp-led body hunt? Once before, when I was still working out of the Dallas office. A guy showed us where he'd hidden his high school math teacher's body." She upped the speed on the windshield wipers. "But I'll tell you, it was a lot nicer day than this one. How about you, Metcalf?"

"Nope. Never had a perp so accommodating. I've been on two body digs, but Stan and Ollie led the way each time."

She smiled. "I love those boys."

Stan and Ollie were cadaver dogs employed by their team.

"I'm surprised Barrett agreed to this," Metcalf said. "I visited him in jail three times in the last few months, and he was never interested in a deal."

"I guess he thought he was going to beat it."

Metcalf shook his head. "I don't think so."

"What makes you say that?"

"You remember when we brought him in? He seemed like he was glad to be caught."

"He did. But that didn't stop him from hiring the best lawyers his daddy's money could buy to try to beat the charge."

Metcalf furrowed his brow. "I know. But every time I talked to him, he seemed...resigned. Like he knew he was never getting out."

"But this isn't about getting out. It's about avoiding a lethal injection. Maybe he didn't like how the jury was looking at him."

"Maybe."

The lead car pulled over to the side of the road, and the others followed. One by one, the cast of characters emerged. Half a dozen forensics team members pulled shovels and a pair of dirt sifters from the back of a police van. A photographer and videographer jumped from their cars with cameras already in their hands. Four uniformed cops placed traffic cones and signs on the slick road, directing passing cars around the parked convoy. A few detectives were also there, with no real purpose other than to be on hand when they finally recovered Dayna Voyles from her lonely grave.

Strode couldn't blame them; there was no way in hell she'd miss this, after years of assuring the grieving parents that they'd never stop looking for their daughter.

She and Metcalf climbed out of the car just in time to see two officers emerging from the department of corrections van with killer James Michael Barrett, adorned in an orange jumpsuit, handcuffs, and leg irons. Barrett looked different than he had when they caught him; his round, bearded face was now clean-shaven, and his long hair was now cut and in an attractive conservative style. A classic defense attorney makeover.

Barrett smiled. "Strode and Metcalf. All the big guns are here."

Strode shook her head. "You're the big gun here today, Barrett."

"You flatter me."

"Never."

The corrections officers pulled Barrett across the tall wet grass bordering the road, toward a clump of trees that looked remarkably like the sketch he'd drawn the morning he entered his plea.

The group was strangely silent, Strode thought, probably sobered by what they knew was waiting for them just ahead. It wouldn't last; she'd visited enough crime scenes to know that the wisecracks would soon start flying. If called on it, the cops and agents would trot out that old canard about their jokes being a defense mechanism. She never bought that. Some of those guys were just sick assholes.

The rain had settled into a fine mist, giving the group's slickers and ponchos a wet sheen as they trudged into the woods. Less than twenty yards in, Barrett stopped and pointed to the ground.

Within minutes, a waterproof canopy had been erected over the spot, and the group circled around. Barrett was still staring at the ground.

One of the forensics officers stepped forward with his shovel. "About two feet down, right?"

"Yeah," Barrett replied. He looked with uncertainty at the barren patch of earth. "But it looks...different."

"It's been over two years," Strode said. "The ground's probably settled."

"Well, it was definitely here, right between that boulder and these two trees."

Metcalf's phone rang in his pocket. He pulled it out, looked at the screen, and stepped away to take the call.

One of the forensics specialists plunged his shovel into the soft earth and emptied the blade's contents onto the wire mesh sifter. He swung the shovel down again, and it hit the ground with a metallic clang.

The digger looked up at Barrett. "Is there something metal down there?"

Barrett just stared at the ground. Before he could reply, the other digger swung his shovel down. There was another metallic clang, and...

BOOM!

A terrific explosion rocked the woods!

A fireball erupted from the earth. The shock wave threw Strode and the other officers back over a dozen feet as a deafening roar overtook them.

Her body crumpled at the base of a tree. Her face stung, and blood gushed over her eyes. Her eardrums were blown, and the odor of gunpowder was thick in her nasal cavity.

She tried to wipe the blood from her eyes and only then realized that most of her left arm was gone.

She could see, she realized, but just barely. Fire everywhere, all around her. And mangled bodies, some writhing in pain, but most just still.

Next to her, Barrett was bloody and wheezing, his orange prison uniform burned and tattered.

"You...son of a bitch," she whispered.

He didn't react. He was now dead, like the others.

As a dark fog crept over her, she realized she would soon be joining them.

CHAPTER

2

SHARP GROSSMONT HOSPITAL
LA MESA, CALIFORNIA

Kendra Michaels pulled open the stairwell door, took a glance to see if the coast was clear, and then ran down the surgical floor's wide hallway.

"Ma'am…Ma'am?" The nurse ran after her.

"Where is he?"

"Ma'am, you can't be back here."

Kendra turned toward her. "Too late. Half the law-enforcement community of Southern California and their families are downstairs. No one is telling us anything. I need some answers."

"I understand. And as soon as we have those answers, a doctor will be down to fill you in. Until then, I have to ask you to—"

"*Please.* Isn't there something you can tell me?"

The nurse cocked her head. "I think I've seen you here before."

Kendra half smiled. "I'm not sure if that's a good thing or a bad thing." She looked at the ID card around the nurse's neck. "Which is it, Holly?"

The woman froze. "You're Kendra Michaels."

"Guilty. Still not sure if it's a good thing."

"I was working at Scripps Mercy the night you brought in the Conway kids. They'd been kidnapped. You saved all three of them."

Kendra's smile faded. There was a fourth she *couldn't* save, but there was no need to relive that awful memory. "Yes."

"But you aren't with the police or FBI at all, are you? You're some kind of music teacher."

"A music therapist. I assist law-enforcement agencies from time to time."

Holly nodded. "I remember. You grew up as a blind person, right?"

Kendra didn't feel like going through her entire bio with the nurse, but every minute she wasn't being forcibly ejected was a good thing. "I was blind for the first twenty years of my life. Now that I have my sight, I guess I don't take anything I see for granted. And like most blind people, I used my other senses— hearing, smell, touch, and taste—to make my way in the world. That has stuck with me. My senses aren't better than anyone else's. I just pay more attention. I've helped out the FBI and several police departments on some of their cases."

"I saw you talking to the police that night. You knew so much about that sicko kidnapper just by looking at him. One of the doctors thought you were psychic."

"Nope. I just pay attention. People tell me about themselves without even realizing it."

"What am I telling you about myself?"

Kendra sighed. At the moment, the last thing she wanted to do was perform her damn party trick. But if she could use it to gain a little trust and perhaps a sense of obligation...

"You live close to work. Close enough to ride your bike, which you did today."

Holly's eyes widened.

"You're an active person in general. You play tennis."

Holly smiled. "Yes."

"I've never played, but a lot of my friends have taken up pickleball. They can't get enough of it. Anyway, on the way in today, you bought a drink from that Starbucks across the street. Pumpkin spice latte. You order from there often."

"You saw me there."

"No. You like to travel, and you've seen a lot of the world. You want to see more. You've recently been to New Zealand. It's beautiful, isn't it?"

"Stunning." Holly shook her head. "But how—?"

"I'll tell you how." She added persuasively, "But first you need to tell me about the blast victims."

Holly looked around to make sure no one else was within earshot. "We have four in surgery right now. Three San Diego PD, one FBI. Two of the cops look like they'll make it. I'm not sure about the other two." She looked at Kendra's tense face. "When you came in here, you said, 'Where is he?' Is there someone in particular you want to know about?"

"The FBI agent. Roland Metcalf. He's a good friend."

"They're working on him. I don't believe his burns were as severe as the others, but he has several serious impact wounds. He's lost a lot of blood."

Kendra closed her eyes for an instant. "Thank you for telling me."

"Sure." She put her hand on Kendra's arm. "I'm sorry."

Kendra was silent for a long moment. Keep her talking. Do the party trick and ease her into telling Kendra more. Finally, she said hoarsely, "Your right pant leg is wrinkled."

"Excuse me?"

"That's because it's been rolled up over your calf, so it won't get caught in your bicycle chain. You rode your bike to work."

"That's right. How did you know I stopped at Starbucks?"

"Coffee breath."

"Ooh." Holly covered her mouth. "Sorry."

"It isn't offensive, but that pumpkin odor is distinctive. And I happen to know Starbucks brought back their pumpkin spice drinks last week. The flavoring syrup is the same, but for some reason it smells different in hot drinks than in cold. It's stronger. You had the latte. You've been drinking it from a thermal cup over there at the nurses' station. The cup is decorated with the logo for the Lake Murray Tennis Club. It's a city-owned club, isn't it? I figure you probably play there."

"How do you know the cup is mine? There are other nurses here."

"The lipstick on the rim matches yours. No one else's."

Holly shook her head in amazement. "You're right. That is my cup, and I do play there. I used to work at the pro shop sometimes. And I do love to travel. How did you know?"

"You're wearing a hairpin. It's jade, which could

mean it's from Asia. But there's a Māori-style twist at the end, which means New Zealand. I saw them for sale there in a few places. You don't really see them anywhere else."

"I got mine at the Auckland Museum."

"As lovely as New Zealand is, it's several notches down on the list of travel destinations for Americans. You most likely visited several European countries before going there. You're well traveled."

"Right again. I'm going to Thailand next winter."

Kendra didn't know how much longer she could go on with this. She wasn't sure if the nurse could tell her anything more and she realized that this idiotic "party trick" wasn't distracting her from the awful thought that Metcalf could be dying in one of those surgery suites beyond the nurses' station. And she'd only just begun to process the fact that Cynthia Strode was already dead. Her body was probably still with the others in that bomb-cratered crime scene.

"I'm sorry," Holly said.

She must have looked more upset than she'd thought. "Thanks."

"No, I mean..." She gestured behind Kendra, where a uniformed security guard appeared from the stairwell door. "I had the floor assistant call security when you first came up here. You should really go back to the waiting room with the others. The doctor will let you know when we know more." She shrugged. "But like we tell everyone..."

"...no news is good news," Kendra finished for her.

"It's true."

Kendra turned and walked toward the elevator. She couldn't tell Holly that she didn't belong down with those other friends and relatives. They'd closed her out, even though she was feeling the same horror and pain that they were. She couldn't go back to that waiting room. That's why she'd bolted up here to get information.

But now that was another closed door.

So, she just had to get the hell out of here.

———◆———

Kendra's hands clenched on the steering wheel as she sat looking at the hospital after she got into the driver's seat of her Toyota 4Runner. She felt so damn helpless. There had to be something she could do. What? It was obvious Cassalas had wanted to get rid of her. He'd been very respectful, but she wasn't FBI and therefore she was an outsider. That waiting room had been crowded with friends and relations of those victims who had been brutally killed and injured. It didn't matter that one of those victims lying at death's door was her friend, or that she had known and admired many of the dead. She didn't belong to the club. She was in the way. She couldn't even go to the crime scene and try to get them answers and closure. All she could do was tell the ones who had been left behind how sorry she was that a monster had decided to take down their loved ones to make his own death more spectacular, she thought bitterly. No, she couldn't even do that, because she didn't have all the facts yet. She had to wait for the FBI to get through with taking care of their own. Lord, how she hated the thought—

Her phone chimed, and she looked to see it was a text from her friend Olivia. It was a simple message: SEE ME WHEN YOU GET BACK.

Kendra felt an immediate rush of relief. She didn't even think twice as she started her car and drove out of the parking lot. Olivia would understand because she'd realize how it was to be closed out and isolated when you wanted to reach out. Besides being Kendra's best friend, they had shared blindness for most of their childhood and young adulthood, and that was a bond that was unbreakable. Even when Kendra had gotten her sight through an operation when she was twenty the closeness and friendship had remained. Olivia was totally brilliant and so was her website *Outasite*, a popular site for the vision-impaired, featuring articles, product reviews, and discussion boards, all accessible by integrated audio screen-reading apps. It was constantly changing and improving and was now a business that generated more than six figures.

Twenty minutes later Kendra parked her Toyota in the condo parking garage. She got on the elevator and pressed the button for Olivia's condo, which was on the floor below her own.

She heard Olivia's dog, Harley, barking as she got off the elevator. Olivia opened the door on the first ring, but Harley got to Kendra before she did. The big, adorable mutt's paws were on Kendra's shoulders, and he gave her ear a slurp before she could push him down. "How's his training coming?" she asked Olivia.

"Splendid," Olivia said. "But he never appears to realize which one of us is in training. I'm working on it."

"I suspected that was what was happening." She gave Harley a pat before she smiled at Olivia. "Well, here I am. Want to go out to dinner?"

"Hell, no." Olivia took a step back. "Get in here."

She pulled her into the foyer and gave her a hug. "I can tell you're about to crack any minute. How bad was it at the hospital?"

"Terrible. I couldn't *do* anything."

"How's Metcalf?"

"I don't know. It could go either way. He could die tonight, Olivia."

"Or he could live. You said it could go either way."

"It could. I know he's your friend, too, Olivia. I don't mean to be pessimistic."

"I've been thinking about him ever since I heard." She gestured to the couch. "Sit down. I'll get you a drink." She went over to the bar. "Maybe after a brandy or two you'll be more positive."

"I hope so." She curled up in a corner of the couch and reached out to pat Harley again. He was looking up at her soulfully, which was peculiar because one eye was blue, the other brown, but he managed to pull it off. "I'm having trouble with positive right now. Did I tell you that I knew one of the agents who was killed? It was Cynthia Strode, and she was always friendly and eager to learn. She'd ask dozens of questions when I'd come up with a deduction. She wanted to go back to Quantico and study forensics. She was a brand-new grandmother, and she was always joking about going back to school when she might be retiring before she could graduate. She was...nice."

"You're tearing up. Drink your brandy." Olivia sat down beside her and sipped her own drink. "It was all pretty crazy, wasn't it? Barrett had to be nuts. You weren't involved with catching him, were you?"

Kendra shook her head. "It wasn't one of my cases. I'm glad I wasn't involved. I'd feel guilty if I hadn't been able to guess what he was going to do." She took a swallow of her brandy. "And of course he was nuts. No one knows exactly how many people he killed. The guesses run anywhere from twenty-eight to thirty-five. It might be even more. He's never given anyone a definite number. He's just teased the FBI occasionally with the location of a body when he wanted something from them."

"And they gave it to him?"

"Closure," she said flatly. "It means everything to a victim's family when a victim has been missing for a long time. It can be agony not to be certain."

"That was what happened out in Pine Valley?" Olivia paused. "Do you want to talk about this? If you don't, tell me to shut up."

"I'll talk about it. I'll be going out to Pine Valley tomorrow morning with Dean Cassalas, the agent in charge of the scene, anyway. Maybe it will help me to get my head straight before I have to examine the crime scene." She smiled lopsidedly. "Though that hasn't happened yet. I guess you'd have to be mentally unstable to be able to think like James Barrett."

"He's a serial killer himself, and he killed himself?" Olivia asked.

"That's what the FBI think happened," Kendra said. "They had enough evidence against him to convict on several counts. Since California has been ambivalent about capital punishment there was always a chance that they'd still give him the death sentence." Kendra added bitterly, "He'd be first in line. Since he was definitely unstable and hated both the FBI and the prison system with a passion, he probably decided that he wouldn't wait. He'd take the decision into his own hands and bring down as many law-enforcement officers with him as he could." She had to take another sip of brandy for what was to follow. "His trial was under way downtown, and he abruptly decided to plead out and show them where the body of Dayna Voyles was buried. Her abduction was probably the one that attracted the most attention from the media. She was twenty-four years old and very pretty, just the kind of young woman that would appeal to the general public and local politicians. Barrett said if they took the death penalty off the table, he'd show them where he buried her. It turned out he'd buried an explosive device with her." Her lips curled sardonically. "He had to have been planning this for a long time. He's been in prison for over two years."

"Vicious," Olivia murmured.

"He got what he wanted. Eleven died with him," Kendra said grimly. "Seven more wounded. Two critical. Metcalf was there with Cynthia Strode, an agent I worked with a couple of times. They played the biggest part in catching Barrett. Cynthia testified in his trial last week, and Metcalf was just about to take the stand when Barrett decided to plead his case out."

"Is Metcalf's family with him?"

"His mother should be there anytime now. She's flying down from San Francisco. Maybe I can stop by and see her before I go out to the valley tomorrow." She made a face. "I'm thinking positive. Everything is going to go well tonight."

"Sure it is." Olivia got up, went back to the bar, and got the decanter. "And I'm going to give you one more drink to relax you, and then we're going to eat the wonderful salad I made for us. Want to spend the night with me and Harley?"

"Nope. I've imposed enough on you."

"It's no imposition." Olivia smiled. "You know, I was just remembering that it was Metcalf who discovered how much Harley loves HGTV. That dog still loves *House Hunters*, but lately he's been wild about *Property Brothers*."

"I remember. But seriously, I don't need anyone holding my hand." She reached out and took Olivia's hand anyway. "Though maybe I did a bit earlier. It was very sad at the hospital tonight."

"Someone to hold your hand is sometimes an excellent thing." Olivia grinned. "Have you heard from Lynch lately?"

"Last week. He called me from Johannesburg. He checks in every now and then." She shrugged. "I don't know why. Actually, he's too busy saving the world to bother with relationships."

"That wasn't my impression," Olivia said. "And I know why. Since you're even more skittish than he is, he's probably playing it cool. And no one can play that game better than Lynch. It's no wonder the Justice Department pulled him out of black ops and sends him out to do damage control all over the world." She topped off Kendra's drink. "But since you're lacking a Lynch, I'll lend you Harley to keep you company tonight."

"Heaven help me."

"He's wonderful. Don't you dare malign him. After all, you're the one who talked me into accepting Harley into my home. It's not as if I needed a Seeing Eye dog."

"We all knew that," Kendra said with a grin. "You rule your world all by yourself, but it made me feel better that you had Harley to protect you in case a burglar tried to break in."

"His idea of protection would be to try to lick the burglar to the point of asphyxiation," Olivia said dryly. "But if they didn't know him, he's big enough to make anyone think twice about attacking me. So, it all works out." She reached down and Harley affectionately nuzzled her hand. "And what he does with the utmost talent and skill is give comfort and remind everyone that there's still goodness and love out there in the world when all you can see is the cold and violence." She added gently, "And I think you might have a little use for that talent tonight. I won't take no for an answer. After dinner you and Harley will go up to your condo. He'll run around and try to get in your shower with you, and then probably steal your towel and jump on your lap when you're trying to dry your hair. Then he'll try to persuade you to watch HGTV while you're relaxing before bed."

"And those are all supposed to be selling points? I don't think so."

"Nah, that comes when you go to bed, and he jumps up beside you and you feel his heart beating and the love he radiates. Then you remember that's what life's really all about, and you might actually sleep tonight." She headed for the kitchen. "Now I'll get your salad. You should go to bed. You'll want to get up early to bring Harley back and have a bite of breakfast before you start out for Pine Valley."

"Any other orders?" Kendra asked.

"Only one. But it bears repeating." She opened the refrigerator. "Think positive!"

8:35 A.M.
NEXT DAY
PINE VALLEY

Kendra inhaled sharply as she stopped and gazed in horror down at the huge crater-like cavity at the bottom of the hill. Even though it was early, there were several agents in FBI windbreakers moving carefully about the destruction area. There were dozens of plastic evidence markers and areas of interest cordoned off by yellow crime scene tape. No one had updated her on their findings overnight, but why would they? she thought in frustration. She wasn't FBI. She was only someone trying desperately to help find out what had happened here that had taken so many lives.

"Pretty grim, isn't it?" Kendra turned and saw Special Agent Michael Griffin coming down the hill behind her. She hadn't expected to see him here. As head of the San Diego FBI field office, he'd been at the hospital when she'd left last night talking to media and relatives of the injured. She'd thought then that he was doing a fairly decent job of it, considering that she'd never considered Griffin to be particularly warm and sympathetic. He was smart and tough and had the experience needed to do what he had to do under usual circumstances. But anyone would have been out of his depth with what had happened here at Pine Valley. He'd been curt to her last night, and he was scowling now. "It's even worse than it looks," he said. "I had to walk on eggs when I was talking to those reporters last night."

"I saw all the forensic and medical vans parked on the hill." She nodded down at the crater. "And the markers. Your team has been busy."

Griffin nodded. "Special Agent Dean Cassalas has been in charge of the scene. He's been out here all night. He wasn't crazy about having you out here, but I let him know how helpful you've been on some of our cases in the past. He wanted to keep it strictly within the Bureau."

"I got that impression." She waved a dismissive hand. "But then so did all the other agents. The FBI can be like an exclusive private club when it closes ranks. I could understand it. I just wanted to help."

"Metcalf? You worked with him on cases frequently." He shook his head. "I didn't think it was professional that he seemed to be that friendly with someone who wasn't in the Bureau. But I liked him, so I let it go." He gazed at her for a moment. "Was it more than…friendship?"

"No." Griffin's curiosity might be harmless, but she didn't intend to trust it. That FBI mentality was too ingrained. "Metcalf and I are just friends. Have you heard anything new? I called the hospital before I left my condo and they said there was no change yet."

He shook his head. "The other agent in ICU died last night but Metcalf had a fair night. He still has a chance."

"I didn't expect to see you out here today."

"It's my job. This is the crime scene. It didn't seem right to be pushing papers back at the office when we lost so many good people here yesterday. This case has already attracted worldwide attention, and people want answers."

"I understand," Kendra said. "People are already wondering how our best and brightest walked into a two-year-old trap that a serial killer set for them."

Griffin shook his head. "How could they have known?"

"I'm not blaming anyone. If I'd worked this case, I probably would have been standing right next to them. That's why I want to find out exactly how this happened."

"That's why I told Cassalas to bring you today. You

have a sterling reputation, and the media will believe everything you say. I can throw a dozen forensics specialists at them, and it won't mean nearly as much as an interview with you."

"Even though it means I'll be talking to those same experts to get my information?" She met Griffin's eyes. "Because I have no intention of sugarcoating your 'mess.' I'm going to do the job I usually do. I'll find answers and the truth however I can."

"That's all I ask," Griffin said. "This is my career; do you believe I'd not be honest in protecting it? I just want you to assure me that you won't let the media influence you into hinting that this investigation isn't entirely aboveboard. They do like sensationalism."

"They won't get it from me," she said flatly. "But I do want to see everything to do with the investigation. I have no desire to get in your way, but, if you're using me, be prepared to have me do the same."

"No problem." Griffin was looking up the hill at a tall, lean, thirtyish man who was hurrying toward them. "And here comes Cassalas. I've told him to cooperate fully with you, so that we can get this investigation wrapped up."

"He wasn't cooperating with me last night when I wanted to come out here and look around," she said wryly. "Though he had a lot of seemingly good reasons."

"One of them was me." Griffin's tone was faintly mocking. "But that was last night." He waved at Cassalas. "And everything he told you was the truth. The only thing I told him to skip was that I didn't want you to see all the body parts we kept finding at this site. It was dreadful. I was keeping that from everyone because I didn't want the stories of gore and blood to appear on Fox News."

"I can understand why." She tried to force herself not to shiver. "But I would have come anyway. It would have been my duty to those agents who had died."

"And to Metcalf?"

"Of course." She turned to Special Agent Dean Cassalas, who was now a few yards away.

He gave her a wary glance. "Good morning, Dr. Michaels."

"Good morning. I've just been talking to Griffin, and he seems to have thought I'd be scared off by this crime scene. I want you to know that I'll respect it, but it won't intimidate me." She told him quietly, "I'm ready when you are. I'm not going to promise you anything. Let's just see what we can do to find out why those good friends of yours died here yesterday."

He gave her a long look, and then nodded soberly. He gestured toward the crater. "After you, Dr. Michaels."

"Kendra," she corrected. "And you should go first, because you're going to get me a good many interviews with the tech people who are going to answer my questions. Okay?"

He smiled and nodded. "Okay." He preceded her down the hill.

She started after him and then looked over her shoulder at Griffin. "I got this. I'm sure you have other things to do here."

"Thank you," he said sardonically. "I know when I'm being dismissed. But I'll be around on the off chance you need anything."

"Fine. But please remember that I don't like to be used. And that I hate the idea that a terrible tragedy could ever be referred to as a 'mess.'"

She turned and followed Cassalas down the hill.

Although the corpses and body parts had already been photographed, tagged, and removed, the stench of death still hung in the air. Dozens of trees still standing on the perimeter were singed and stained with blood.

"Are you okay?" Cassalas asked.

"Yes. More than anything, I'm just…angry."

"We all are." He motioned toward the dozen or so evidence collection techs still working the scene. "We knew these people. They were family." He consulted a clipboard and pointed to the base of a tree, where a yellow marker rested with a bold black "9" on its face. "That's where we found Cynthia Strode."

Kendra looked at the bloodstained tree root. Damn. She gazed around, realizing that the yellow plastic markers scattered around the scene represented the location of corpses.

Cassalas pointed to another marker just six feet away. "Barrett was there."

Kendra turned. Farther from the blast crater, she saw half a dozen blue plastic markers scattered around the scene. "What are those?"

"Survivors."

She shook her head. "I'm amazed anyone could have lived through this."

"Well, two of these people didn't make it to the hospital. And, as you know, another didn't make it out of surgery."

"Where was Metcalf?"

Cassalas consulted his clipboard and stepped back a few feet. He pointed toward a blue marker. "Here. Number five."

Kendra crouched next to the marker. "I know

he arrived down here with Cynthia, but the nurse told me he was somehow spared the burns that the others had." She looked at the distance separating Metcalf's and Cynthia's markers. "I wonder how that happened."

"It might have been the phone call," Cassalas said.

Kendra's head lifted sharply. "*What* phone call?"

"A lab tech had just called Metcalf with test results from another case he was working. He was still on the phone with her when the bomb went off."

Kendra stood up. "That could explain it. He may have stepped away to take the call, which saved his life." She continued around the crater and looked at the surviving trees. Pieces of clothing and hair still hung from the higher branches, along with shreds of what she suspected was human skin.

She turned and looked at the sea of markers, which looked almost like tombstones. She pointed to a red marker in the middle of the blast site. "What's that?"

"It's to mark what was left of his victim who was buried here."

"You have a positive ID?"

"Not yet, but we're assuming it was Dayna Voyles, just as he promised. There wasn't much left of her even before the explosion, but we recovered clothing fragments that match what she was wearing when she was abducted."

Kendra turned away. Poor Dayna Voyles had become an afterthought in the wake of the horror that had been unleashed at her grave site. "Who was left to call it in?"

"Uniformed officers at the road. They were directing traffic around the cars parked up there. They came down here to help, but there wasn't much they could do. I talked to one of them last night, and he was pretty shaken up."

Kendra nodded. "I can imagine."

An agent called out from the clump of trees behind them. "I got something here!"

Kendra and Cassalas joined the agent, whom she vaguely remembered from a previous case. She believed his name was Kollar. He was holding a long telescoping pole attached to a net, which he was using to try to snare something caught in the tree.

"What is it?" Cassalas asked.

"Not sure," Kollar said, still trying to capture the object. "It looks like metal of some kind." He tried to use the rim of the net to pull it free of the branches.

"Can you extend the net any further?" Cassalas asked.

"No dice. I'm already all the way out. Eighteen feet." He concentrated on the object, then finally pulled the trigger on his pole. The net zipped closed. "Got it!"

He lowered the net and pushed the trigger to unzip the net's rim. Cassalas, who had already slipped on a pair of plastic evidence gloves, reached in and pulled out the metallic object.

"What is it?" Kendra asked.

Cassalas showed her. "A video camera. More accurately, *half* a video camera. We had a videographer and a still photographer here. Neither survived." He turned the device over in his hands. "Fortunately, I think this is the half with the data card." He pried open the cover to reveal the SD card.

He looked up at Kendra. "We have a tech van parked on the road. Wanna see a movie?"

CHAPTER

3

Less than ten minutes later, Kendra was crowded into the black-panel windowless FBI tech van that always reminded her of something a serial killer might drive. The inside, however, was filled with all manner of surveillance equipment and other gear. A twenty-five-inch video monitor was mounted on the left rear side, which now had everyone's attention. Cassalas was there with her, along with Griffin and three other agents.

The tech supervisor slid the card into a countertop reader. "Everybody ready?"

"Roll it," Griffin said.

The image flickered, and they immediately saw the procession of agents and cops walking from the cars down to the site she had just visited. Kendra's breath left her as she saw Cynthia exchanging words with Barrett. The woman had no idea she was living the last minutes of her life.

The camera panned toward the overgrown pathway

a few seconds before the group followed Barrett toward the burial site.

Kendra suddenly leaned closer toward the monitor. "Interesting," she whispered.

"What?" Griffin asked.

"I'll tell you later."

It only took a minute or so for Barrett to point out the location of Dayna Voyles' body, and the camera remained on as the officers erected the tarp and sifters at the site.

"The resolution is incredible," Kendra murmured. "Is this 4K?"

"It's 8K," Griffin said.

The agents gathered closer to the site as the first shovel swung down.

Kendra studied their intent, eager faces. None of those poor people had any idea what was waiting for them in the next few seconds.

Metcalf abruptly turned and stepped away. He raised his phone to his ear.

"You were right," Cassalas said to Kendra. "That phone call saved his life."

The shovel came down again. There was a white flash, a burst of static, and...

Nothing. The recording was over.

The agents huddled around the monitor were silent.

"Impressions?" Griffin finally said.

After a long moment, Kendra finally spoke. "Barrett didn't put that bomb there. That charge was set during the last few days."

The agents turned and just stared at her.

"What makes you say that?" Griffin asked.

She leaned toward the tech supervisor. "Rewind this to where Barrett is pointing out the site."

He scanned back the video and let it play from the spot she indicated.

"Watch Barrett here," Kendra pointed out. "It's been a couple of years, so he may not remember everything exactly. But something's not right. You can see it on his face. And watch him when the first shovel comes down and seems to hit something metallic. I'm guessing it's the bomb's strike plate. He's more surprised than anyone. Barrett isn't expecting that."

"Maybe," Cassalas said.

Kendra leaned toward the tech supervisor again. "Show from when everyone leaves their cars."

He scanned back and played the scene.

Kendra pointed toward several places in the overgrown brush. "Look here. Several broken bush branches. The brush has been disturbed. These are all fresh breaks. There are no hiking trails around here. No hunting. Whoever came out here had only one thing in mind: setting this bomb to go off when Barrett brought the police and FBI out here. This bomb was set in the last few days."

Griffin slowly nodded. "It's certainly something to consider."

"You'll need to do more than consider it," Kendra said flatly. "I hate to destroy the neat little picture you were going to present to the media of Barrett killing himself and taking all those agents with him. But I'm afraid there's still a mass murderer out there, Griffin."

———◆———

It was almost dark when Cassalas walked Kendra back to the parking lot to retrieve her Toyota. "I believe we covered the entire area, and we didn't find out that much," Cassalas said ruefully. "I guess we'll have to wait for lab results and then put it all together."

"Perhaps not," Kendra said. "Maybe we'll manage to do it ourselves. Once we put what we saw and sensed and felt together." She shrugged. "And *then* we might have to go to the lab. It could go either way."

"You seemed to be very certain when you were talking to Griffin earlier. I know he shut you down right away, but he never likes to be told what to do." His eyes were narrowed on her face. "But that wasn't the first time today you were very intense while you were looking over the scene. Are you shutting me out, Kendra?"

"No, I'm trying to make sure you're going to keep your job. Griffin isn't very fond of me, and I don't really know anything at the moment. He wouldn't be pleased if we came up with anything that might be controversial without being able to substantiate it. I'll have to think about everything we saw and researched and let it come to me." She had reached her car and she turned to face him. "But when it does, I promise I'll share it. Now go away and find a buddy to drink with tonight. Lift a glass to all those men and women who nearly broke our hearts while we were down in that crater today."

"Want to come along? You might qualify as a buddy."

"Thanks, but I've got to do a little more research. It's obvious Griffin is going to take some convincing. I believe I can do it, but I need to look over those shots of the terrain and maybe bring in a tracking expert or two."

He was still lingering. "Controversial? You're the

one who made it controversial. Griffin and several other agents were convinced it was an open-and-shut case when Barrett blew himself and our people to kingdom come."

"Which is why Griffin was edgy about exposing the Bureau to criticism today. We'll just have to be a little careful."

"Yeah? Like you were right before you left him this morning, or later when we looked over those videos?" He was grinning as he lifted his hand. "Not that I object. He's not my favorite person. But I wouldn't have done it."

Kendra watched him as he strolled across the parking lot and started back down the hill. Cassalas was a good guy and he had been very helpful easing the way for her with all the detectives and forensics techs today. It had made her even more eager to keep him out of Griffin's bad books. She hated corporate politics in any form, and she was lucky enough not to have to pay any attention to it either in her role as a music therapist, or when she dealt occasionally with the FBI. But people like Cassalas and Metcalf had to handle it constantly and risk not only their lives but their livelihoods on a daily basis. It was too bad that they didn't have the freedom to—

"Your car or mine?"

Lynch!

Kendra whirled to face him.

Adam Lynch was walking out of the trees of the pine forest, and he was smiling. "Maybe it should be your car. You're looking a little tousled and dusty today, and I believe you have a smudge on your cheek. I'm not sure you're worthy of my Lamborghini Aventador. It takes a certain style to carry it off. The Toyota is much more fitting your presentation today."

"Damn you." She started walking toward him. She shouldn't be this glad to see him. Every time she was away from him, she told herself that she should keep their relationship on a more platonic basis. But it never worked when she saw him. How could it? When he looked like a blasted movie star, and she knew all the intelligence and charisma that he could weave without even trying? There was definitely never anything platonic about how she felt about him when he was smiling with that hint of mischief. "Are you finished? What are you doing here, Lynch? Weren't you in South Africa last week?"

"You sounded bored. I thought I'd wrap up that business in Johannesburg and come back and keep you company." His smile vanished. "And then I heard about the butchery that happened here. I'm sorry. I thought you could use one more person in your corner right now."

"Funny you should say that. Olivia told me last night that I might need someone to hold my hand."

"It doesn't surprise me. Olivia is always incredibly wise."

"But as usual she knew you weren't around, so she gave me the perfect substitute."

"And that proved to be?" he asked warily.

Kendra looked him in the eye. "Why, Harley. Who else would be that perfect?"

He clutched his chest. "Stabbed to the heart."

She chuckled. "You'll survive. You always survive."

He nodded. "That's my reputation." Then he asked soberly, "But I heard Metcalf was one of the victims. I called Griffin when I got to town, and he said he's still critical."

"ICU. The head nurse said he was doing as well as

could be expected." She made a face. "Whatever that means. When they brought him to the hospital, they expected to lose him." She held up her hand. "I've got to stop that. Olivia said that I had to be positive."

"So, you spent the entire day trying to find something to be positive for in that crater?"

"No, I spent the entire day looking for some reason that a human being could do what they say Barrett did."

"Did you find it?"

"Maybe." She rubbed her temple. "Or maybe not. I'm thinking that he might be as crazy as everyone says, but self-preservation is a powerful deterrent. I just have to find out what drove him."

"And you're very tired, and right now you're sick of the human race." He took a step closer and then she was in his arms. He could feel her stiffen and began to rock her. "Shh. Pretend I'm Harley. We're both hanging around to make sure that you have everything you need and nothing else." He cradled her face in his two hands. "Well, maybe a little something else." He kissed her, slowly, gently. "And then we'll go out to dinner, and I'll take you home. But if it's all right with you, I'll stick around at your place in case you hear something about Metcalf and need me. I'll even forgive the tousled hair and dust and let you ride in the Lamborghini."

"How self-sacrificing." She buried her face in his shoulder. He felt strong and solid, and it seemed too long since he'd held her like this. "Where did you park that fancy chariot? I didn't notice it?"

"I parked it on the other side of the pine forest. This wasn't a place to bring a hot toy like the Lamborghini. I had to respect what happened here."

And how many people would have thought to strike that balance? It meant too much that she knew he had probably done it instinctively. "Yes, you did." She added mockingly, "You're all heart, Lynch."

He was silent, studying her. "Just trying to compete with Harley." He pushed her back and looked down at her. "How am I doing?"

"Pretty well. Except for your eyes. Yours are just a kind of boring blue. Don't you remember? Harley has one blue eye and one brown. They would be difficult to duplicate."

"I admit I'd forgotten that I had such a serious discrepancy to overcome. Do you suppose you could overlook it?"

"I could try. Since you came halfway around the world to pay me a visit." She turned away. "But I'll take my own car back to the condo while you go and get us something to eat. I need to shower and change so that I won't be tempted to sock you if you make any more cracks." She headed toward the Toyota. "We're not all expert fixers like you, who corporations and governments pay to go into hot spots and straighten out their disasters. Some people actually have to get their hands dirty occasionally to accomplish a decent day's work."

"Really?" he said mildly. "I've heard that's true. How unfortunate. It would be even more unfortunate if I thought you believed what you were saying. Do you?"

She looked back at him. "No. I had no reason to strike out at you. You do a job that no one else could dream of doing and I respect that. I'm just tired and sad and I hate like hell that you thought you had to come back because you were worried that I couldn't handle the situation. Another project to fix. It just underscored the helplessness I've been feeling since all those innocent people got blown up."

"There's nothing that's helpless about you, Kendra," Lynch said quietly. "I've always known how strong you are. I have no intention of trying to 'fix' you. I came because I couldn't take the thought of you having to face the death of a friend alone when I could be here. I realize that you've been trying to take a step back where we're concerned, and I'm not pushing. Who knows where we'll end up? What will be, will be. But I do know that even if it's not as lovers, we've been through too much together not to work at keeping the friendship alive and well." He paused. "So, stop being on the defensive, and think about what you'd do if our situation was reversed." He smiled. "And then tell me where you want me to pick up dinner."

He was doing it again, she thought as she stared at him. Taking the situation and bending it to suit himself. The ultimate fixer. But she could tell he was sincere, and she found she was relieved and grateful that he'd made it easy for her to accept without making any commitment. Reversal? Yes, she would have gone to him if she'd known he might lose a friend he cared about. She hadn't the slightest doubt she would have been on the next flight. The reason? The many cases they'd solved as partners? The romantic sparks? Friendship? Perhaps a dozen other reasons in a relationship as complicated as theirs. Pick one.

Or don't. And just accept that he was here where she wanted him and do whatever was necessary to survive whatever was to come.

"I don't care where you go." She got into her 4Runner. "But I'm in the mood for Chinese…"

———

Kendra was blow-drying her hair when she heard the front doorbell ring.

"Open the door," Lynch called. "I come bearing gifts from the Middle Kingdom."

She opened the door and he whisked into the condo carrying two huge shiny red sacks with white firecrackers all over them. "Li Po's," he said over his shoulder as he headed for the dining room table. "I'll set up the table while you finish drying your hair."

She shut the door. "You rang the bell. Why didn't you use your key? Did you lose it?"

"Nope." He pulled cartons from the first sack. "But I thought that it might be a good idea not to use it until you tell me to. When I left here the last time, it was because I thought it was safer for me to be able to reach you at any time. But it has to be your choice. I don't want to ever have you feel that I'm violating either your independence or your privacy. I'll always ask you and I'll never take you for granted." He smiled. "Or you'll tell me. That would be even better." He started delving into the other sack. "You'd better finish drying your hair. You don't want Li Po's special to get cold."

"No, I don't." She headed for the bathroom. "I won't be long. I'll just run a comb through it and let it flop."

"Good. I always liked it like that. It's all honey brown shot with sun streaks, but it certainly doesn't flop. No matter what you do, it always turns out rather sculpted. And it shimmers."

"Shimmers?" She looked over her shoulder. "Where on earth did that come from? I could understand if you were talking about Olivia. She has that gorgeous brunette hair."

"True. But I prefer sun-streaked. 'Shimmers' perfectly describes the hair and you."

"Okay, I'll take it. How did things go in South Africa?"

"It's still ongoing. I'm helping to arbitrate an agreement between energy producers and politicians. There's corruption to deal with on all sides. It's an ongoing struggle just to keep the grid up."

"Really?"

He nodded. "And I'll tell you about it at dinner if you don't let the food get cold."

"Deal."

She disappeared into the bathroom.

◆

The food was excellent, and Lynch's stories kept her amused throughout dinner. His background was always colorful, and his experiences were equally fascinating. Everything was entirely different from the darkness and blood that had been surrounding her for the last couple of days. Tonight, Lynch was in fine form, and she just let herself flow with the stories. She even found herself laughing a few times.

"That's what I wanted." He got her a glass of red wine and then sat down again. "Now it's time for you to perform. Are you ready?"

"Ready?" She took a sip of wine. "Perform? I don't have any tales to tell you."

"Yes, you do. I've heard you tell me about your wild days, and the times you and Olivia almost closed down that school you both went to." He poured himself a glass of wine. "But that's not what I want you to tell me right now. What did you find down in that crater today that made you so intense while you were talking to Cassalas?"

She stiffened. "Eavesdropping, Lynch?"

"I admit I was watching you for that couple of minutes before you sent him on his way. I could tell you were almost exhausted, but you were still generating that electricity. It was…interesting."

"Why?"

He shrugged. "I wanted to see exactly how you were doing before you confronted me. Sometimes lately I've had to fight to get you to show me what you're thinking. I thought it might help me to know how to handle our situation."

"Situation?"

His brows rose. "Kendra."

She nodded. "I grant there is a situation. And how did you decide to handle it?"

"The way we always do. Working together and then going from there. When I saw that you'd probably discovered something in that crater today, I was relieved. I knew I was going to have something familiar to hold on to." He smiled. "It will be easier this way."

"You're very sure."

"No, I'm not." He coaxed, "Make me sure."

"I'm not sure myself."

"But you're almost there," he said. "Don't leave me out in the cold. Talk to me. What did you find in the crater?"

She told him about the disturbance in the terrain and the expression on Barrett's face when he was watching the digging.

He gave a low whistle. "It wasn't Barrett who set those explosives?"

She shook her head. "And if he didn't do it, then we have another murderer who killed both Barrett and all of those other cops and FBI agents." Her lips tightened. "That's mass murder. The question is why? Is it a single atrocity? Or how long has he been killing?"

"And why pick James Barrett's grand exhibition to stage his launch?" Lynch murmured. "He had to know where Barrett was going to bring those agents."

"So where do we start?" Kendra's hands were clenching into fists. "All those deaths...He thinks he's gotten away with it. We can't let him do it." She was thinking. "Barrett. I think we have to begin with Barrett. He was the one who took the plea deal and arranged to go to Pine Valley. Why? And how did anyone else know where that body was buried so they could booby-trap that area?"

"You're all in," Lynch said softly, his gaze studying her face. "I've seen you when you get like this. Yes, Barrett would be a good start."

"You're damn right. Even if we have to go back to—"

Her phone was ringing. She glanced at the ID.

"Griffin." She punched the access. "Hello, Griffin. What's happening?"

"You don't deserve this." His voice was gruff. "Particularly after you made things difficult for me today. But I did promise you that I'd let you know. I just heard from the hospital. Metcalf is awake and he's being allowed limited visitors. The doctor said he's going to make it."

"Thank God."

"Yeah, he's a good man. Anything else to report on your work today?"

"Not yet. Look, I have to hang up. I need to go to the hospital and see Metcalf."

"I'll let you go. The media will love that we have at least one survivor." He ended the call.

She turned to Lynch. "You heard him. I've got to go to the hospital."

"I'll go with you," he said. "That's great news, Kendra."

"You bet it is." She smiled brilliantly. "And I'll even let you drive me to the hospital in that Lamborghini. Because this is definitely the time to show off toys and celebrate."

CHAPTER

4

Y ou look...great." Metcalf's voice was a little slurred as he gazed up at Kendra. "This is terrible stuff, huh? I couldn't believe it when they told me...what had happened. All those people...dead. So glad...you weren't there."

"Terrible." Her hand tightened on his. "I won't tell you not to think about it because it's all any of us can think about right now. But we're all happy that you're on your way back. The doctor said that a few more days and you might even be able to go home."

He shook his head. "I have to get back to work. We're probably short of agents. So many died...We all knew Barrett was...crazy."

She nodded. "But you can afford to take a few days off. We've got to find out everything that happened. Once you're rested, I'll need you to help me. Griffin wouldn't like you to overdo it before that."

He made a face. "I'll go crazy sitting at home. I need to be out there."

She knew how he felt, but she just patted his arm. "Right now, you just need to relax."

He glanced around the room. "My mom's here. Have you met her?"

"Not yet."

"It's just as well. She can be a bit…bossy. She's probably driving everyone here crazy."

She smiled. "I might have some research work for you to do. I'll drop it by if that will be okay. Maybe I'll bring Olivia with me. She's been worried about you."

"Terrific. Love to see her." His eyes were closing. "Sorry. I'm having trouble staying awake. They gave me something…"

"I'm leaving anyway. They only said I could stay five minutes. Take care, Metcalf. I'll be in touch."

"Yeah, do that…"

He was asleep.

Kendra gazed at him for another moment. He was pale and bruised, but he had been fully conscious during most of the time she'd been here and that was great. She gave his hand a squeeze and left the hospital room.

Lynch stood up from the hall bench. "Okay?"

"Better than I expected," she said. "He wants to go back to work. I told him I'd give him something to do while he was recuperating."

"Sounds like Metcalf. It will be good for him. I could never stand to be cooped up when I was wounded."

"I remember." She also remembered that when she'd visited Lynch in the hospital, she'd been shocked to glimpse all the scars on his body. "Maybe we can convince Metcalf to be more sensible."

He shook his head. "Don't count on it. He'll

probably try to impress you with his stamina. May I take you home now?"

"In just a few minutes, I want to talk to his mother." She indicated the red-haired woman sitting in a chair by the coffee machine. "This must have been very hard for her."

"It was. I had a talk with her when you were in Metcalf's room. But she's tough, and she doesn't think you deserve him."

Her eyes widened. "What?"

He shrugged. "Evidently Metcalf has spoken to her ad nauseam about you. She's his mother, and she could see he has a thing for you."

"Thing?"

"Crush, infatuation, whatever. I just thought I'd warn you not to expect a warm welcome."

"Thank you." She braced herself, painted a smile on her face, and strode across the room to Metcalf's mother. "Hello, I'm Kendra Michaels, I'm so glad to meet you at last. I wanted you to know how much we all appreciate your son."

"Thank you." The woman looked away.

"He's smart and very brave. It's a privilege to have him as a coworker and a good friend."

She stayed there chatting for a few minutes longer and then made her way back across the hall to Lynch.

"Escape?" he murmured as he punched the button of the elevator. "You didn't stay long, but I could see you were making a valiant effort. Cold?"

"Very cool. But I'm not sorry I tried to reach out to her. She's the mother of a friend. I wouldn't want Metcalf to think I wasn't courteous to her."

"And it's not your fault that you don't have the good sense to appreciate her son."

"I do appreciate him. I just can't..." She got on the elevator. "Drop it, Lynch."

"It's dropped," he said as he pushed the DOWN button. "But you've had a couple of rough days, and I didn't want you to feel you had to be everything to everyone. You have a tendency to do that."

"Not your business."

"It's dropped," he repeated gently. "Now, what time do you want me to pick you up tomorrow?"

"Eight. But we'll take the Toyota."

"No more celebration?"

"Since I want to first stop at the security prison to talk to the warden and ask to search Bennett's cell, I'd think that a more modest car would be more suitable."

"Whatever you like," Lynch said. "Personally, I prefer the celebrations, but I'll let you choose when and where. Let's see, I'll drop you at your condo and then go to my house and wait to make a few calls to Johannesburg to make certain negotiations haven't totally broken down. After a few hours' sleep, I'll join you tomorrow morning for a boringly suitable drive out to the prison."

"I thought you'd wrapped up Johannesburg," Kendra said.

"Mostly." He opened the door leading to the parking lot. "I can handle the rest long-distance." He added quietly, "I wanted to be here with you. Well, I'm here. We'll take care of everything else, starting tomorrow. Okay?"

Kendra hesitated only for a moment. She wanted this horror of a case over as soon as possible. And she didn't want to do it alone. Lynch was always incredibly intelligent and could sometimes even be ahead of her given his zillions of contacts on both sides of the law.

She nodded slowly. "Okay."

———◆———

Lynch showed up at Kendra's parking garage at seven forty-five the next morning with two cups of coffee from Starbucks. He handed her a cup as she got off the elevator. "Are we in a hurry? Or do we have time to stop for breakfast?"

"We can eat later." She got into the driver's seat of the Toyota. "I want to get these interviews over. I phoned Griffin last night and asked him to call Jonas Rollins, security director of the jail, and see if he'd give us an interview about Barrett. Together with permission to examine the contents of his cell. It was not only nearly midnight, but I had to ask Griffin to do it as a favor. He wasn't pleasant." Her lips tightened. "Though he enjoyed having me come to him. I've been having a little trouble with Griffin lately."

"I thought you were getting along better with the FBI lately," Lynch said as he got into the car. "What did you do to Griffin?"

"He annoyed me. I suppose I let him know it."

"You usually do." His lips were twitching. "You really should leave the executives alone. You manage to terrorize the agents by showing them up in front of their superiors, but the Griffins of the world can cause you difficulties."

"You never seem to have any problems. You can get Griffin to jump hoops for you."

"That's a question of expertly applied pressure, not intimidation. You've never been good at pressure."

"Because I hate to do it." She shot him a glance. "But you must not mind. You're a specialist or you wouldn't be able to pull off all the hijinks you manage. I take it the Johannesburg power grid is still up and running?"

He smiled and shook his head. "Evidently, I'm not as essential as I thought. They were probably glad to see the last of me. But you're right, I don't mind applying pressure. It's a game that most people play in one form or another." He added softly, "Except you. You don't even understand the rules. That's why you should leave it up to me."

"I wouldn't do that. It wouldn't be honest."

He sighed. "I told you that you didn't understand the rules. Honesty doesn't usually enter into it. To win the game it's just my job to play it better."

"You're honest with me."

"How do you know?"

She looked him in the eye. "Aren't you honest with me?"

"Yes. But that's because I can't bear you losing because you won't play the game."

She looked back ahead. "And that's honest, too."

He laughed. "Have it your own way. But you'd still be better off letting me do the questioning of this security director. I'm sure he has an entire history in the art of pressure."

"But all I want is the truth from a public servant. Pressure isn't an issue." She took a swallow of her coffee. "So I'll do it, Lynch. Griffin would have prepared him to talk to me." She saw the building ahead and turned into the parking lot. "I'm sure he'll be very cooperative."

Jonas Rollins was not at all cooperative. He was a sleek, white-haired man in his sixties, and he reminded Kendra of every blustery politician she had run across since she had registered to vote. He started by keeping them waiting for thirty minutes, and then when they were permitted into his office, he lectured them on why the FBI should not have tried to interfere with the workday of private citizens.

Kendra interrupted him in mid-sentence. "We won't keep you long, Mr. Rollins. Just a few questions, please. I'm sure Special Agent Griffin told you that we're just tying up loose ends on this investigation."

"This entire investigation is a waste of my valuable time," he said coldly. "Our prisoner Barrett is deceased, and we've had nothing but media knocking on our doors trying to stir up trouble since that unfortunate incident."

Kendra had had enough. "'Unfortunate incident,'" she repeated. "You and Griffin must think very much alike. Only he referred to it as a 'mess.' Neither description describes a tragedy of that magnitude. I'd hate to quote you to any of the media you're talking about." She heard Lynch smother a chuckle but ignored him. "Now, I've been told to get the total information available to complete an in-depth report on the conditions this prisoner dealt with while incarcerated. So why don't you just answer my questions, and we'll get out of here."

"I'm listening," Rollins growled.

"Has Barrett had any visitors since he's been here?"

"Lawyers, a few representatives from the Death Penalty Litigation committee, a pastor."

"Family?"

"No, never, though they funded his pricey defense team."

"Friends?"

"No one who visited him." Rollins was becoming impatient. "What difference does it make now?"

"Letters? Did he have a phone?"

"No phone was permitted, of course."

"We know that prisoners and greedy guards often have a way around that."

"I assure you, he had no access to a cell phone. And all letters were confiscated and examined and photographed before they were given to him. Anything else?"

"If there is, we'll be sure to come back and ask it. Now I believe we're ready to be taken to his security cell to examine it."

"I don't have the time for this."

"That's perfectly fine, I'm sure that officer at the front desk will be happy to take us to the cell."

"I tell you it's a complete waste of time."

"But we won't know that until we examine the cell." She met his eyes. "Perhaps the conditions were so bad here that they contributed to him committing suicide and taking all those other agents with him. We should know if that was the case, don't you think?"

Rollins's face was flushed. "His cell and other conditions were perfectly in line with the standards of any facility in the state. You'll find nothing wrong."

"But I won't be able to make my report to that effect until I see it," Kendra said. "So please authorize that officer to take us to his cell so that I can file my report."

"It's nonsense," Rollins grumbled. Then he went to the door and shouted. "Officer Kopt! Take these people down to Barrett's security cell and stay with them while they take a look around. Then escort them out of the building to the parking lot." He turned back to Kendra. "Take your look around," he said curtly. "But I want a copy of your report sent to me."

"Of course." She sailed past him to the officer waiting in the outer office. "Officer Kopt? Sorry to trouble you like this. We'll try not to bother you for long."

"No problem," Kopt said as he headed for the elevators.

Lynch fell into step with Kendra as she followed the officer. "Griffin wanted a report?" he murmured. "You didn't mention it."

"I'm sure someone at the FBI will want a report sometime or other. I was just doing a little advance work."

They stepped into the elevator. "Because he wasn't being cooperative?"

"That might have had something to do with it." She paused and then said in a low voice, "I didn't really expect to learn anything from Rollins. But the cell might be different. Sometimes people tend to keep items that can tell interesting stories."

"And you want the opportunity to get a good look around."

"That would be helpful."

The elevator doors slid open, and Officer Kopt stepped out and waited for them to exit.

Lynch winked. "No one can say I'm not helpful."

He moved forward to catch up with Kopt, and Kendra heard him start to chat up the officer as he led them down the dark corridor toward the Barrett security cell.

◆

The Barrett cell was nine by twelve and with a single bunk bed and no window. There was a narrow desk jutting out from the far wall on which a couple of paperback books had been tossed, a utilitarian steel office chair that was fixed permanently to the floor in front of it. One overhead light was the only illumination in the ceiling, and the interior of the cell was almost as dim as the corridor.

"Not much to see," Kopt said as he threw the door open a little wider. He glanced at Lynch. "But the son of a bitch managed to get whatever he wanted. Do you know six months ago he made one of his deals with the prosecution and they brought a big TV in here so he could watch the World Series? I was stuck working upstairs and I missed the last three innings. It just goes to show you that life's just not fair."

"Sure does." Lynch's voice was warmly sympathetic. "That was a great series." He moved to stand in front of Kopt. "Did you manage to at least see the final?"

Kendra waited until she was certain Lynch had Kopt absorbed in the conversation before she moved deeper into the cell. *Keep it casual.* She moved over to the desk and began to glance at the paperback books. They were all porn, which didn't surprise her. Almost all of his female victims had been raped. She looked through all of them to make certain there were no hidden compartments.

Nothing.

She opened the single drawer in the desk. Nothing but pens and a notepad. She checked the pad for visible indentations. Nothing. It looked as if he'd never written on it.

She knelt down on the floor and looked underneath the chair. Clean. Nothing affixed beneath it.

She went to the bed and examined the blanket, mattress, and pillow. Nothing. She knelt down and examined the bed's steel frame. Nothing.

Or maybe... While she was lying on the floor, she'd caught sight of something across the cell in the corner...

She glanced at the door. The guard was still talking to Lynch. She got to her feet and moved quickly to the corner.

It was nothing really. Just a small wisp of a feather. But it smelled... weird. It was familiar, but she couldn't quite place it.

And why over here in the corner, not close to any mattress or pillow?

She went back to the bed and examined the mattress. Airtight. She took the pillow and ran her fingers over the edge. It also seemed airtight... until she came to the upper right corner. Then the two sides parted, and she was able to slip her hand into the interior! She froze for an instant and then she began to carefully explore. She was able to only go a small distance before she felt a small object embedded in the feathers. She gave a quick glance at the door.

Keep him busy, Lynch. Just a little longer.

Her hand closed on the object. Small. She was holding it in the palm of her hand. Rubber... Glass... What the hell was it? She carefully pulled the object from the pillow and looked down at it. The light glittered on round glass... They were eyeglasses of some sort. She brought the object closer so that she could get a better look.

And then she caught the smell again. It was overwhelming her.

Shit!

She quickly wrapped the glasses in a tissue from her pocket and stuffed them in her jacket pocket. Then she closed the opening in the pillow itself and pulled and drew the cloth case over it again. She straightened the bed and then whirled and leaned back against the wall. What was she going to do? She knew what she wanted to do. Get out of here right now. But she couldn't do it. Not yet.

She took out her phone and punched in Griffin's number.

"Griffin." Then he followed it immediately with, "What the hell do you want now, Kendra?"

She kept her voice almost low enough to be a whisper. "I want you to send an agent and at least one forensics specialist down here to Barrett's cell now. I want you to tell them to obey my instructions and not let Rollins intimidate them."

"What are you up to?"

"I'm trying to be legal. I found something here and I don't want Rollins to conveniently lose it to save his ass."

Silence. "Evidence?"

"I don't know. You can tell me after your labs take a look. Get them here *fast*." She cut the connection.

Now she could only hope Griffin would do as she'd told him, and they'd get here as soon as possible. She took the tissue-wrapped glasses out of her pocket and replaced them in the pillow. *Give them a little time.* She waited another ten minutes. Then she moved over to the desk and sat down on the steel chair. Lynch gazed at her inquiringly. "Are we finished?"

She shook her head. "Not yet. I had a little trouble and I need a forensics expert to come and examine my findings. It might not be long."

Kopt was frowning. "You found something? Maybe I should call Mr. Rollins. I don't think he expected you to—" His phone rang. "Kopt." Then he quickly said,

"I just heard about it, sir. No, I won't let her take any-thing." He hung up and turned to Kendra. "He just got a call from an Agent Griffin, and he bit my head off. What have you got? I may have to search you."

Lynch stepped forward. "I wouldn't do that," he said quietly. "You don't want that kind of trouble."

Lord, the last thing she wanted was to have Lynch step in and take down this guard. "No, he doesn't," she said quickly. "If he'll just realize that the FBI will have authority to—"

"What's happening, Kendra?" Agent Bill Carmack was coming down the corridor from the elevator followed by another agent. "Griffin told me to get here double quick before you caused him a major headache."

"I'm grateful for the double quick. Did he also tell you to do what I told you?"

He nodded. "He might have mentioned that."

She nodded at the pillow. "I want FBI forensics to examine the contents of that pillow and take posses-sion of it. I want you to give your colleague authority to do that and then get out of here."

Kopt took a step forward. "I can't allow that. I'm sure Mr. Rollins will object to—"

Bill Carmack interrupted harshly, "You're talking to the U.S. government and we're investigating a multiple murder case. I'm sure we'd have authority to take any evidence we need. If you want to complain, do it to Agent Griffin." He nodded to the forensics agent. "Go get it, Sara."

The woman he'd called Sara was already care-fully and methodically handling the pillow. Agent Carmack turned to Kendra. "And the second thing Griffin told me to do was to get you out of here the minute we took over." He jerked his thumb to the elevator. "Move it, Kendra."

"I want to stay and watch as she—"

"No, you don't." Lynch took her elbow and was gently pushing her toward the elevator. "You wanted them here or you'd never have called Griffin. Let them take care of it now." He nodded at Carmack. "Thanks, take good care of whatever it is. We'll contact you later."

"Whatever it is?" Kendra repeated. "It's a pair of goggles."

"Well, you'll remember you didn't see fit to tell me."

"There wasn't time, and you were keeping Kopt out of my way."

"Now that's Carmack's job, and it isn't a bad idea to get you out of here." He shut the elevator door. "You'll probably be the one Rollins blames if he decides he's been persecuted."

"This is an enormous bother." She made a face. "It would have been much easier if I'd acted on my first idea."

"And what was that?" When she didn't answer he studied her face and then chuckled. "You were going to steal the damn thing."

"Borrow," she corrected. "I couldn't trust Rollins. And then I would have known the research was done properly because I would have done it. It's not as if I wouldn't have given it back to the Bureau as soon as I got the results."

He was still laughing. "Then why didn't you do it?"

"Because if I didn't involve the Bureau and their forensic expertise, anything I did might not have stood up in court." She added gloomily, "You have to go through proper channels."

"I've noticed that. How unfortunate."

"But when have you ever gone through proper channels?"

"When I can't do anything else." The elevator door opened, and he said quickly, "You didn't want to leave until you were sure Carmack and company were safely out of the building. We'll park down the street and watch to see the FBI van when it leaves. I don't believe it will be long. Carmack evidently had his orders, and he wouldn't have wanted to cause any more trouble than you managed to do."

"I only did what I thought I should do. No trouble whatever."

"Tell that to Griffin."

———◆———

Lynch was correct. They only had to wait another fifteen minutes before they saw Carmack and Sara leave the building, get in the FBI van, and drive out of the parking lot.

"Mission accomplished." Lynch turned to gaze at Kendra as she was driving out of the parking lot. "Okay, you found a pair of goggles. Is there something special about them?"

"Wait until we get to that park a few blocks up the road. I don't want to be anywhere near Rollins and his officers. I still think they'd probably lock me up if they got the chance."

"I promise I'd break you out."

"Shut up. It's not funny. That's why I had to turn all of this over to Griffin and the FBI. I decided Rollins would be more difficult to deal with than Griffin. I thought Griffin would be bad enough. He's eager to make this entire crime go away or at least delay any investigation until the media goes on to another story. I wanted to be able to prove that he can't ethically do it before I let him have anything that he could stuff in file thirteen and forget."

"Now you see why I couldn't stay in the FBI," Lynch said. "It can be extremely political."

"When I ran into Rollins, I realized that he was cut from the same cloth as Griffin, but he'd be even worse to deal with. He definitely would have used any excuse not to let anyone in the world know that the story about Barrett's suicide might not be totally true if it damaged his own political career. Griffin has at least a modicum of integrity where his job is concerned. If he were shown that his agents had been deliberately targeted, he'd go after the person who did it."

"He definitely would," Lynch said. "Whatever Griffin's failings may be, there's no denying that."

Kendra pulled over to the side of the road. She turned off the car, reached into her jacket pocket, and pulled out her notebook. She rapidly made a sketch of the goggles. "This is what was tucked into Barrett's pillow. They're swim goggles. And after examining them I think the lenses might be prescription. At first, I wasn't sure what they were or why he'd have them. But the styling of those rubber frames and those lenses... They look like high-performance swim goggles."

He nodded. "The FBI lab will pull any DNA present on them. And they'll also ID the company that made them."

"That's what I'm hoping. If those are prescription lenses, the manufacturer probably custom-made them. The company should be able to give us the name of the purchaser."

"And then we contact the owner?"

"We can try." She bit her lip. "I don't know if the owner is still alive. It might be a souvenir of one of Barrett's kills. But I don't know how the goggles could have gotten into that cell. Barrett would have been searched thoroughly before being incarcerated and he had no visitors. It goes without saying that he couldn't have made the kill after he was jailed." She paused. "But I'm still leaning toward the idea that it was a souvenir."

"Why?"

"The way he treated them." She was still looking down at the sketch of the goggles. "His scent was on them." She swallowed hard. "I could *smell* him."

"What?"

"I could smell him on that tiny feather I saw in the corner that led me to the pillow, but I wasn't certain what it was. But after I had the goggles in my hands it was much more clear. He didn't just keep them tucked away in that pillow. He took them out, he fondled them, he rubbed his thumbs and fingers over them in a kind of caress. He transferred his body oils when he did that." Her voice was uneven. "It was as if he were in that cell with me today. He liked what he did to that victim. He wanted to always keep the memory. I could almost see him lying there and reaching into the pillow to bring out those goggles so the victim would have to be close to him again." She took a deep breath. "We can check, but, as I said, I'm not sure what they'll find."

He reached over and squeezed her shoulder. "Neither am I, but we'll find out together."

"No, we won't. We'll have to sit and wait and hope that Griffin will keep on those agents who are doing the work. It's going to frustrate the hell out of me."

He nodded. "I can see that. And you'll probably be calling those agents and doing a little prodding yourself."

She smiled reluctantly. "I might. I figure that since Griffin knows I'll probably be harassing him until I get answers, he'll put a rush on it. That means I might have what I need by late this afternoon or early evening."

"And if you don't, heaven help them. But no doubt the prodding will continue."

"I have to know why those goggles were in Barrett's cell. The rules concerning Barrett were very strict because of his background. Anything connected to him either would be evidence or could lead to another victim."

"Which means that the answer was yes."

She nodded. "But maybe it won't be necessary." She changed the subject. "I might not have had a chance to search thoroughly and find that damn thing if you hadn't been able to distract Kopt and keep him from hovering over me and getting in my way. I meant what I said back there to Kopt. I'd almost forgotten how helpful you could be. I won't do it again."

"You hadn't forgotten, you just blocked it out. Sort of a defensive measure. Now I'm on the scene and I'll keep reminding you." He took out his phone. "I'll make some calls and talk to a few savvy people about how a prisoner in solitary might have been able to get his hands on those goggles. Sound okay?" He didn't wait for an answer. "But right now, it's time you took me to lunch. Somewhere outdoors, bright and sunny, overlooking the ocean. I think we both need to get away from dark corridors and the thought of jails, craters, and men like Barrett." He snapped his fingers. "The Del Coronado. A golden-era hotel and restaurants with take-me-away allure. Plus, beautiful celebrities running around in bikinis. Perfect."

"And why should we run away to a place like that just to eat lunch when we need to be working?"

"Because they have a fantastic buffet, and it's great for people-watching." He paused. "And it might be a way I can distract you from nagging those agents at the Bureau and keeping them from doing their work. It would also take the edge off, and make the afternoon pass faster for you." He tilted his head. "Well, have I convinced you or pissed you off?"

"Let me think about it."

"What's to think about? As I said, it's perfect. Shouldn't I have mentioned the babes in bikinis?"

"Not if you wanted to lure me into going there." Oh, what the hell. She was suddenly grinning. "Wrong bait, Lynch. You should have mentioned the Navy SEALs who train and work out on the beach there. I can't tell you how often I've enjoyed watching them." She pulled away from the curb. "Of course we'll go to the Del Coronado. Like you said, perfect…"

CHAPTER
5

After a perfect lunch at the Hotel del Coronado, Lynch dropped off Kendra at her condo so she could spend a few hours rescheduling appointments for her practice. Some of that time, however, was consumed by an enlightening call from the FBI.

When Lynch returned, she greeted him with a large mug of coffee. "Come in and sit down. We need to get to work."

"What's the urgency?" He took a sip of coffee and strolled over to the couch. "Did something happen?"

"No, I just realized after I got home that we spent half an afternoon playing in Neverland and I need to make up for it." She made a face. "And you need to tell me that you didn't waste time after you left me a few hours ago."

"Ahh, now I get the picture," he said solemnly. "Major guilt trip. I should have known you'd have an attack. You were having entirely too good a time out on the beach after lunch."

"Guilt trips are foolish," she said. "I did have a good time, but I could have stopped it at any time. I didn't choose to do it, but it shouldn't interfere with the work we agreed to do today."

"Absolutely not." He smiled. "Totally logical, Kendra."

"Is that a smirk?"

"I wouldn't think of it. I have far too much respect for you. I did make those calls exploring ways to get contraband items to prisoners. It's fairly common for prisoners to be able to get their hands on phones if they pay enough. Some of those methods are quite inventive." He shook his head. "But slipping anything to a high-profile prisoner like Barrett in solitary would be different." He held up his hand when she started to speak. "But not impossible. I'm still exploring who would do it, and how. I'll make some more calls tonight."

"Good. Then I'll tell you as much as I've learned so far." She took a notebook out of her pocket and flipped it open. "I got most of the report on the goggles from the Bureau a few minutes ago. The only fingerprints on them belonged to Barrett. The same goes for any DNA. I was right, there was Barrett's body oil on them. But every inch of those goggles had been scrubbed and sterilized before Barrett handled them. Wherever there wasn't a print, there was absolutely nothing. Whoever gave those goggles to Barrett made certain they couldn't be traced back to them by any means."

"Sterilized," Lynch repeated. "I can see them being wiped clean, but that's going to an extreme."

She paused. "And you said they were probably given to Barrett. Why couldn't they be a souvenir?"

He shrugged. "Maybe they could. If that was the

case, it makes sense the person who gave them to Barrett wouldn't want to be connected to the goggles or to Barrett." He added, "An extreme solution from an exceptionally careful person."

"We don't even know how those goggles got to him in that prison yet, much less who managed to bring them," Kendra said. "But I do know who they belonged to. I told you I only got a partial report, but the forensics specialist managed to trace them after she hung up, and she left me a message. They were high-performance goggles custom made by the manufacturer with prescription lenses. They were sold two years ago to a Tricia Walton, an eighteen-year-old freshman at UC San Diego."

"Very good," Lynch said. "Now for the big question. Is she still alive?"

"I don't know. I hope so. As I said, the agent left a message, but it was only about where the goggles were issued. He said he'd call me back later with more info." She shook her head. "There was no way I was going to wait for him to get back to me. I was about to call this Tricia Walton when you came to the door."

"Then by all means go ahead and do it," Lynch said gently. "Let's put that souvenir question to rest."

She nodded. "Maybe I was hesitating because I didn't want to know. I kept remembering the scent of that bastard on those goggles. Only eighteen, Lynch."

"She'll be older now. Maybe it wasn't a souvenir. Call her, Kendra."

"Don't nag me." She was already dialing the number. "I just want to—"

"Hi, this is Tricia and you guys know I can't have the phone by the pool when I'm practicing." The voice on the other end of the line was vibrantly alive and filled with amusement. "Which is forever and ever. I'll call you as soon as I get through here if you'll leave a message." She was laughing. "Hey, do what I tell you. You know I'm worth it." She ended the call.

"Encouraging," Lynch said. "But it's not uncommon for family members to keep a cell phone account active for months or even years just so they can call and hear their deceased loved one's voice."

"You're right, but I want to think she's still alive." Kendra stared at the phone in her hand. That voice had been full of humor and warmth and vitality. "I like her."

"So do I," Lynch said. "But I believe it's time to try to see her in person and ask her a few questions about Barrett."

"We don't want to frighten her," Kendra said.

"She didn't sound as if she'd be easily frightened. I think we have to know how Barrett got those goggles. We can't ignore that she and Barrett evidently had a connection."

"Of course we can't," Kendra said. "I'd just like to find out more about that connection before I spring any of this on her. The Bureau will have someone checking her out, but I don't want to wait around for them. I think I'll do a bit of research on her myself and see what I can find out."

"May I help?"

She shook her head. "This is just preliminary. I only want to try to get to know her. But you can go with me to see her tomorrow at the university."

"You might have to make an appointment. It sounded as if she was pretty busy with her training."

"If we have trouble, I'll see if I can get my mother to pull rank. She teaches at the university, and she might be willing to help me influence Tricia's coach."

"I'd forgotten Diane still teaches. I thought she was going to take a diplomatic post in South America."

"She decided she'd get too bored. She loves to interact with those college kids."

"And keep an eye on you?"

"I'm the one who has to keep an eye on her," Kendra said. "I was relieved when she decided not to go down to Chile. I could see her demonstrating in the streets with the entire student body."

"And you would have gone down to bail her out when they threw her in jail."

"Of course. If I couldn't get her out any other way. I'd prefer to negotiate. What's a daughter for?" She was already thinking ahead. "Maybe I'll call my mother tonight and see what she knows about the swimming team. She follows most college sports, and she likes swimming. Maybe she's even met Tricia."

"Aren't you becoming overinvolved?" Lynch asked. "All we wanted to know was why Barrett had her goggles."

"'Overinvolved,'" she repeated. Then she shook her head vehemently. "You didn't smell Barrett's scent on those goggles. And you just told me that it could have been someone else who brought the damn things to Barrett and gave them to him as a present."

"I didn't exactly use those words." He got to his feet. "I don't know what happened, and I certainly don't have your nasal sensitivity. So, I'll get out of here and let you run your own show. I still have some more checking to do on how Barrett got hold of those goggles while he was in solitary." He smiled down at her. "But I want to know. Will you call me after you do your research on Tricia Walton and fill me in?"

She nodded. "Yes." She paused and then said, "She might have been even younger than eighteen when he went after her, Lynch. I can't stand the thought of anyone victimizing kids."

"I know you can't." He leaned forward and brushed his lips across her cheek. "I'll be waiting for you to call and tell me what's been happening to Tricia. Then we'll decide what to do about keeping her safe." He headed for the front door. "If I can do anything before tomorrow, let me know. I'll be here for you." Then he was gone.

She knew he'd be here for her, but she was feeling a responsibility to do everything she could herself. She'd felt almost as helpless in that cell as she had when she'd been at the hospital. There'd be no way to escape that feeling until she felt totally in charge of the situation. She just didn't *know* enough. Not enough about Tricia Walton, and not enough about Barrett. She hadn't researched Barrett as much as she could, because the bastard was dead, and she'd instinctively thought good riddance. But the minute she'd had a hint that he wasn't a suicide she should have explored his death the way she would have anyone else's.

So, catch up, call the Bureau and get to know as much as they did about James Michael Barrett. Then call anyone at the university, including her mother, who could tell her anything about Tricia Walton.

Kendra sat down at the table, took out her phone and notebook, and punched in the number for the FBI.

———

"I'm reporting in as ordered, Lynch," Kendra said when she phoned him over three hours later. "The good news is that not only is Tricia Walton alive and well, she's a champion swimmer. Not that I learned all that much about her. I got hung up finding all I could about Barrett. Tricia is from a solid upper-middle-class family who brought her up in Seattle, Washington. She has excellent academic grades and won an athletic scholarship that enabled her to get into one of the best colleges in the country for her swimming specialty. She may even be Olympic-caliber." Kendra grimaced. "But Barrett's career was every bit as twisted and ugly as I'd heard."

"You dove into Barrett's past, too?"

"I had to do it. It wasn't fun. But since he had her goggles, I had to explore how he'd gotten them." She paused. "And the son of a bitch had to have been practically drooling over them. He was treating them as if they were his toy."

"And did you find out how he got them?"

"Not yet. I suppose Tricia might have given them to him, but I doubt it. And I wasn't able to get through to her to question her. I'll have to try to do it tomorrow," she said. "But I found out why he might have been obsessed with her."

"Ahh, now we get to the twisted and ugly. How bad was it?"

"It was bad, but not as terrible as it could have been. Though she must have been terrified, and he must have been really pissed off."

"Kendra."

"I'm getting to it. Barrett attacked her when she was living down here with her parents at their lakeside summer home when she was only fourteen. Evidently, he'd been stalking her for some time because he waited until her parents had gone to town one day and left her at home alone. She was working out when he showed up and attacked her. He was clearly trying to rape her, but she put up a hell of a fight. She hit him in the balls with a hand weight and broke free. She got to the fire alarm in the house and set it off. When he caught up with her, she hit him again with the weight, this time on the head, then ran out and hid in the hills. He was gone when the cops and fire trucks showed up a short time later."

Lynch chuckled. "Yes, I'd say that would have pissed him off."

"The FBI records say that Tricia was the only one known to have escaped alive from Barrett. He was a suspect even then, and they gave her surveillance protection for some time after the attack. It only stopped when he was arrested and incarcerated."

"Is it possible he stole the goggles when he attacked her?"

"I don't know. One more question for Tricia Walton." Kendra leaned wearily back in her chair and added, "I'm too tired to worry about that right now. I'll figure it out later. I'm going to remember every one of those murders Barrett committed after spending two hours listening to every single detail. But those details were so horrendous, I just want to go to bed and pull the covers over my head."

"Then go ahead and do it." He paused. "I could come and keep you company if you need me. Any way you want it."

She was tempted. She did feel as if she needed him. She needed warmth and distraction and the intense sexual diversion that Lynch could bring her. The world seemed very cold and barren at the moment. But it wasn't fair to use him, and it might only complicate the situation. "Thanks, but I might be able to sleep. I called my mother and she's going to contact Tricia's coach and set up an interview in the morning. I'll see you tomorrow, Lynch."

"Okay, but I'm only a phone call away." He ended the call.

Kendra looked down at her notes for a moment then turned and moved toward the bedroom. She would go to bed and try not to think of that monster on the attack. Instead, she'd try to remember a young girl who had desperately fought off the monster and come out victorious.

———◆———

10:15 A.M.
NEXT DAY
UC SAN DIEGO MAIN CAMPUS

Diane Michaels was waiting for Kendra when she drove into the parking lot in front of the aquatic center. She crossed to the car and opened the driver's door. "Come on. There's not much time, Kendra. You said you wanted to interview Tricia Walton as soon as possible. I talked her coach into letting her skip thirty minutes of the morning session. But you're not going to get another chance today." She gave Kendra a quick hug and glanced at Lynch as he got out of the car. "Hello, Lynch. Good to see you. I'm glad you're tagging along with Kendra on this one. I didn't like the sound of that massacre in the valley."

"Hi, Diane, you're looking well." He grinned. "Always happy to tag along with Kendra when she lets me. She does make things interesting."

Kendra wondered what any of the powerhouse figures who paid enormous sums to Lynch would have thought of the way her mother had referred to him. "I'm hoping that it will be Tricia Walton who makes things interesting for us. You couldn't get her coach to give us more time than that?"

"It was Tricia who set up the boundaries for the interview. Coach Lydecker said that at this point of her training she lets Tricia set her own schedule. She has to balance both her training and the fact that she's working with a think tank to get an advanced degree in computer statistics. She said Tricia's a workaholic and the only thing she has to do is keep her from overdoing it." She smiled. "You're lucky Tricia gave you the thirty minutes. Lydecker said she's determined to make the next Olympic team and she'll bet Tricia will take gold. She's been dominating all the meets she's entered in the last six months."

"Then we'd better not be late," Kendra said as she headed for the main entrance. "Do you have time to have coffee with us after we're finished with Tricia?"

Her mother shook her head as she turned away. "I've got a packed day. Call me later this evening and we'll talk and set up a lunch." Then she turned back and said to Lynch, "I don't like this. I know Kendra can take care of herself, so I won't insult her. But I'll be very upset if you don't perform in a way that I approve. You'll do well to remember that."

"No problem. I never forget a word you say to me."

"Excellent." Diane was already walking away. "Keep it that way."

Kendra shot a glance at Lynch. "You said exactly the right thing."

"I was too terrified to do anything else." His eyes were dancing with sly mischief. "I always try to stay on her good side."

"Bullshit."

She opened the door, and her nostrils were immediately assaulted with the scent of chlorine and the thick humidity of the pool area. "Now, where is this—"

"Dr. Michaels?" A tall, slender woman with short dark hair was approaching them. "I'm Shirley Lydecker." She shook Kendra's hand. "I'm glad you're on time. Now let's get this interview over." She nodded at a door a few yards away. "Tricia is in my office waiting for you."

"Thank you for your cooperation." Kendra gestured to Lynch. "This is Adam Lynch. He'll be present at the interview."

The coach nodded impatiently. "Whatever. Let's just get it done." She strode toward the door and threw it open. "Your visitors are here, Tricia. I'll be waiting when you're finished."

"Thanks, Coach. I won't be long."

Kendra was at the door, and she saw Tricia smile warmly at Lydecker. She was tall, slim, and tanned, and her short curly hair was dark blond and sun-streaked. She wore flip-flops, and the short, loose print robe that covered her swimsuit made her look vaguely like a young gladiator. When she turned to face Kendra, the smile was still there and lit her face with that same warmth.

"Hi, I'm Tricia." She crossed the room and shook Kendra's hand. "I'm so sorry I have to cut this interview short, but I'm working." The smile deepened and caused a crease to frame her dark blue eyes. "But you know all about that, don't you, Dr. Michaels? Between your music therapy job and your work with the FBI, you must be busy all the time." She didn't wait for an answer but turned to Lynch. "And you are?"

"Adam Lynch." He shook her hand. "But you don't

have to pay any attention to me. I'm just here to listen and observe. I'm very good at that."

"I bet you are." She smiled again. "And I always pay attention." She laughed. "That's one of things that *I'm* very good at." She turned back to Kendra. "Shall we sit down and have our talk?" She perched on the corner of the desk. "Shall I start? I've actually been expecting someone from the FBI to come around to see me, but I never thought I'd rate a visit from you. I knew they'd want to tie up the last details on the case after that asshole blew himself up, but I'd judge you to be more a celebrity than a regular cleanup agent." She shrugged. "Oh, well, what do you want to know? This is really a waste of time for all of us. I've no complaints about the Bureau's handling of my case. Everyone seemed very efficient, and the most important thing is that they kept me alive, isn't it?"

"Yes, they did," Kendra said quietly as she dropped down in the visitor's chair beside the desk. "But I believe you've misunderstood my purpose in coming here. I wasn't sent here to get your stamp of approval on the handling of your case. I'm afraid it's an active investigation. I need to ask a few questions regarding your relationship with Barrett."

"Active investigation?" Tricia's smile disappeared. "What the hell do you mean, my relationship with Barrett? I'll tell you what my relationship was with that bastard. He wanted to kill me. I wanted to stay alive. I won. He lost. End of report." Her voice was suddenly fierce. "And now he's dead and I'm going to try to forget about him. I've fought that battle for over four years. After I first got away from him, I just tried to make certain that I'd be able to defend myself if I was ever in that position again. First, I only used my mind because I realized you have to start with outthinking someone like Barrett. Then I took judo and karate and I got better and better. After that I learned about weaponry. Then I discovered swimming and I realized my body was getting stronger and stronger. When I began swimming in competition, I learned how good I was. Now every time I win a swim meet or ace an academic test, I show the world what I can do out there and how wrong Barrett was to try to take it from me." She drew a deep breath. "Does that answer your question?"

"No." Kendra grinned. "But I can see why he was obsessed with you until the day he died."

"Ditto," Lynch murmured.

"I don't know what you're talking about," Tricia said. "I did my best to put him out of my mind since the day he tried to rape and kill me. And, since I had the FBI shadowing me, he gave up and left me alone."

"Wrong," Kendra said. "You're saying that you had no communication with Barrett after that day when he attacked you?"

She shook her head and said bitterly, "I suppose he was a little busy when they started digging up his other victims."

"That could be true. But it's become clear that he never forgot you."

"You think he had some sick obsession for me? Even if that's the case, his only goal was to murder me once he had raped me."

"How do you know for sure?"

"Because he had a butcher knife pressed on my throat, and he was telling me all the ways he was going to cut me into pieces," she said sarcastically. "Don't you believe that would be proof enough?"

Kendra nodded. "I had to ask."

"Well, now you know. If your curiosity is satisfied, I'd like you to leave."

"It's not satisfied. I'm afraid I've just begun. If you've had no contact with Barrett, how did he get hold of your swim goggles?"

"What?" Her eyes widened. "My goggles?"

Kendra held up a photo of the goggles she found in Barrett's cell.

Tricia squinted at the photo. "I lost those about a year ago." She inhaled sharply. "*He* had them?"

"You said you lost them about a year ago," Kendra said. "Is it possible he got them before then? Or maybe even back when he attacked you?"

She shook her head. "No. No way. I just started using that style in the last year and a half. Barrett was already in jail when I lost those."

"Are you sure?"

"Positive. I know exactly when those went missing. It was a big deal. They had expensive prescription lenses. How would Barrett get hold of them?"

"That's what I'm trying to figure out." Kendra leaned forward. "Can you tell me the approximate time and place you found out they were missing? Were you aware of any strangers in the vicinity? Or did you take them with you when you went somewhere?"

"Stop." Tricia motioned for her to be quiet. "I realized they were missing the day after the fall meet here at the university. I had a practice session, and I couldn't find them. Yes, there were all kinds of strangers here that day. It was a meet, for goodness' sake. I didn't take them with me anywhere. The last I remembered they were in the waterproof kit in my swim bag. Any other questions?"

"Not right now."

"Well, then I have a question. How the hell did

Barrett get those goggles? You must have some idea, if you're here asking me about them?"

"We don't know. That's why I'm asking the questions. I found them in his cell yesterday and turned them over to the FBI. We're searching for answers."

"Why? He's dead, isn't he? Tell me he's dead."

"He's dead. No doubt about it." She paused. "But when I went to the blast site, I found something that led me to think that he might not have been the one who planted that bomb. It's possible he may have been working with someone else."

"Shit," Tricia whispered. "I had no idea."

Kendra nodded and handed her a card. "That's what I thought. But I had to be sure. If you can think of anything else, will you call me?"

"I will." She closed her eyes for an instant. "I thought I was through with him. But he's back, like a ghost hovering over me." She straightened and lifted her chin. "It won't make a difference. I won't let him win. I don't know what's happening, but we'll find out." She looked into Kendra's eyes. "*You'll* find out. I know about you. You're smart and if anyone can solve this nightmare, you can. It *is* a nightmare, isn't it?"

"Yes. A lot of people died out there."

"Then don't let anyone else die." She got off the desk. "If I can help, notify me right away. You can't stop fighting, you know."

"I realize that's your philosophy. It's mine, too." She added, "I'll try to get the Bureau to reactivate your protection until we're sure that you're safe."

"That would be good. But safe from whom? It's more difficult this time." She smiled and lifted her hand. "If worse comes to worst, I'll just take care of myself. Thank you for coming. Goodbye." She left the office.

"You promised her protection," Lynch said. "It might be difficult to persuade Griffin. We don't have a proven murderer on the loose. Flimsy evidence at best."

"I'll call him right away, I'll persuade him," Kendra said grimly. "Or I'll do the job myself. There has to be a reason that she's still involved in this. I won't let anything happen to her. I *like* her."

"I got that impression. But it might not be an easy job." His gaze followed Tricia as she shed the robe and dived into the pool. "I was just wondering how good you are at swimming."

———

For the first time in a long while, he felt *alive*.

Milo adjusted his backpack and took cover behind the gum trees near the campus aquatic center. He'd been doing his homework, logging Tricia Walton's comings and goings and pinning down her daily schedule to the minute. Intelligence wasn't enough; it took patience and discipline to gather the necessary information to formulate a plan and execute it with grace and precision.

Only the best for you, Tricia.

He'd been given an unexpected bonus with the arrival of Kendra Michaels and her tough-looking friend. They'd spent at least fifteen minutes with Tricia. For what purpose?

Information gathering? A warning? Maybe a bit of both.

Either way, he had a new variable to consider. It couldn't be more perfect.

The moment he'd been waiting for was finally here.

The game was on once more.

CHAPTER

6

Surveillance?" Griffin repeated. "You can't say I haven't been cooperating, Kendra. But now you're out of bounds. You haven't given me any proof that Tricia Walton would need it. You haven't given me any proof, period. Except..."

"Except?"

"You were right. There's no way Barrett could have planted that bomb."

"How do you know?"

"The Evidence Response Team found fragments of a blast cap. It was of a type that has been manufactured only in the last five months. There's no way Barrett could have put that there. Someone else did it. But you still haven't given me any evidence that Tricia Walton is in danger."

"We're working on it. You'll have proof as soon as we do," Kendra said. "What if I'm right? And what if some enterprising reporter finds that out, but it's too late for Tricia Walton? That wouldn't look good for the Bureau. Why not assign an agent to keep her safe for the next week and give us a chance to get that proof?"

Griffin was silent. "Three days. No more."

"I'll take it," Kendra said. "But I'll be knocking on your door if that's not enough time."

"I won't be answering," Griffin said sourly. "You really believe this, don't you?"

"I believe it's worth our best shot. I keep thinking of Metcalf and Cynthia and all those other agents. You should be, too."

"You know I am, and I always will. But I need proof, Kendra." He cut the connection.

Kendra turned to Lynch. "You heard him; we've got three days."

"And you managed Griffin very well. I could even detect a certain softening. Amazing."

"I only got three days. He'll be tougher if I have to go back and plead my case again."

"I have faith in you. But just in case, we'd better get busy. Drop me off at your condo. I have to pick up my car so that I can chase down a few prison contacts that might help with info."

"You show up in that car and your prison contacts might take it away from you," she said dryly.

"Attempt to," he corrected. "But that would only make it more interesting. They'd be much more likely to furnish me with anything I wanted afterward."

"You're not inviting me to come along?"

"You might be a distraction. After all, I let you question Tricia."

She shrugged. "Then I'll go my own way. I do have my own informants."

"Really? Who?"

"Jackie Gabert. A perfectly charming woman who might be a wealth of information about Barrett. She's one of the persons of interest the FBI told me about when Griffin had them fill me in on Barrett's background."

"If you thought she'd be a wealth of information, you would have told me about her sooner. You didn't even bother to tell me about her."

She made a face. "Because the FBI has eliminated her as either a Barrett accomplice or someone of interest in the suicide/murders in Pine Valley. She had cast-iron alibis and wasn't around at the time Barrett was having his killing sprees. At first, I thought I might be able to squeeze her for information, but I didn't even want to talk to her after they told me her background."

"Indeed? What is her background?"

"She was Barrett's fiancée. Evidently, she is one of those women who become fascinated by criminals in prison. She wrote him and then she visited him constantly during the first few months after he was arrested and still being allowed visitors. Later when the charges started piling up, they stopped all visitations, but by that time they were engaged."

"Maybe she *can* tell you something," Lynch said. "He might have spilled his guts when true love struck."

"That's why I'll go see her this afternoon. But I can't imagine Barrett telling her anything that might hurt his chances in court. Maybe he was just trying to set her up to help break him out." She grimaced. "She must be either a criminal herself or a complete nutcase. The idea of her wanting to get close to a homicidal maniac like Barrett makes me shudder."

"Maybe you'll get lucky, and she'll turn you down for an interview," Lynch said. "Or maybe she'll convince you that everyone was wrong about him, and she's going to write a million-dollar tell-all book that will prove it to the entire world."

"I'll take option number one," Kendra said gloomily. She'd drawn up in front of the condo and watched him get out of the car. "I'll call you later and tell you how it went."

"I can hardly wait." He waved and disappeared down the ramp leading to the garage.

Stop hesitating. Tricia only had three days. Kendra sighed and reached for her phone.

———▸———

"Adam Lynch, get your ass in here."

Lynch smiled. He was on the sidewalk outside the closed Sapphire Dance Club when a familiar woman's voice boomed from a pair of speakers over the glass front doors. He'd know that Filipina accent anywhere.

He looked up at the overhead security camera. "The door's locked, Ula. Exactly how am I supposed to get my ass in?"

The door buzzed, and he heard the lock disengage. Lynch pulled on the door and entered the empty nightclub.

It was dark except for a few spotlights over the long bar. Oddly, the club appeared smaller than it did when packed with hundreds of drinking and dancing revelers, as it was almost every night of the week.

"Welcome, Adam Lynch!" Ula appeared in a stairwell doorway at the back of the club. She was a well-coiffed Filipina in her seventies who on this after-noon wore a formfitting purple dress. Thirty years before, Ula had run one of Manila's most ruthless criminal organizations, but she'd left that life behind to pursue her dream of owning a club in America. Her stateside activities still weren't completely legal, but law-enforcement agencies largely left Ula alone due to her willingness to share information when needed.

"Ula, you haven't changed." He hugged her.

"Liar. But I'll accept your compliment anyway." She gestured toward the large white booths just off the dance floor. "Have a seat, my friend."

They sat down, and Lynch motioned around the room. "The place looks good. You've remodeled."

"We must move with the times, no? I only have a few years with each set of customers. Then they get married, buy homes, and have kids. I always have to keep an eye on what the next generation will want."

"You'll outlive them all, Ula."

She cut loose with a high-pitched laugh that was uniquely her own. Lynch tried to imagine the bearer of that laugh ordering brutal revenge killings against rival gangs in Manila. It didn't fit, but he had no reason to doubt the Justice Department dossiers he'd read about her.

She patted his hand. "It's good to see you, but I don't think this is just a social call."

"You're right, Ula. I need some information."

"Ah, I see. Somehow, I don't think you want to know about the most dependable liquor wholesalers."

"No. I'm more interested in how one might move contraband to an inmate inside the McArthur Deten-tion Center."

She raised one of her thin sculpted eyebrows. "And you think I could help you do such a thing?"

"I know you could, Ula. And you know that I know. You have connections everywhere."

She smiled. "Three questions for you: What do you want to smuggle inside, who do you want to get it to, and how much are you willing to pay?"

"I don't want to smuggle anything. I'm just looking for some information. How would something get to someone inside?"

She shrugged. "A guard is the easiest way, of course. But unless you know which guards are open to such transactions, it can be tricky. If you happen to pick a Boy Scout, you might find yourself under arrest. Not ideal."

"I'm guessing you know which guards to approach."

"Not offhand, but I know people who would."

"There's a particular transaction I need to know more about. The FBI is making inquiries, but I'm quite sure no one there will want to talk to them. Where would I start?"

She thought for a moment. "I do know there's an inmate there who runs things. He's called Adelmo. Some members of his old gang used to spend time here."

"I should talk to him."

She cut loose with that laugh again. "No, not you. Someone he trusts."

"You?"

"No. But someone I know. Give me some specifics."

"I need to know who smuggled something to an inmate there. James Michael Barrett."

Her eyes widened. "The serial killer? The man who blew himself up?"

"Yes. There may be another killer out there, and this might help us find him. We need to talk to whoever smuggled a certain object to him. This person may be able to help identify this second killer."

"That's what this is all about?"

"Yes. We're not looking to jam anybody up for smuggling contraband."

"What did he have? Narcotics? A cell phone?"

"No. A pair of stolen swim goggles."

She looked at him in disbelief. "Swim goggles."

"Yes."

"Well, no one's likely to get in much trouble for *that*."

"Exactly. I just want some information. Who arranged it?"

She sat back in her chair and shook her head. "Swim goggles. Hmm. I'll make some calls and get back to you."

"Thanks, Ula."

"Anything for you, Lynch."

───◆───

"You're Kendra Michaels?" Jackie Gabert threw the door open. "Welcome. I've been wanting to meet you ever since I started to read those newspaper articles about you. I thought you and I would be on the same wavelength. Come in, come in."

Kendra came into the foyer. "Really? And would you care to tell me what that wavelength is?"

"Certainly. Two women who have intelligence and the power to force other individuals and situations surrounding us to give us what we want." She smiled. "I could see that in you the moment I read those articles about you, and now I see it in person. Do you see it in me?"

"Perhaps." What Kendra could see in Jackie Gabert was an attractive brunette woman in her thirties with a personality that was as powerful as she claimed. Kendra could almost sense the vibrancy of that self-will reaching out to enfold her. "I do see you're a woman who wants her own way, Miss Gabert."

"Jackie." She threw back her head and laughed. "You're being careful. I usually am, too, with strangers. But I don't feel you're a stranger. Why do you think I permitted you to come and interview me? I realized we were soulmates and I wanted someone to talk to." Her voice lowered. "I'm in mourning, you know."

"I understand that you were engaged to Barrett."

"And you don't understand why I would mourn him?" She motioned toward two chairs across the room. "Sit down. I've made tea. We'll talk and I'll tell you. There are all kinds of mourning, you know." She brought the teakettle and poured tea into the two cups. "And reasons for a person to mourn that may not be in the usual vein."

"Other than sorrow?"

"Rather the knowledge of things lost."

"What things?"

"It depends on what is of the most value to you." She smiled. "First, you must realize what that is. I came to that conclusion when I was a teenager. After that, it was merely a question of going after it." She paused. "You're not drinking your tea."

"I've been too fascinated with what you've been saying." It was the truth, she thought. This woman was like trying to open a Chinese puzzle box, but she felt she was getting closer. "You knew I was coming here because of Barrett's death, and you permitted it. You're obviously intelligent and I understand you have a respected background as a freelance feature writer. You must have known that there was no way I could approve of your relationship with a murderer like Barrett. What are you trying to tell me?"

"I'm trying to tell you I don't care if you approve or disapprove of my relationship with Barrett." She smiled. "Because the only reason I allowed you to come today was because I wanted to interview *you*. I thought I'd allow you to ask me whatever questions you chose and in return I'd get to know if you suited me."

"Suited you? I beg your pardon."

She laughed with genuine amusement. "But you never beg anyone's pardon. You say exactly what you mean and you let everyone accept or reject it. I told you I'd studied you."

"What do you mean, suited you?"

"You're very strong and determined. You'd be a magnificent challenge. I wanted to know if it would be worth my while to concentrate on training you to replace Barrett."

Kendra stared at her, stunned. "What the hell do you mean?"

She shook her head. "You're thinking about sex? You underestimate me. That was never why Barrett was drawn to me. Though it might have been a weapon I might have used later. It certainly wasn't why I was drawn to him."

"Then why were you drawn to him?"

"Ahh, the interview begins." Jackie took a sip of her tea. "It was all about power. I pretended to believe he was innocent, but I'm smart and I did my research. Before I visited him that first day, I knew that he'd killed all those women. It was what attracted me to him. The numbers intrigued me more than anything else. One or two deaths aren't unusual, but he kept on. I thought that might indicate a stamina and power worth tapping. So, I decided that I'd experiment with the control factor."

"Control factor?"

"You haven't found how fascinating control can be?" She leaned forward. "I could teach you," she said softly. "You choose someone strong and then you use your mind and what other skills you have to make them do exactly what you want them to do. It can be thrilling."

Kendra couldn't believe this woman. "Or sickening."

"You'd learn to love it. It's completely exhilarating. I started to experiment with it when I was a teenager. By the time I went to the university, I was very, very good."

"Good enough to hypnotize Barrett?"

"That nonsense has nothing to do with control. It's all about mental acuity and determination."

"Barrett?" she prompted.

"I was almost there," she said impatiently. "The timing was wrong. They stopped allowing me to visit him."

"How do you know you were almost there?" Kendra asked. "Did he confide in you?"

"No, but he'd mention things now and then. I could tell he was beginning to trust me."

"What things? People? Tricia Walton?"

"Tricia," she repeated. "Yes, that was the name."

"What did he say?"

"Nothing much. Just that he'd taken care of her."

"Nothing else?"

She shook her head. "I never asked questions. That wasn't the way it was with us."

"That's right, it was all about power. I'm afraid I haven't seen an example."

"Are you making fun of me?" Jackie was suddenly no longer amused. "That isn't wise. Everything I've told you is the truth. It wasn't my fault that I wasn't able to quite complete what I started. First, it was the timing, then it was Barrett himself. He shouldn't have listened to anyone but me or he wouldn't have ended up in the morgue."

Kendra stiffened. "Who *did* he listen to, Jackie?"

"How do I know?" Jackie asked bitterly. "He'd never talk to me about him, but I knew there was someone in the background. Sometimes I thought he might be using me as a front." Then she vehemently shook her head. "No, I won't believe that. I almost had him."

"Maybe you did," Kendra said. "But it would help if you could remember a little more about anyone else in Barrett's life."

"There's nothing to remember," she said curtly. "If I'd asked questions, I would have lost any chance of maintaining my influence over Barrett. It's a very complex game, and I never lose."

"I rather think you did this time," Kendra said. "And I'd be careful about indulging in any other power plays. You might not be as adept as you think."

"You know nothing," Jackie said. "I was foolish to think I might be able to teach you anything."

"I thought the entire point was to dominate, not teach," Kendra said. "And there's no way I would have let you get near me no matter what you decided." She got to her feet and headed for the door. "You're bad news, and I think Barrett may have deserved you."

"You're wrong, he didn't deserve me. Or he wouldn't have been on that hill getting himself blown to pieces." She was trying to smile. "You don't deserve me, either. But if I change my mind, I'll let you know."

Kendra shivered with distaste. "Please don't."

She slammed the door.

———◆———

Lynch was leaning against the wall beside Kendra's front door when the elevator opened forty minutes later.

"Oh, for goodness' sake, what are you doing?" she said in disgust. "Why didn't you let yourself in?"

He gestured toward her condo. "Because I told you I wouldn't." He watched her unlock the door and throw it open. "I thought you'd probably be back soon." His gaze raked her face. "You probably wish it had been even sooner. Do I detect impatience and perhaps disgust?"

"You do." She threw her handbag on the couch. "And you should have opened the damn door. I didn't need to see you leaning out there like an orphan. You make rules for yourself and then I'm supposed to feel rotten when you end up like that. I refuse to feel rotten."

"That's good, I'd hate it if you got any worse-tempered." He smiled. "Could I get you a drink?"

"No, people seem to be continually pouring alcohol down me." She went to the refrigerator and got a Coke. "Though that idiot woman gave me tea. Maybe she wanted to prove something or other. That seemed to be her plan for the day."

"Jackie Gabert? She apparently pissed you off."

"How did you guess?" she asked. "The woman was certifiable. I couldn't decide if she was hitting on me or just spinning a tall tale. Perhaps a little of both."

"Hitting on you?"

"I don't really think so. It was all bullshit about power and how Barrett should never have paid attention to anyone but her." She grimaced. "Like I said, certifiable."

"Nothing about Tricia Walton?"

"Only that Barrett said that she'd been taken care of." She took a swallow of Coke. "The only thing that was interesting was that she thought that Barrett was paying attention to someone else's advice, and she didn't like it." She shrugged. "I got the impression she might have been jealous of him."

"Him?"

"That was how she referred to him. No name. Evidently Barrett didn't give her any details about anyone in his past. If she thought she was succeeding in controlling the bastard, she had a long way to go." She had a sudden thought. "She didn't like it that Barrett listened to anyone else. Listening? Controlling? I believe that she was thinking of it as the same thing. She believed that the mark she'd chosen was being controlled by someone else. It would have been a bitter blow to her."

"Could you go back and try to squeeze a little more out of her?"

She slowly shook her head. "She kept saying that she never asked questions. She was clearly walking a tightrope even if she swore she was making progress in her game with Barrett. But it's something to know that there might have been someone out there who could make Barrett jump through hoops. It almost makes putting up with Jackie worth it." She dropped down on the couch. "Thanks for listening to me vent. Did you have any luck with your contacts?"

"A strong possibility that I might be on the right track if Ula comes through for me."

"Ula? A woman?"

"An exceptional woman, but not one that I'd want to compare with the lady you spent the last couple hours with. Well, perhaps in one category. Ula isn't as much into control as she used to be, but there still lingers a bit that may prove valuable to us. But any control she exerts is always razor-sharp and clearly defined. Actually, you might like to meet her. She could act as a palate cleanser after what you went through with Jackie Gabert."

"You could have taken me with you before." She shrugged. "But I did learn a few things." She smiled. "And I wouldn't have wanted to get in your way while you were dealing with your 'exceptional' friend."

"I believe I could tolerate it." He got to his feet. "Now do you want to go out to dinner, or should we go downstairs and see if we can persuade Olivia to make us one of her fantastic salads? I vote for Olivia. I think you need to be exposed to sanity and affection after your bout with a crazy megalomaniac."

"I'll vote for that, too." She finished her Coke and threw the can in the recycling bin. "Now all we have to do is persuade Olivia. But she's usually willing to—"

Lynch's phone rang.

He held up his hand and punched ANSWER. "You've got it, Ula?" He listened. "Okay, I'm on my way." He ended the call and looked at Kendra. "Olivia and sanity? Or are you coming with me?"

She was already heading for the front door. "Where are we going, Lynch?"

———◆———

Lynch and Kendra stopped at BB's Café in National City, a Filipino restaurant on one of the community's main thoroughfares. The place was busy even though it was well after lunchtime.

Ula waved from a table near the back of the dining room. "Over here, Adam Lynch."

Kendra smiled. "Does she always call you by your first and last names?"

"Always." As they approached, he made the introductions. "Ula, this is Kendra Michaels."

Ula waved to the seats opposite her. "Please, please sit down."

Lynch glanced around. "I've never been here. How's the food?"

"Excellent, of course!" Ula threw her head back and laughed. "I own the place!"

"Seriously?" Lynch said. "I thought you just had the club."

"Oh, no. I own three other restaurants in this neighborhood. They're all good, but this one is the best. But if you have a problem with the food, I wouldn't mention it to the chef. He used to work for me in Manila. I won't tell you about his previous line of work, but trust me, you don't want to get on his bad side."

Lynch and Kendra looked toward the back of the restaurant, where a large, muscular man in a dirty chef's apron appeared in a doorway. He wore a surly expression.

Kendra raised her eyebrows. "Is that blood on his apron?"

"He was cutting fresh beef for the asado. But let's just say he's comfortable wearing that."

"I believe it," Lynch said. "You have some information for me? I was surprised to hear from you so quickly."

"It isn't like the old days. Now there are probably twenty cell phones hidden among the inmate population there. Information can flow quickly if you know the right people."

Kendra smiled. "I understand you know all the right people."

"I know enough. Including who got those goggles inside the jail."

"A guard?" Lynch said.

"No. A construction guy."

"Really?"

"Yes. There's been remodeling work going on there for the last couple of years. New flooring, drywall, things like that. It's an outside construction crew, and some prisoners have been allowed to join the team. Someone on the outside contacted one of the craftsmen and paid him to get those goggles to your serial killer."

Lynch nodded. "It would help if we could get the construction guy's name."

Ula reached for a takeout menu on the table and flipped it over. "A name like this one?"

Kendra and Lynch leaned forward to see *Stewart Dusenberry, Avalon Construction*, written in purple ink.

Ula looked at their amazed reactions and cut loose with yet another high-pitched laugh. "Ula delivers, yes?"

"Yes." Lynch took the menu. "Again, I'm amazed you got this so quickly."

"I told you, there's little that happens in that jail without Adelmo knowing about it. One of his crew arranged the transfer from this man."

Lynch took the menu and stood up. "Thanks, Ula. This will be extremely helpful."

She looked disappointed. "You won't stay and have something to eat?"

"Sorry. Perhaps another time. We need to find and talk to this man."

Kendra stood and gestured toward the still-glowering cook. "Our regrets to the chef."

———◄———

Lynch pulled out his phone and thumb-typed through a variety of search screens before they even reached his car. "Got him. Stewart Vincent Dusenbery. He has his own flooring installation business. Some residential, some commercial, but he also contracts out to other construction companies." Lynch leaned against his car as he continued typing. "You don't mind if I violate this man's privacy rights, do you?"

She crossed her arms. "I know I *should* mind."

He smiled. "Of course you should. But since there's a mass murderer on the loose, and I'm not presently working for any government agency…"

"Enough rationalizations. What are you doing?"

"Saving us time and legwork."

"How?"

"By tapping into the tracking device he carries in his pocket."

"His phone? You're accessing his phone?"

"Not yet." Lynch's fingers flew across his screen. "Give me another forty seconds or so."

"What's scary is that you're using government tools to do this. Tools you're obviously accustomed to using."

"Lucky for us."

"Hmm. What does it say about me that I'm going along with this?"

"I don't know…Maybe that you want a killer off the streets as quickly as possible?"

She thought about it. "Okay, we'll go with that."

He showed her his phone screen. "Got it. He's in Cherokee Point."

"His home?"

"No, he lives in Lincoln Park."

"Of course, you would already know that."

"I can also tell you how much he owes on his mortgage."

"And not his Mastercard balance?"

"Visa. A little over eleven thousand dollars."

"Unbelievable."

"I take that as a compliment."

Kendra climbed into the passenger seat. "Let's go talk to him."

CHAPTER

7

Their drive to the Cherokee Point neighborhood took less than fifteen minutes, and the phone's map app immediately directed them to a construction site near the intersection of the I-805 and I-15 freeways. It was a six-story office building with what appeared to be a large central plaza. The complex still appeared to be several months from completion.

"It doesn't look like anyone's here," Kendra said.

"It's almost six. Almost every construction crew I've ever known clears out at five on the dot. But according to my tracking app…" He nodded to a white pickup truck parked near a construction trailer. "That's Dusenberry's truck."

"Are you sure?"

"Positive. That's his license plate."

They stopped next to the truck and climbed out. It was almost dusk, and a cool ocean breeze had begun to blow over the construction site. Kendra looked inside the pickup's driver's side window.

"Does that tell you anything?" Lynch asked.

"Not much. Other than he *really* likes Taco Bell."

"Anything else?"

She took another look. "Well, he's probably shorter than average height, a somewhat intense driver, maybe even prone to fits of road rage. And he travels up the I-15 freeway toward Escondido fairly often."

"Whoa. Okay, I figure you got his height from the position of the seat. What about the road rage?"

"Look how worn the leather on the wheel is. He grips that thing to within an inch of its life. Definitely not a relaxed driver. Almost every angry driver I've ever known has a steering wheel that looks just like that."

"I-15?"

"He has a FasTrak freeway electronic toll tag clipped to the visor. No one would go through the trouble of getting one unless they used it regularly. The I-15 is the only major local freeway that uses the FasTrak payment system."

Lynch nodded. "Between the two of us, we know everything about him except the one thing we really want to know."

"Then hadn't we better get it out of him?" She pointed to the construction trailer. "Should we start there?"

They approached the structure and tried the door. Locked. Lynch peered through warped blinds covering the windows. "No one here. I'm starting to get the feeling that he may have gone out for an after-work beer with his coworkers. If that's the case, we may be waiting here until someone brings him back here for his truck."

"Maybe not." Kendra cocked her head. "Do you hear that?"

He listened. "Footsteps?"

She pointed toward the building. "From that direction. Let's go."

Before they could move, a man's scream echoed across the empty plaza!

Lynch pulled out his gun. "Hurry!"

They bolted across the plaza and climbed an uneven set of cement stairs. They entered the building's large ground-floor opening, which would obviously one day become a grand foyer.

"Oh, God." Kendra stopped short. Just a few feet in front of her, a man was lying on his back, throat cut and impaled on three lengths of iron rebar protruding from the concrete floor.

Lynch knelt beside him. "It's Dusenberry. I recognize him from his driver's license photo."

Kendra spun around as she heard something. Then she went still. "Whoever did this is still here."

"Which way?"

Her gaze was already searching deep into the bowels of the dark building, where concrete dust was swirling in the air. "There."

They ran into the shadowy corridor, slowing only to listen for footsteps echoing ahead.

The footsteps stopped.

Kendra put her hand on Lynch's arm. "Hold up." They stopped to listen.

Silence.

Lynch raised his gun and stepped forward. The last tinges of daylight crept around the tall pillars, casting long shadows over the concrete corridor. He motioned toward the right side. They ducked low and moved from pillar to pillar, watching for any sign of their prey.

No trace. Damn.

Kendra froze. Had she just heard the sound of someone breathing up ahead? Maybe slightly to the left…

She glanced at Lynch and cocked her head toward the shadows before them. He nodded and raised his gun again.

He took one step, then another…

BLAM-BLAM-BLAM!

Gunfire rained from the dark corridor. Lynch went one direction, Kendra went another, each taking cover behind a different pillar.

BLAM!

She turned back just in time to see Lynch's body fall in a heap onto the cement floor. His eyes were closed, and blood trickled from his head.

No!

She stifled the impulse to cry out. She needed to go to him, to hold him, to help him…

But she couldn't.

Not with that maniac still out there.

"Hello, Kendra." A voice with a deep-throated rasp came out of the darkness ahead. "I didn't expect to see you here."

She froze, shocked.

Don't speak. He wanted her to respond and give away her location.

"Oh, I know exactly where you are," he said as if reading her mind. "You're directly catacorner from me. Let's have a civilized conversation, shall we?"

She finally spoke. "There's nothing civilized about you."

"Come now. We both know better than that. I'm sure your profilers have told you you're dealing with someone of significant intellect."

When he spoke, she slowly moved into the shadows. Maybe, just maybe, his voice would mask the sound of her movements.

Significant intellect? Significant ego, she wanted to tell him. But she didn't want to give away her new location.

"Talk to me, Kendra. If you talk to me, maybe I'll let you take care of your friend. He might still be alive. I'm usually very accurate, but you didn't give me the opportunity to check."

Mustn't let him get under her skin. His words had brought a picture of Lynch lying there helpless. But that had been exactly his intention.

Use this opportunity to figure out who the hell this was.

Close your eyes. Concentrate.

He was probably a man in his thirties or forties, likely from the Upper Midwest. He'd seemed to have a slight shuffle in his walk. An injury? But that wasn't enough.

Surely there was something else…

"I'm impressed by you, Kendra. Do I impress you?"

Don't answer. Resist the urge to tell him how totally repulsed she was by him.

"If you won't talk to me, perhaps I should go see if your friend has any words on the matter."

She'd been continuing to move whenever he spoke, but this stopped her in her tracks. Even if she could get away, how in the hell could she leave Lynch alone with that monster?

She couldn't.

But without a weapon, how was she supposed to—

Wait.

Coiled on the floor in front of her was a long red

hose. But not for water, she realized; it was attached to a four-foot tank of compressed air.

The other end was attached to a large device she knew would take both hands to lift and operate. She'd seen one before at Habitat for Humanity building projects where she'd volunteered.

She listened. The killer was now moving toward Lynch.

She gripped the tank's top nozzle and turned it counterclockwise. The hose shook and shifted on the floor, making more noise than she'd expected.

She'd given away her location. Shit. She'd better make this count...

His voice was sharper now. "What are you doing, Kendra?"

She picked up the heavy device and looked it over. It was a pneumatic nail gun, an industrial-size unit capable of driving small spikes. She had no idea how to check and see how many spikes were in the feeder chamber.

She uncoiled the hose and looked back toward the entrance. The sun had finally set, casting the area in almost complete darkness.

Good.

She walked as quietly as she could, pulling the hose behind her.

The killer wasn't talking anymore. He was obviously trying to get a bead on her position.

Now if only she could get a bead on *his*.

She heard something. Not a footstep, but a rustling of fabric. He was now a few yards to her right.

She felt for the spike gun's power switch and switched it on. It hummed to life.

She heard those familiar shuffling footsteps.

Heading her way.

Closer.

Still closer...

She raised the gun.

Now!

She fired half a dozen steel spikes into the void, making sure to avoid the area where she knew Lynch was still lying.

The man screamed! At least one of the spikes had made contact. He dove behind another pillar. His breathing was labored; he was clearly in pain.

Perfect.

"Just go," she said. "Now!"

"Sorry, Kendra. I'm not finished here."

She fired another spike. "Go!"

He was on the move again. It wasn't toward her, and it wasn't toward Lynch. Had she convinced him?

She listened for another moment. He was still nearby, crouched not far from where she'd just been.

She raised the spike gun and zeroed in on the movement. Then, out of nowhere, there was an ear-shattering sound of escaping air.

She took aim and squeezed the trigger.

Nothing.

She tried again.

It still didn't work.

He'd cut the hose!

Footsteps. He was now walking toward her. Slowly at first, then quickly. She threw down the still-humming spike gun and backed away.

BLAM! BLAM!

Gunshots. But not from him.

From Lynch, she realized. He was alive! Thank God!

BLAM!

Lynch's third shot must have hit the killer. His firearm clattered on the concrete as he dropped it.

He backed away. "Not the end. Until later, Kendra."

He disappeared into the shadows, and his running footsteps receded to the far side of the building.

She ran to Lynch and crouched beside him. "Be still. Your head is still bleeding."

He tried to sit up. "Guess that's what happens when a bullet grazes your skull."

"Are you sure that's all it is?"

"We wouldn't be having this conversation otherwise. But I have a *monster* headache."

She pulled out her phone. "I'm calling for a paramedic."

"Never mind that. Call the cops and the FBI. They need to find this guy."

She gently pushed him back down. "Absolutely. I'll phone them all."

———◆———

Griffin showed up before the medical team. But he'd brought a forensics crew with him. He took a quick look at Lynch's head wound. "You're okay. I always knew that you were hardheaded. Where's the body?"

"I'll show you," Kendra said. "I don't think Lynch needs to be walking around until he gets clearance from the EMTs. Though I agree he does have a very hard head." She saw the ambulance coming toward the site. "I'll be right back, Lynch."

"Take your time," Lynch said.

"Why? We've done his job. Now Griffin and his forensics teams can give us what we need. We almost both got killed. I'm a bit pissed off."

Lynch chuckled. "You heard her, Griffin. You don't want to get Kendra pissed off."

"Don't I?" he asked sourly.

"I'll be right back," Kendra repeated as she strode after him. "Come on, Griffin."

Kendra was as good as her word and was back with Lynch and the EMTs in eight minutes. They were in the ambulance and on their way to an ER for X-rays five minutes later.

"What did you tell Griffin?" Lynch asked curiously.

"I told him that he said he wanted proof that there was another killer out there and we'd given it to him. Dusenberry's corpse was self-explanatory."

Lynch laughed. "And what did Griffin say?"

Her lips were twitching. "Lots of gruff obscenities. But they ended with him saying he'd think about it. That was good enough for me for the time being." She paused. "But that bastard knew who we were. He recognized me and called me by name. I'm wondering exactly how much he knew about what we've been doing since that first explosion."

"No telling. It's been slow and painstaking for the most part."

"Not like it was tonight."

He shook his head. "No one could call tonight by that description under any circumstances. Personally, I was encouraged."

"Even with that bump on your noggin?"

"It showed he wasn't that good a shot. And you were much better with the nail gun."

"Until he went after the tubing with—" Her phone was ringing, and she was about to get rid of the call when she saw the ID.

She stiffened. "What the hell?"

Lynch's eyes narrowed on her face. "What?"

"Jackie Gabert. I wasn't going to take the call. But now I can hardly wait. It seems weirdly suitable to be talking to a nutcase like her while I'm in an ambulance on the way to an ER." Kendra pushed ANSWER and SPEAKER. "Hello, Jackie. I thought we'd agreed to disagree. Why do I have this honor?"

"You're being sarcastic, but it is a compliment to you that I decided to give you another chance to change your mind. You didn't really give me an opportunity to explain why I do what I do. You just assumed that I was totally self-absorbed and didn't care anything for Barrett. That was completely wrong. I did care for Barrett, and, if by some chance he'd been released from prison, he would have been very content with me."

"If he'd been released from prison, he would have started murdering again. You'd have probably been first on the list."

"That's how little you know," Jackie said impatiently. "Barrett was weak, the quintessential Beta personality, and he needed an Alpha, someone to control him. I recognized that from the moment I started studying him. When I met him in person, I realized he had all the traits. As long as he had an Alpha person as a partner, he wouldn't have been a threat to anyone. He would have waited for a command. Since I take no pleasure in the kill, I wouldn't have given the command."

"You actually believe that?"

"I do. Do you think I'm the only one out there who runs their lives to suit themselves? I can't tell you how many couples I've found who play my game. I've been an Alpha partner to any number of people over the years. It can be breathtakingly thrilling. I could have had an exciting life with Barrett. He could have had a satisfactory life with me. I was looking forward to a new experience." She paused. "But I might have come into his life too late and missed out. I hate when that happens."

"Is that all you wanted to say to me?" Kendra asked.

"Other than that, you were a mistake. I thought that because you were strong, you might be a challenge, but you would never have given in."

"No, I wouldn't. I'm glad you realize that, Jackie."

"I don't like people not to understand me. It wasn't my fault that Barrett died. I was just too late. He must have already found his Alpha."

She cut the connection.

Lynch looked at Kendra and shook his head. "I can see why you were a bit irritated with her. Jackie Gabert is definitely…unusual."

"She did irritate me the last time, but she didn't just now. I just felt as if I was being caught up in some kind of cult. She didn't think there was anything wrong with the way she was thinking or behaving. She was even trying to convince me there was a world out there like her." She shivered. "I don't want to live in that world. There's no way on earth I could understand it."

"I can understand it," Lynch said wearily. "But I don't want you to live in it, either." He sat up and his hands were cupping her face. "I know that you're not going to stop until this is over, but how about planning a vacation and forgetting about mass murderers and kooks who want to rule the world and things that go bump in the night?"

"Sounds good." She smiled. "But we both know that you're too in demand for Justice to let you get away for too long. Maybe I'll just forget about the FBI for a while and get back to my music therapy work. Last time I checked, my kids didn't want to rule the world."

———◆———

"If you don't want to help, I'll understand, Metcalf," Kendra said after she'd explained what she wanted on the phone. "You're just out of the hospital. I could get Griffin to assign someone else to go through those cold cases and see if I can see any similarities that might give me a clue."

"Don't you dare," Metcalf said. "I've only been home for two days and I'm bored out of my mind. My mom is hovering and won't let me do anything but watch TV. Besides, I have a resource better than whatever files you're sending my way. I have Trey Suber."

Kendra smiled. Trey Suber was one of Metcalf's fellow agents at the San Diego FBI office, and he'd distinguished himself as one of the world's foremost serial killer experts while still in his twenties. A self-professed "serial killer geek," Suber created and maintained an exhaustive online serial killer database in his teenage years, and his self-published serial killer trading card set was in its ninth printing. Kendra had worked with him a few years before when he was at his previous post at the Florida Department of Law Enforcement, and Griffin had lured him to the San Diego FBI office less than a year later. But now Suber was in demand all over the country—and occasionally overseas—and the Bureau higher-ups were making noises about wanting him full-time in Washington, DC.

Kendra clicked her tongue. "Then I shouldn't even bring you the files. Suber knows everything in them and much more."

"Yep, I've told him that many times."

"And I'm sure Suber appreciated that fact," Kendra said dryly. "No one can say he doesn't have an amazing ego to match that exceptional memory."

"I thought you liked him."

"I do. That doesn't mean I don't occasionally get annoyed with trying to pin him down when I need an answer right away. Griffin has a habit of lending him out to other law-enforcement organizations. This time it was Scotland Yard, and I couldn't get a callback from him." She grinned. "But I'll bet you'd get a callback since he works just a few cubicles over from you. Griffin said he even sent you a gift basket at the hospital."

"He did. I guess the one you sent got lost in transit."

"Well, it happens. What did he send? Chocolates?"

"Better. The latest set of *Star Wars* Black Series collectible action figures."

"Wow. From one geek to another."

"You know it."

"Well, if the two of you can tear yourselves away from your *Star Wars* figures and his murderer trading cards, maybe you can identify any patterns that can help us with our case. But I really wish you'd just try to get some rest."

"Not an option. Not after what happened to Cynthia Strode and all the rest. I'll call if we come up with anything."

Metcalf ended the call.

Kendra turned to Lynch. "He could hardly wait to get rid of me. I believe he may be turning into as much of a geek as Suber. I'll bet we'll hear from one or the other of them very soon."

"Maybe," Lynch said. "But it takes a certain drive to maintain the geek mentality. Don't think you're out of the woods where he's concerned. He may be caught up in Suber's mystique at the moment, but that'll fly out the window the second you walk into the room. Geekdom might go down the drain."

"Cynic."

He shook his head. "Realist."

"Well, I'm sure his mother is also a realist and will make sure that he knows I'm not worthy. By the time he's no longer bedridden, she will probably have arranged for him to meet someone she does approve of." She was heading for the door. "I've no intention of worrying about it either way. We never did get around to going down to Olivia's and asking her to fix us that salad. We got too busy that night."

"You could say that," he said grimly. "We're going to try again?"

"Unless you don't want to."

"I always want to see Olivia." He opened the door. "And I haven't paid my respects to Harley lately. I wouldn't want Olivia to be offended…"

<hr />

10:40 A.M.
NEXT DAY

"Really, Kendra, I would have returned your call," Trey Suber said the minute Kendra picked up the phone the next morning. "It would have been discourteous not to, and you shouldn't have intimated to my friend Metcalf here that I was being rude because I'd made new associates at Scotland Yard. You know that you and Lynch come first with me."

"Of course," Kendra said. "And Metcalf defended you and insisted on calling you and proving how cooperative you'd be if you realized how we needed your help. Did he tell you the problem?"

"Naturally, and he's on this Zoom call with me because we tackled your problem and worked all night to solve it."

"Indeed?" Kendra said. "Then I'm doubly grateful. Hello, Metcalf, I believe I told you not to work too hard."

"It wasn't like work," Metcalf said. "It couldn't have been more stimulating. Is Lynch there? He'll want to hear what Suber has to say."

"I'm here," Lynch said. "Kendra called me and told me she'd had a text from you, Metcalf, setting up this call from our old friend Suber. I drove right over. But I admit I'm ready to hear this solution…immediately."

"Well, perhaps not quite a solution," Suber said. "But I might be able to give you more of an idea on what we're dealing with here. Until recently, we thought Barrett was working alone on his murders. Now we're faced with the likelihood that he was working with someone else. Are you familiar with the Alpha-Beta partnership dynamic?"

"We're just beginning to be," Kendra said. "A team in which one partner allows himself to be dominated by the other."

"Exactly. It's rare in the serial killer world, but not unheard of. The silent partner stays in the background, pulling the strings. Their first step is to find someone with an intense interest in serial killers and their crimes."

"Someone like you?"

"You joke, but I got a lot of creepy attention after I started my serial killer website. I was only sixteen, and I didn't know how to deal with some of the weirdos who came out of the woodwork. The Internet has made it easier for these people to find each other. The idea is for the dominant one to nurture that fascination with serial killers to the point that the other one is willing to participate in murders. Like I said, it's not common, but it happens. But I'm sure you've already considered this."

"There have been a few events in this case that have led us in that direction," Kendra said. "What we need to know is if it's likely that a man who has a record of homicides like Barrett would take a partner for just one massacre or if it would more likely have to be an established relationship before it would take place?"

"It could go either way," Suber said. "It depends on how strong the relationship between the two partners is. But it usually takes a long time to develop a complicated arrangement that would support a life-or-death decision." He paused. "Unless both parties are natural-born or psychically damaged killers. Then it only requires that one can overpower the other emotionally or mentally and get their own way."

"The Alpha personality," Kendra said.

"Like I said, that's usually how these duos manage to come together. A stronger personality goes looking for someone to conquer and they usually find them. Character traits can determine how deadly the relationship can be. Sometimes there are no murders involved. But more often the stronger individual wins the day. If they demand deaths, then there will be deaths."

"But you wouldn't think that Barrett would be the weaker considering his background," Lynch said.

"You can never tell. How do you know what kind of background the person who killed Barrett had? Perhaps he'd murdered even more people than Barrett. But the only difference might be how clever he was since he wasn't caught. Or if I were to make a guess, I'd bet that this was a longtime relationship and Barrett's partner killed at least a few of the victims Barrett was charged with when he was arrested."

"And Barrett didn't give him up, but took the hit?"

Suber smiled. "But that's how the relationship works. The Alpha dictates the rules and may kill if he wishes or may designate a kill."

"And still get off scot-free? I can't believe Barrett didn't try to take him down."

"Perhaps he was planning on it," Lynch said suddenly. "Either giving him up to the law or finding another way to get rid of him. Maybe his Alpha partner realized he couldn't trust him any longer and that was the reason he set those charges."

"Actually, that's quite reasonable," Suber said. "These relationships are very secretive by both parties. No one outside the duo ends up knowing about them, not family, priest, or friends. You can see why? Shame or death must be fairly common."

And Suber said that almost without expression, Kendra noticed. It was just an exercise to him. Well, who was she to criticize? Because he studied and became knowledgeable about these monsters, he could tell the rest of the world how to rid themselves of them. "You were studying case files from the last ten years last night. Could you weed out a few of the more likely ones that help us to understand them?"

"Or perhaps pick out one that might zero in on your killer?" He chuckled. "I told you that I wasn't able to do that. Though I wish I could, for the sake of Metcalf and all those other victims. But I'll be glad to try to point out a few that managed to catch the attention of family members or our own agents. I particularly remember one college student, David Spalman, who lived in San Luis Obispo."

"I remember that," Kendra said. "He killed several members of his high school football team."

"Four. He died in an accident before he could be arrested. What you may not remember is that his father swore that he had fallen under the influence of someone else. Someone who practically forced him to do it. According to his dad, Spalman never would have become a killer if this mysterious 'someone' hadn't come into his life."

"Did the father have a name?"

"No. And investigators' attempts to find this person went absolutely nowhere. Either he was amazingly good at covering his tracks, or he never really existed. The agents I spoke to tend to think the father was just looking for someone else to blame. The father had no proof, and the FBI couldn't find anything to substantiate the claim. The question was moot because the kid drove his car off a cliff just as law enforcement was moving in. It sounds like there may be a similar dynamic at work in your case, so you may want to at least talk to this guy and a few others. Metcalf will give you the paperwork." He added, "Good luck catching your monster. Be sure and give me credit when you lock him up."

"It will be our pleasure," Lynch said. "We'll give credit to both you and Metcalf."

"Oh, yes, that's what I meant," Suber said. "Let me know if I can help you again." He ended the call.

"That came very close to what Jackie Gabert said," Kendra said. "And it didn't sound any better coming from Suber. In spite of his very educated accent, it's still nasty stuff."

"All the more reason for us to try to wrap it up," Lynch said. "Come on, we'll drive over to Metcalf's and pick up those files. I'll even volunteer to go to the front door and brave his mother while you cower in the car."

———◆———

3:40 P.M.
HOME OF GERALD SPALMAN
SAN LUIS OBISPO, CALIFORNIA

Kendra and Lynch had made stops at the homes of three other families whose files Metcalf had given them before they ended up at the Spalman residence that Suber had told them about.

Everything about the Spalman home appeared to reflect a typical middle-class California subdivision: red-tiled roof, stucco construction, scarlet hibiscus plant growing in a pot beside the front door.

Everything but the ten-foot chain-link fence encircling the property, and the faded graffiti marks on the walk approaching the front door.

A thin, gray-haired man met Kendra and Lynch as they reached the front porch.

"I'm Gerald Spalman, and I don't know why I said

you could come. You'd think I'd learn." Spalman was frowning as he gestured impatiently for Kendra and Lynch to come into the foyer. "I know that you're not going to do anything. I've been through it all." His eyes squinted on Kendra's face. "You're that lady who was blind. I read all about you. I guess maybe I thought that you might have a different viewpoint than those guys at the FBI who think they're so tough."

"I'm Kendra Michaels." She reached out and shook his hand. "And this is Adam Lynch. We appreciate you letting us come to see you. I'm sure the agents at the FBI did what they could during the investigation. But there was no real evidence."

"And now there is?" Spalman's lips twisted with bitterness. "I don't think so."

"I can't blame you for being cynical. You're right, there's still no proof. But we're looking at the cases from a different viewpoint." She added, "And we're trying to fit your testimony into what we've learned since your son took his own life."

"Because that mass murderer Barrett killed himself, too?" he asked harshly. "It was all over the TV. My David wasn't anything like that Barrett. Barrett was a monster; my David was a good boy before someone got hold of him and messed with his head."

"Have you found out anything more about the person who might have done that?" Lynch asked. "Since you told the FBI that your son had confessed to you that he'd killed those football players, I'm sure you tried to find out who would have tried to influence him."

"Of course I did. After he drove off that cliff, I searched his room and his locker at school, and I found nothing. But I know there was someone in his life...he changed that last year. He didn't talk, and he broke with his old friends. He mentioned the name Milo a couple of times."

"Milo?" Kendra said.

"Yeah. But there's no evidence he even existed. An FBI profiler had a theory that it may have been a figment of David's imagination." Spalman snorted. "Like an imaginary friend. I never believed that. But whatever was happening, David seemed...tormented. He wasn't the same boy."

"In what way?" Kendra asked. "How did he change?"

"Night and day." There was pain, not bitterness, in his expression now. "He loved sports. My wife wouldn't let him play football because she was scared of all those head injuries, but he watched every game. He played hockey and was on the track team." He wrinkled his brow. "Those four football players he killed; they were his heroes. He'd watched and admired them from the time they'd started playing in high school. He always talked about how great they'd do when they made the NFL."

"Sometimes emotions become twisted," Kendra said gently.

"Not with him." His voice was hoarse. "He loved those guys. If they became twisted later, it was because something happened to him that shouldn't have happened. Someone..."

"Anything else?" Lynch asked.

"Little things," his father said. "He had secrets. He'd bring home objects, small gifts, and tell his mother and me that he'd bought them himself." He was silent for a long moment. "And I found he'd burned photos of those four football players in his room. I felt sick."

"I can see why. Would you mind if we searched your son's room?"

"Why should I? There's nothing there that has anything to do with David any longer. He was taken from us, and we'll never get him back. Go ahead. His room is the second one to the left at the top of the stairs." He suddenly turned back to them. "But I should probably tell you our house was broken into a week after David died. The only thing that we found stolen was one of those small objects I told you about. David kept it on a shelf facing his bed. It was the statue of a woman in an old-fashioned outfit. My wife said she remembered she'd seen it when she cleaned his room. There was a plaque on the bottom with her name. NAIAD."

"Did you report it missing?"

He nodded. "I called them once. They didn't seem interested. By that time, I was sick of the FBI. My wife had left me. My son was dead. The neighbors hated us and scrawled graffiti all over our property. What did it matter if some sicko had decided to steal from me? I just built my fence out front higher."

"I'm sorry that you've had such a terrible time," Kendra said as she started up the stairs. "I promise we won't be long."

He didn't answer but went back out on the porch.

And Kendra tried to keep her word. The last thing she wanted was to stay in that sad room that seemed to be weighed down with melancholy. She and Lynch made a perfunctory search, but there didn't appear to be anything that could be considered evidence. Would she have recognized it if she'd found it? Before they left the room she lingered at the door, her gaze circling the bedroom and ending at the empty shelf facing the bed. What had been so important about it to David

Spalman that he'd wanted it to be the last thing he saw before he closed his eyes?

"Kendra?" Lynch asked.

She nodded. "I'm ready to go." She followed him out of the room. "More than ready. What a complete tragedy to strike a family. I wish we'd found—" She suddenly broke off as a thought came to her. "But maybe we did." She hurried down the steps. "Let's get to the car!"

They quickly said goodbye to David's father and then headed for the car. "Give me a minute before you get on the road," Kendra said. "I need to look up something."

"Don't you always?" He got in the driver's seat and turned to look at her. "The statue?"

She nodded, her fingers flying over her phone's touchscreen. Then she found it. "Shit!"

"Bad? Good? Indifferent?"

"Definitely not indifferent. It could be bad or good." She read from the text. "Naiad, a female nature entity. Sometimes they could be considered dangerous because they could take men underwater when fascinated by their beauty. Those men were never seen again."

"Underwater," Lynch repeated.

"Right," Kendra said. "A naiad is a water nymph." She put her hand on his arm and stared him straight in the eye. "She's a swimmer, Lynch."

CHAPTER

8

A swimmer." Lynch had caught the connection immediately. "You're thinking about Tricia Walton. You're reaching, Kendra. It could be coincidence. The same man who was James Barrett's prime influencer also David Spalman's Alpha? Barrett a mass murderer, the Spalman boy a college kid. What are the chances?"

"How the hell do I know?" Kendra's hand tightened on his arm. "As far as I've heard, there aren't any firm statistics that would tell anyone what kind of choices a power-hungry monster with a passion for molding everyone's lives to suit himself would make. I can only look at the similarities and possibilities." She was trying to quickly mentally separate and go through both. "First, we can't be sure when he made contact with Barrett. We do have to assume that his meeting with Spalman was within the last couple of years. For that matter we don't know how many subjects this Alpha would have at the same time any-way. Jackie seemed to think that the Alpha had all the rights and privileges in the relationship."

"What are you getting at?" Lynch asked.

"I'm thinking that if this Alpha wanted to maintain both relationships, he could have decided to use Spalman to pacify Barrett. If Barrett wanted Tricia punished or killed, the Alpha might influence Spalman to do it for him. The killing of those four football players may have been a method to prepare Spalman for the murder of Tricia Walton. It could have been more difficult for Spalman to kill a young woman. The Alpha had the kid position the statue in his bedroom so that he had to look at it every night…He chose a naiad because the legend had already designated her as a killer."

"But he didn't do it," Lynch pointed out.

"He didn't have time. Because he knew the police suspected him of the other killings. His father said they were closing in on him the night he drove off that cliff. He killed himself before he could be arrested." Her gaze was searching his face. "I realize it's fairly thin, but it could have happened that way. He did want to keep Barrett pacified or he would never have arranged for Dusenberry to smuggle those goggles into Barrett's cell." She frowned, feeling her way through the puzzle. "I think he might have done it as a kind of promise. He knew Barrett wanted Tricia dead, and giving Barrett her goggles would have been proof that he'd make it happen."

"All supposition, Kendra," Lynch said. "But very good supposition." He grinned. "All we have to do is figure out who the Alpha is, and a few other small items like when, where, and how."

She made a face. "I don't see any other leads on the horizon, so I'll go with these until you come up with something else." Then she shook her head, troubled. "Or maybe even a bit beyond that time. I don't like the idea of that statue of the swimmer. This creep has already made two promises that Tricia Walton would die. The first were the goggles sent to Barrett, the second the statue given to Spalman."

"So? Both men are dead. Wouldn't that make the promises null and void?"

"I don't *know*," she said. "Neither do you. All we know is that this guy is probably crazy, and we don't have any idea how he thinks." She added bitterly, "Oh, yes. And he kills people. We have to remember that."

"We will," Lynch said. "You've got a three-day promise of surveillance from Griffin. We can build on that."

"That's not enough. We'll have to warn Tricia, too. I have to be honest with her." She was frowning. "And I want to call Jackie Gabert."

"Why?"

"Because if anyone knows how those crazy Alphas think, it would probably be her. She obviously regards herself as belonging to the club. I'll tell her what we discovered here today and see what she says."

"I can't imagine she'd be helpful."

"Neither do I, but I've got to try." She fastened her seat belt. "You go talk to Griffin and see if you can persuade him to extend the agent surveillance time he'll give Tricia. Drop me off at the condo. I'll see what I can get out of Jackie."

"You want me to spin the tale you just concocted about the Spalman kid to Griffin? I thought you'd want to do it."

She shook her head. "Griffin's more likely to believe it coming from you. You're the golden boy as far as the Bureau is concerned. I get a certain amount of respect, but they definitely don't believe I'm one of the crew. I always have to talk them into accepting anything I say."

His gaze searched her expression. "And you're tired of it, and you can't see why they can't see what you see. Sometimes it's worse than others. This is one of those times."

She shrugged. "At least I'm not alone. You could see what I saw this time."

"Even if I question you?"

"Questions are good. They keep us honest. I question you, too."

"True." He was driving away from the house. "If we're being honest, we both know I don't always see what you see right away. There are times when I have to probe and analyze."

"But even then, you don't turn your back and leave me alone with it," she said. "That's important."

"I can understand how it could be," he said quietly. "But you don't have to worry about that. As long as you'll let me stick around, that kind of loneliness isn't going to be a problem for you...."

———————

"All that power," Jackie murmured when Kendra had finished speaking. "Really incredible, and terribly exciting. What did you say was the name of the victim?"

"David Spalman." Kendra's hand tightened on her phone as she concentrated on Jackie's response. It wasn't easy, since they were complete opposites. The woman's reaction seemed to be a mixture of fascination, absorption, and tension. "Do you know him?"

"David Spalman," Jackie repeated. "No, of course not," she added quickly. "I believe I heard something about him when he killed those football players. It caused a big stir, all kinds of stories on all the sports TV stations. Why would you think I'd know anything about it?"

"Because you recognized Tricia Walton's name when I mentioned it," Kendra said. "You told me that Barrett said that she was going to get hers. Spalman had a statue of a woman swimmer in his bedroom on the night he died, but it was stolen from the house a week later. Strange coincidence…"

"Not particularly."

"I disagree. David Spalman's behavior had changed over that year, and his father thought that he was being forced to do those killings. I immediately thought about all you'd said about Alphas, how you'd claimed to be one yourself."

She laughed. "That was all bullshit. You totally fell for it. I was really amused."

"I don't think you were. I think you were telling me the truth. And that boy's father definitely thought he'd been influenced to do those killings."

"Fathers always want to believe their sons are innocent. It doesn't mean they are. Did he give you a name?"

"No." Kendra was trying to be patient. "He didn't know it. So, I thought I'd ask you."

Jackie laughed. "Why? I told you that Barrett rarely talked to me about anyone he knew. We hadn't reached that point in our relationship yet."

"And I believed you. But that doesn't mean that you weren't familiar with other Alphas in this area. You've been involved with this weird cult for years. You can't expect me to believe that you hadn't interacted with other Alphas or their subjects during that time."

"I don't expect anything of you, and you mustn't expect anything of me. Because it was all lies, Kendra."

"And you just want me to go away and leave you alone." Kendra was silent, trying to work a way to get what she needed from the woman. "But you wasted a good deal of my time with your tall tales, and I believe you owe me. Suppose we come to an agreement. I'm not going to try to browbeat you into admitting you might know anything about what Spalman was doing that might incriminate you. All I want you to do is give me the benefit of your expertise to help me get to know what to expect from this particular Alpha. I don't want to make a mistake and get someone killed. I don't know how they think, how any of you think, it's utterly foreign to me. If you help me, I'll give you what you want and leave you alone."

Jackie didn't answer for a moment. "You realize I'd only be guessing since I don't actually know this Alpha?"

"I do. But you're clever, and I'd expect your very best guess. You should be able to accommodate me. I've told you everything we know about how he handled Spalman."

"Yes. It was really fascinating."

Kendra was once more aware of that excitement and admiration in Jackie's tone. But was there also envy?

Another silence. Then Jackie asked, "You won't call down the Feds on me?"

"I wouldn't have grounds. I'm only going to ask you a few questions. I'm just tapping your knowledge about the personality of a certain type of individual you might have run across."

"Then I don't see why I shouldn't help you out. Go ahead, ask your questions."

Kendra released her breath. "Thank you. I'll try not to take too much of your time."

"No problem. I'm actually glad you ran across an Alpha like this. You can judge how much better I would have been if you'd taken me up on my offer."

"I don't believe we got as far as an offer," Kendra said dryly. "I remember I shut you down fairly quickly."

"That's because you didn't realize how natural and healthy it was to have two separate but equal partners in a relationship. One would always dominate and the other would always surrender. Unless permitted to temporarily take precedence by the Alpha." She added earnestly, "I'd have given you that gift frequently. It would be the intelligent thing to do with a partner who has so many Alpha qualities. I wouldn't be like that Alpha of Spalman's. That must have been total domination."

"You're not being convincing," Kendra said grimly. "Let's forget about any weird plans you had for me and concentrate on answering my questions. I didn't realize there were differences in the amount of power exerted by the Alpha. You guys don't have some kind of standard rule?"

"Of course not," Jackie said impatiently. "It's all about intelligence and how far an Alpha can push the Beta subject. Most of the Alphas I've run across have taken extensive courses in psychology to train themselves."

"That's bizarre."

"But it has rich dividends. If you're good, you can write your own ticket. I'd bet Spalman's Alpha is very, very good. It sounds to me as if he took a long time preparing and then setting the kid up."

"And twisted him from being a normal student to something tortured and ugly," Kendra said harshly.

"I said that he was good at what he did," Jackie said. "Not that he had any kind of moral compass. That's always up to the individual. And, in a way, that choice is part of the excitement."

Kendra didn't know how much more of this she could take. "The most important questions I need to ask concern what you believe this Alpha would do about his promise to Barrett about getting rid of Tricia Walton for him. Barrett is dead, and so is Spalman. Would he just forget about any revenge against Tricia?"

Jackie was silent. "I'm not sure. Let me think about it."

"I need an answer, Jackie. Everything you've said about this creep screams that you're pretty damn sure which way he'd jump. I believe you even admire the son of a bitch."

"Not exactly. But you're right, I do feel as if I know him. I just think that he'd be an enormous challenge."

"Tell me if Tricia is going to be safe."

Jackie still hesitated. "I told you it would only be guesswork." Then she said in a rush, "Why should she be safe? This Alpha put in a hell of a lot of time and effort with Barrett and Spalman using her as bait to get what he wanted. It doesn't really matter if he won't get a payoff from them now. He'd have the satisfaction of completing what he started. That would still make it a win in his book."

"You believe he'll go after her," Kendra said flatly.

"I'm saying that he wouldn't see why he shouldn't. I don't think he can bear to lose, and he doesn't care about moving people out of his way." She added, "He killed Barrett, too, didn't he? He was balancing and pitting them against each other to get that Walton girl. Maybe he decided Barrett wasn't worth his trouble any longer."

"That's a possibility."

"Selfish bastard," she swore beneath her breath. "Barrett was going to be *mine*. He should have left him alone."

An opportunity seemed to be presenting itself. "You're sure you don't know who he is?"

"I told you I didn't," Jackie said curtly. "Now I've answered your questions and I'm going to hang up. I kept my word and you can keep yours. I don't want to hear from you or any of your FBI buddies again." She ended the call.

Kendra hadn't even put down her phone when she received a call from Lynch. "Griffin was more cooperative than I hoped," he said when she picked up. "He gave us until the end of the week before he cuts the surveillance for Tricia."

"That might not be enough time," she said. "We might have to go back and work on him. Jackie said she believes that Tricia is going to be a target."

"You think she's right?"

"Jackie thinks she is, and she appears to be familiar with this breed of tarantula." She thought about it. "More than familiar. She could almost tell me what he was thinking. She said she had no idea who this Alpha was, but I was beginning to have a few doubts about that by the end of the conversation. She was clearly putting together the details of the entire scenario by the time she tried to get rid of me." Kendra was going over the conversation in her mind. "It might be a good idea for me to call her back. Though she obviously had no desire to talk to me again."

"I could call her," Lynch said. "Or I could drop by her apartment if you're that uneasy."

"No, I'll do it. I'm not exactly uneasy, I just want to know why she was in such a sudden hurry to get rid of me. I'll call you back."

Kendra hesitated, gazing down at her phone after she'd pressed the disconnect. She wasn't certain that she'd told Lynch the truth. She *was* experiencing a faint uneasiness about Jackie's response to the story she'd put together that bridged Barrett to David Spalman and ended with the same mysterious monster hovering over both of them.

Because the moment Kendra had invited Jackie Gabert into that scenario was the moment she had opened it to whatever Jackie chose to do. What if she hadn't been telling the truth about not knowing who the murderer was who had tormented Spalman?

Barrett was going to be mine. He should have left him alone.

Her tone as she'd said those last words had been angry and bitter…and *intimate*.

Dear God, and very, very familiar.

Kendra felt a bolt of pure panic as the ramification of what that might mean hit home to her. She quickly dialed Jackie's number.

Voicemail.

She tried again.

After a minute, she tried once more.

Still no answer.

She called Lynch, and he answered immediately. "What's up?"

"I've been trying to call Jackie, and she's not answering her phone." She grabbed her jacket and headed out the door. "I don't like it. It could mean she just doesn't want to talk to me. Or it could mean she knows the Alpha and she's making a move. Meet me there."

"I'm already on my way," he said. "If you get there before I do, wait for me."

"How near are you? I think I'm closer to her apartment."

"I don't care how close you are." Lynch's voice harshened to sudden roughness. "Wait for me!"

CHAPTER

9

The first thing that Kendra noticed when she parked her Toyota in the parking lot in front of the apartment building was that she could see lights in Jackie's apartment. The second thing was Lynch's Lamborghini screeching into the parking lot behind her and Lynch jumping out of the vehicle and coming toward her.

"Good." He opened her car door for her. "You did what I told you for once."

"No, I just got here myself," Kendra said. "The lights of her apartment are on. I was going to give her one final call and then go up and knock."

"You make the call. I'll go ahead and pound on the door. What floor?"

"Third." She nodded at the lights of the apartment as she started across the parking lot. "The one with all lights blazing. And it appears more like she really didn't want to be bothered by me than that anything was wrong."

"Possibly."

She glanced at him. "But you don't think so?"

"No, it's you who don't think so. You're still on edge." He took her elbow and nudged her gently toward the building. "Make that call."

She was already phoning Jackie. "There's still no answer."

"Now, that does worry me." He opened the front door for her. "Will you let me go up and check the apartment out first?"

"No." She punched the elevator button for three. "I'm not that on edge."

But she couldn't say that when she reached Jackie's door and rang the bell. Something seemed very wrong.

Come on, Jackie, open the blasted door.

But Lynch was stepping in front of her, his hands moving over the lock. Then he threw open the door.

And Kendra heard the first desperate, grunting sounds.

Then she saw the blood.

So much blood. Lynch was following it across the room toward the small coffee table where Jackie had served Kendra tea that first day.

Kendra ran after him and saw that Jackie had been manacled to the chair; the grunting sound was her trying to talk through the gag tied around her mouth.

And the blood was pouring from her lower back.

Lynch turned to Kendra. "Get out of here. She needs help. There was a fire alarm box beside the elevator. Go pull it."

Kendra didn't question him. She ran for the hall and a few minutes later the fire alarm was blasting through the apartment building. Then she was running back to Jackie's apartment. But Lynch was no longer beside Jackie, he was coming out of the kitchen. "The apartment is clear." He was striding back toward Jackie. "And I called 911 after I took off her gag."

"But you still had me set off the fire alarm." It had been his first instinct to make certain no one else was in that apartment and to raise enough hell to make sure that the entire apartment building was on the alert. "How is she?"

He shook his head. "Knife wound in the kidney. She's been bleeding out."

"Can we do anything?"

"I tried pressure, but it's too late. He knew what he was doing. She's almost gone."

"Ken…dra…" Jackie's eyes were opening. She reached out desperately toward Kendra, trying to get to her.

Kendra instinctively took her hand and held it tightly. "We're trying to help. Hold on, Jackie."

"Damn…son of a…bitch…Hurts…All he could…think…about was making you know how helpless…you were…"

"Don't talk. We called 911."

"Too late…Milo…always been too…smart. Damn his…soul."

Kendra shared a quick glance with Lynch before turning back. "Milo? Did you say Milo?"

Blood trickled slowly from the corner of Jackie's mouth. "Vicious…knew…should…stay away from…" Her eyes rolled back and then fixed on nothingness.

She was dead.

Kendra stood. "She said Milo. That was the name the Spalman boy mentioned."

"Come on," Lynch said gently. "You're shaking like a leaf, Kendra. I need to get you out of here."

"We shouldn't leave her alone," she said numbly.

"Yes, you should. You can't help her. Griffin and the police are going to be asking us mega questions. But you need a break right now." He held out his hand to her. "We'll catch up with them later."

She released Jackie's hand and got to her feet. She let him draw her out of the room, through the crowds in the hallways to the parking lot.

"We'll take my car." He was tucking her into the Lamborghini, but he'd grabbed tissues from the dashboard and was doing something with her hand…

She looked down in confusion.

Blood. Her hand was covered with blood, and he was carefully wiping it with the tissues. Jackie's blood. "I can drive my car."

"You could, but you won't." He was wiping the blood off his own hand he must have gotten when he pulled her to her feet. "Hush. We'll talk when we're back at the condo." He got in the driver's seat. "Just try to relax. I'm going to call Griffin and try to give him a heads-up so that he can get agents out to that apartment before the police declare jurisdiction."

He was already on the phone by the time he exited the parking lot.

Relax? Kendra thought incredulously. *No way.*

TWENTY MINUTES LATER
KENDRA'S APARTMENT

"Go wash up," Lynch said after unlocking Kendra's door and giving her a gentle push into the foyer. "I'll start the coffee and then go into the guest room and clean up myself. Griffin said he'd need statements, but I told him I'd call and tell him when he could have them. I've put him off until tomorrow for mine. But he said he'd see you tonight, so you'll be hearing from him."

"Stop ordering me around, Lynch," Kendra said. "I'm okay. I can do anything I have to do."

"I know you can," he answered quietly. "But you don't have to do it right now. You can take the time to wash away the blood and get your thoughts together. Then we can talk." He smiled slightly. "As for not bossing you around, may I remind you that it wasn't long ago that you were doing the same to me when I was on my way to the ER? It's my turn, Kendra."

"No one shot me in the head."

"But tonight was a blow even so." He was heading for the kitchen. "Stop trying to be a tough guy. No one expects you to be anything but what you are. Let's just get this over so that we can move on."

She hesitated and then turned and moved toward her bathroom. He was right. She had to block out what she had seen in that apartment and try to function normally. She couldn't deny that she was shaken. Not only by Jackie's death, but by how it was done…

She was doing it again. Block it out for now.

When Kendra came back into the living room twenty minutes later, she'd taken a quick shower and slipped on the terry-cloth robe she kept in the bathroom.

"That's better." Lynch was standing at the bar, shirtless, naked to the waist, and looking tanned, powerful, muscular, and vaguely like an ancient Roman warrior. "Got anything for me? I had to get rid of my shirt. It was splattered with blood when I tried to stop her bleeding." He poured her a cup of coffee and handed it to her. "But if you don't mind, I don't."

"You didn't leave any of your clothes here when you left last time. But I notice you used your key to open the door tonight."

"I was only concerned with getting you inside as soon as possible."

"I don't give a damn about that blasted key. And I don't care if you want to stride around buck naked." She took a sip of coffee. "I didn't even notice your shirt was spattered. I was a little upset."

"I'm aware of that." He poured himself coffee. "And you should have been. It was a particularly brutal murder."

She nodded jerkily. "He stabbed her in her lower back, and then he manacled her in place and let her bleed to death. And it was aimed at me, wasn't it?"

"According to Jackie Gabert. Though some of it might have been directed at Jackie. We don't know what transpired that brought him to her apartment. She obviously had known this Alpha in the past. She might have contacted him because she was angry at Barrett's death. Or he might have been monitoring your movements and it led him back to Jackie. It could have gone either way." He smiled sardonically. "And I suppose we should stop calling him the Alpha. We can ask Griffin to do a trace on Jackie's past and see if a Milo pops up. It's about time we had a break. Plus, there could be DNA evidence in her apartment."

"That bastard's very careful. They didn't find anything at that construction site," Kendra said. "And he had time to clean her apartment before we got there."

"Everyone makes mistakes," Lynch said. "And if

anyone could spot one, it would be you. Are you ready to give it a try?"

She tensed. "What do you mean?"

He leaned closer to her. "Make that woman's death mean something. Think about what you just saw in there."

Dear God, she didn't want anything to do with the scene she'd just witnessed. It seemed as if the agony and blood was still right there before her.

She looked away. Well, that might not be bad. It might bring it closer, clearer. What was she thinking? There was no way it wasn't going to be bad. She braced herself. She knew she'd have to face this sooner or later. It was one of the things that only she could do.

And she *could* do it.

Close your eyes. Concentrate.

Lynch was right. She had to make it count.

Kendra's eyes suddenly sprang open. "The killer wore gloves. Disposable."

"Latex gloves?"

"No. Nitrile. The kind that medical personnel use. Or law-enforcement officers at crime scenes. We should tell Griffin to search dumpsters nearby. I might even be able to tell him what color to look for. I need to send a couple of texts first."

Lynch nodded. "This is good. What else?"

"She may have opened the door for him, but she didn't invite him in."

"Are you sure?"

She closed her eyes again, picturing the scene. "Yes. He stabbed her in her foyer, then dragged her into her living room. Quickly, before she really started bleeding out."

"Anything more?"

"When the police and Griffin's agents do their canvass, they should concentrate on the apartment beneath Jackie's." She frowned. "Maybe even more than the apartments next to it."

"Okay..."

She thought for another moment. "The killer may have some military training, possibly special forces experience."

"I concur. You're referring to the kidney stab wounds?"

She nodded. "The reach-around might have been awkward for anyone else. I suspect you've probably had that training."

"It's a favored method for eliminating sentries."

"Hmm. You're speaking with uncomfortable authority on this topic."

"Uncomfortable for the sentries, maybe. So how did you know about the gloves?"

"Disposable nitrile gloves give off a distinct odor. The intensity varies from batch to batch, depending on the manufacturing impurities. You used them in your FBI days. I'm sure you know the smell."

"Actually, I do. But I never thought the odor was that strong."

"Like I said, it depends. When I was blind, I often knew what doctors were in the room based on the brand of gloves they wore. My dermatologist now uses a purple grape-grip style that is especially recognizable."

"'Grape grip'?"

"I have no idea what it means, except they're purple. Grape grip is what it says on the box."

"Huh."

"Anyway, that smell was still in the air at Jackie's apartment," Kendra said.

"Very good. I guess it's good he chose nitrile rather than latex."

"Latex has its own odor. Chlorine, mostly, that gets left over from the cleansing process in manufacturing."

Lynch gave a low whistle. "How can you possibly know that?"

"It's like I've told you, when you don't have vision to make your way in the world, everything else becomes that much more important. And the hows and whys become much more interesting to find out."

Lynch nodded. "To you more than most, I suspect. But please go on."

"There were two fresh blood droplets on the ceiling just inside the front door. Nowhere else. They were tiny, but I'm pretty sure that's what they were. Probably splatter wounds inflicted from a killer standing in the open front doorway. If the killer had merited an invite, he probably would have waited until he was safely in the apartment."

"Reasonable."

"After she was disabled, he closed the door, moved her, gagged her, and let her bleed out where we found her."

"Okay, but why should we pay special attention to residents in the apartment downstairs?"

"When we were in there, I could easily hear footsteps and movement upstairs, but almost nothing from the apartments surrounding it. The building obviously has very little noise dampening between floors, so we'd be much more likely to get useful information from the downstairs neighbors than from those next door."

"Good. I'll pass these along to Griffin. You did a great job," he said gently. "He might want to follow up with you on some of these things."

"I did the best I could. In the meantime, I'll keep thinking and analyzing." She shivered. "I just don't want to be the one to make a mistake if it means he'll be able to zero in on Tricia." Her hands tightened on her cup. "Jackie said that she'd be a target, and after tonight, nothing could be more clear than that she knew how this particular demon thinks." She felt sick. "Every time I think about what he did to Jackie, I want to run out and gather Tricia up and hide her away. I didn't even like Jackie Gabert, but no one should be able to inflict that kind of punishment and death on another person." She had a sudden panicky thought. "How do we know he's not going after Tricia while we're sitting here?"

"Because I checked on her living arrangements and she lives at a dorm on campus with another girl," Lynch said. "He'd have to make special arrangements to go after Tricia, and he was busy tonight. Take it easy. We'll face that problem tomorrow."

"Yes, we will. First thing. I'm going to be at that pool when it opens tomorrow morning," she said. "I'll call and leave a message on her phone that I want to see her before she starts practice. And we need to talk to Griffin about surveillance for her. She appears to be principally at the pool area, and that should be checked out."

"Then we'll do it," Lynch said. "It's going to work out, Kendra."

She nodded. "I know." She corrected herself. "Not true. But I know I'm going to try like hell. When am I supposed to expect Griffin?"

He checked his watch. "In about five minutes. Do you want to handle him by yourself, or do you want me to stay?"

"I don't need you. Stop coddling me." She tossed him a burgundy velvet throw from the couch. "Drape that around yourself and get out of here. You may look a little flamboyant, but it's better than having Griffin and his detectives running into you parading around here half naked." She called after him, "And I don't want to have this problem again. Use your damn key, and don't come here without bringing a change of clothes." She held up her hand as he opened his lips. "Stop being so weird. I realize you don't want to pressure me. That's not going to do it."

"I didn't think so." He grinned at her as he draped the velvet throw around his upper body, tossing the end dashingly over his shoulder. "But I didn't want to take a chance. See you tomorrow morning."

And he left the condo with that outrageous grin and a swirl of burgundy velvet.

7:55 A.M.
NEXT DAY
POOL DECK

"My God," Tricia whispered. "I was hoping it wouldn't be true. You're sure?"

"I was there when she died," Kendra said. "I was holding her hand. I couldn't be more certain, Tricia. And she told me that she thought that you'd be targeted. We have to protect you. We're trying to arrange for surveillance from the FBI. But you're also living at a dorm and that could be chaotic. It would be hard to protect you. I'd like you to come and stay at my condo until we catch this killer." She nodded at Lynch. "And Lynch has agreed to be present during your training during the day. He's fully qualified and you should be absolutely safe."

"Absolutely?" Her lips twisted. "I don't know what that means any longer. I do know I should be safe with my friends at the dorm. They care about me."

"But they wouldn't always be with you," Lynch said quietly. "They're young and have their own lives. There would only have to be a shift of schedule and you'd have a problem. We're trying to put you in a position where there would be no problem. But we have to have your permission to protect you."

Tricia was frowning. "Look, do you think I'm not scared?" She turned to Kendra. "But right now, I'm going through the most intense training of my life. I can't have anything interfere with it. I feel very safe at the pool. And I'm sure you're very nice and well meaning, but going to live with you would upset whatever social life I've managed to salvage. I'd have to think long and hard about what I should do. You said I'd have the FBI keeping an eye on me anyway?"

"As much surveillance as we can arrange." She paused. "It may not be enough."

"I don't want to be unreasonable," Tricia said. "And Lord knows I don't want to end up dead. Could we try to keep on my present schedule for a few days with the addition of those FBI guys and see how it works out?"

"It's not the best solution," Kendra said. "It scares me. It should scare you."

"It does...a little. It's not that I'm not grateful. But

Barrett is dead, and we only have that woman's word that she thinks I'll be a target." She was nibbling at her lower lip. "I'd like to just see if she might be wrong. Could we please?"

"A couple of days?"

She nodded. "I went through weeks of FBI surveillance after that attack by Barrett, and they seemed to keep me safe. If I see any problem, I'll be knocking on your door."

"We can't force you to do anything," Kendra said. "But we'll be keeping an eye on you during that period. Get used to it."

"No problem." She headed for the door. "I'm sure we'll work something out. I've got to get in the pool now. Thanks for everything."

Kendra stared after her in despair as she murmured to Lynch, "I didn't think it would be so difficult. I know she's scared. Why won't she listen?"

"She's listening," Lynch said. "But she's young and she has a life. So far, it's not been such a terrific one. She's probably trying to desperately squeeze every bit of pleasure she can into it."

"I just want her to stay alive," Kendra said. "Last night after I went to bed, I was looking down at my hand and remembering the blood on it. I don't want it ever to be Tricia's blood. I realize what she's feeling, but if she'll just be patient…" She shook her head. "And I know the answer to that, too. People who live on the edge…" She shrugged. "Well, we'll have to throw together a schedule to keep her safe."

"Then we'd better talk to her coach and get me permission to take a look around this facility," Lynch said as he started toward the door. "Since this seems to be her home away from home. Why don't you call

Griffin and see if he's managed to pull together any preliminary info on Jackie Gabert?"

"He didn't leave my condo until almost midnight."

"I guarantee he wouldn't do any of the grunt work himself, when he could get his team to do it, but the FBI is twenty-four seven." He smiled. "And he knows that we're going to keep on his ass."

"He told me last night to be patient."

"And that isn't going to do any more good than you telling Tricia the same thing."

He was gone.

And she was reaching for her phone.

"I think I owe you a sincere thanks," Griffin said when she reached him.

"For what?"

"Lynch passed along your observations. They were helpful."

"Wow, Griffin. I think it actually pained you to say that."

"Not at all. Trust me, we need all the help we can get on this one. Gabert's apartment was clean as a whistle. Forensics is still working on it, but this guy did an immaculate job."

"DNA?"

"Nothing yet. We're hoping the woman might have struggled and we can get autopsy evidence. But your picking up on the nitrile disposable gloves could make a difference."

"You found them?"

"Afraid not. We've been searching public waste cans and dumpsters in the area, but haven't come up with anything yet. If we had, our lab would be swabbing them for DNA as we speak. But our canvassers have been asking neighbors about anyone seen wearing disposable gloves, specifically purple ones. We got a hit from a dog walker a couple of blocks away."

"Someone was wearing them?"

"Close. Someone was holding them bunched up in his hand. The dog walker remembered them because of the color. Even with just the streetlight, he could see they were purple. Sounds like you made a good catch there, Kendra."

"Tell me you got a description of the man."

"Not a good one. Caucasian, dark hair, medium height. That's about the extent of it. But he did have a distinguishing feature: a small tattoo on his neck, just under his left ear. The dog walker thought it was a circle superimposed over a triangle."

Kendra thought about this. "It isn't much to go on."

"It's a lot more than we would've had if you hadn't come along. Thank you."

"Did you do a background trace on Jackie?"

"That will take days to do in-depth." He sighed. "Yes, we checked on anyone named Milo. So far that's a big zero, too." He added impatiently, "I'll let you know when I do have something for you."

"I'm sure you will. But I'll also be in touch."

"That goes without saying." He paused. "Good work on following up with Jackie Gabert. Her murder appears to link her directly with Barrett and the Bureau murders. I just wanted you to know that I felt the Dusenberry killing could have been attributed to someone else, but this one convinced me that you and Lynch are on the right track."

"That's encouraging, Griffin." She carefully kept the sarcasm out of her voice. "Then can we count on you to help us?"

"Of course," he said brusquely. "It would have been

simpler if Barrett had worked solo, but truth is truth. We have to catch that son of a bitch. Call on me anytime." He added warily, "With any reasonable request."

"Thank you, I'll keep that in mind."

He hesitated. "Oh, and there appears to be a threat to you. I've been thinking about it. Ordinarily, I'd tell you to back off, but I wouldn't be doing my duty to my people who have been killed by that son of a bitch if I didn't use every weapon I possess." He added gruffly, "So I'm going to do it. If the occasion presents itself, can I use you to bait and bring down the perp?"

She thought he meant what he said, and for the first time since this nightmare had started, she was feeling genuine respect for him. "It depends on the occasion and how much control I have of the situation. We could look into it."

"I thought you'd cooperate. Lynch said it was out of the question. Not in your job description."

"Then you should have asked me."

"I will in the future. Lynch can be negative on some subjects, and you appear to be one of them. Good talking to you, Kendra." He ended the call.

Kendra put away her phone. The call had not been informative, but it had been interesting.

And she would definitely have to have a discussion with Lynch.

Lynch took one look at her expression when he came back a few hours later and said, "You're bristling. Griffin hit you with the bait proposition, didn't he? I was hoping that I'd squashed it when he brought it up to me."

"I'm not bristling. Though I let him know that you don't control anything about my life. He won't make that mistake again." She met his gaze. "Neither will you. I don't know why it happened this time. It's not like you at all."

"I didn't think so, either." He shrugged. "But it appears that this is turning out to be a groundbreaking case in a number of ways. I had a hunch it might be when I heard about the explosion. That was why I shifted everything around and was on the next plane out of Johannesburg. I realized how it would affect you to see all those agents you'd been working with blown to kingdom come. It would have been different if you hadn't known them. You would still have cared, but it wouldn't have struck that deep. I knew it was going to tear you up and I had to be there for you."

"It hurt, but I was handling it."

"I wasn't," he said simply. "I could see that you were diving in and there was no way you were going to let go. And with every new development that popped up you sank deeper, and I was watching it pulling you in. I could see that damn Alpha beckoning to you, and I knew that you'd go after him."

"Of course I would. You knew that from the beginning."

"But I didn't realize that the fact that you're keeping me at a distance would bother me that much. Ordinarily, I could have dealt with it, but I was worried and scared about what you'd decide to do at any given minute and that I might not be able to give you support when you needed it the most." He ruefully shook his head. "And then I screwed up and did something I knew would piss you off. What are you going to do about it? Banishment won't work, because I'm not going anywhere. You'd do better to just forgive me for being a manipulative asshole and keep an eye on me." He grimaced. "Because you might need me if Griffin does come up with a plan that doesn't suck. You know you can count on me, and Griffin is an unknown quantity."

"He seemed sincere this time."

"He might be. He does care about his agents. But that doesn't mean he's brilliant, only efficient. We might need more than efficient to outsmart that Alpha who killed Jackie Gabert."

Kendra shuddered. "I just want to catch him soon. This Milo must be fairly intelligent if he's managed to maintain relationships with Barrett and no one knows how many other cult followers. It sounds as if he kept them spinning around him like balls he tossed in the air."

"Then you obviously need me. I'm an expert at shooting down balls or drones or any other flying object. I assume that means that I'm forgiven?"

"It might." She was gazing at him in resignation. He was smiling and he was the Lynch she had always known: charming, intelligent, witty, and sexy as hell. He had been honest with her when she'd called him on how he'd tried to sidetrack her from cooperating with Griffin. And how could you not forgive someone for wanting you to be safe? "Though it can't happen again. That came close to being an insult, Lynch."

"It was actually a compliment. It's all how you look at it."

And he could make black look snowy white. It was better not to go into any details with him. The last thing she wanted right now was to cause a rupture that would send him away from her. It was enough that she'd stated her displeasure and made it clear she wouldn't tolerate it again. "Did you find any hazards while you were looking around the pool area?"

"A couple. But the place is enormous. I haven't had time to go through the entire facility. I'll just keep watch over Tricia for the next two days while I'm checking it out and see if it's manageable."

"It had better be manageable," Kendra said. "It might be the difference in the color of a medal to her if she can't train here. We'd have problems persuading her to budge."

"We'll worry about that when it happens," Lynch said. "In the meantime, I'll shadow her when she goes back to her dorm and make certain that's safe for the next couple of days."

"And I'll go back to the condo tonight and tell Olivia about Tricia, see if she'll help out occasionally. It would help to have someone in the same building on the alert."

He chuckled. "That sounds a bit peculiar considering Olivia is blind."

"Only if you didn't know how sharp Olivia is," Kendra said. "I'm surprised you'd even mention it."

"Just preparing you for Tricia's possible reaction. The world you live in is different from practically any other you might run across. It requires a certain indoctrination into its subtleties."

"Then she'll have to learn to accept all the nuances and she should feel lucky to be able to do it. Not only are the people in my world extraordinary, but most of them had to fight to reinforce those differences. It causes them to become a unique breed of human being." She smiled. "Like you, Lynch. So don't knock it."

"I wouldn't think of it. I like living in your world, Kendra. I'm delighted you permit me inside the gates." He turned toward the door. "One can't say it's not stimulating." He winked mischievously. "And sometimes *fantastically* satisfying."

CHAPTER

10

I didn't expect to see you here tonight," Tricia said warily when she saw Kendra coming from the parking lot. "I saw Lynch inside checking out the area and he asked me to wait, said he'd take me back to the dorm. I told him what I'm telling you. I'm going to stroll down to a coffee shop a couple of blocks from here and meet a few friends. I don't need you. I thought I was clear that I'm going to try it with just the FBI surveillance. Lynch said they're on duty."

"You were very clear." She smiled. "And Griffin's men are keeping their eye on you. But when Lynch told me what you planned, I thought you wouldn't mind if I went with you as far as the coffee shop. I don't think I really look like law enforcement, and I wanted the chance to explain why you should let us help you."

"No, you don't look like a cop." Tricia made a face. "But you're semi-famous. Someone might recognize you." She sighed. "Look, I know you're only doing what you think is best for me. I appreciate it. But I want this chance to see if the Gabert woman was wrong. I like everybody thinking I'm normal and not shying away from me because they can't be sure they might become collateral damage. The only way I want to be famous from now on is in the sports pages. You said that you'd give me time."

"I didn't believe you'd be strolling around the city."

"With a couple of Federal agents behind me. Give me a break."

"Will you let me drive you?"

"Kendra." Tricia's lips suddenly curved in that appealing smile as she turned and headed for the street. "You're a busy woman. Give it up. It's only two blocks. Let me live my life."

"This isn't the end," Kendra called after Tricia as she started to cross the street. "I'll keep trying."

"I realize that," Tricia said. "I think we might be soul sisters. I don't give up either, and I—"

A roar of sound.

A black Cadillac Escalade.

Tinted windows.

Going very fast.

Too fast.

And heading straight for Tricia!

"No! Tricia, move!" Kendra leaped forward into the street without thinking. She only caught a light-ning glimpse of Tricia's terrified expression before she launched herself in a tackle to push her out of danger. The fender of the car grazed her and knocked her to the concrete.

Pain.

Blinding headlights.

Hard concrete...

"Are you okay?" Tricia's voice. "Are you hurt? The car hit you, didn't it? Dear God, why did you do it? Can you sit up?"

Kendra opened her eyes, but Tricia was just a blur kneeling above her. She had to shake her head to clear it before Tricia's pale, panicky face sharpened enough for her to be sure who it was. Her gaze flew down the street, but the Cadillac Escalade was no longer in view.

A heartbeat later, a UC campus police car swerved out of an adjacent parking lot. To Kendra's surprise, Lynch leaned out the driver's side window. "Get her inside. I'm going after him!"

He spun out as a campus police officer appeared from the lot on foot with his gun drawn. The cop was shouting into his radio.

But Lynch was gone.

Tricia now looked even more disoriented. "Was that—?"

"Yes." Kendra knew she must have looked even more shocked than Tricia. "I think Lynch just stole a police car."

Lynch gunned the squad car's engine and roared down the dark campus streets. There were a few students walking to and from the library and residence halls, but otherwise the coast was clear. Up ahead, he saw the distinctive taillights of an Escalade. It was turning left onto a street that would quickly take it toward the I-5 freeway.

Damn. Gotta catch it before it gets there.

Even before Lynch reached the intersection, he heard the squealing of brakes and the gunning of an engine. Seconds later, the Escalade came roaring back in the opposite direction.

What the hell?

Lynch looked left and saw that two police cars had pulled across the roadway, blocking access to the neighboring streets.

Looking for him and the stolen squad car, no doubt. It was totally expected since he'd yanked that poor officer out of his car and taken off with it.

Lynch was impressed at how fast the campus cops had mobilized. He made a mental note to give his compliments to their commander. Later. When the timing was more convenient.

Because one of the police cars blocking the street had turned and peeled out after him. He'd been spotted.

Uh-oh.

He turned the wheel right and sped after the Escalade.

They roared down La Jolla Shores Drive, one of the campus's main thoroughfares. For a stretch, there was an odd mixture of student housing, campus athletic facilities, and multimillion-dollar homes, with residences becoming larger as they neared the campus's western side that bordered the Pacific Ocean.

BLAM!

A bullet shattered one of his windows. Was the pursuing cop shooting at him?

BLAM!

No. The gunshots were coming from the Escalade's driver's side window.

Shit. Time to put some pressure on.

Lynch hit the accelerator hard and rammed the Escalade's rear bumper.

The larger vehicle swerved from the impact. He knew the tank-like Escalade was unlikely to sustain any real damage, but the hit might be enough to make this bastard put down his gun for a moment.

Lynch rammed it again. Again the Escalade wavered only slightly.

A blinding light lit up the window behind him!

It was the pursuing police car's roof-mounted spotlight. Its blue flashers were on, and the PA was blaring an unintelligible message.

Probably something about wanting their police car back.

Lynch grabbed the radio mic and raised it to his mouth. "Heads up. I'm assisting the FBI in a murder investigation. I borrowed this squad car in pursuit of a suspect driving the black Cadillac Escalade with California plates 2HXW100."

The police car rammed him with its push bumper.

Lynch dropped the mic and gripped the wheel with both hands. Either they didn't get the message, they didn't believe him, or they didn't care.

He sped past a series of campus tennis courts and approached the Scripps Institution of Oceanography, a complex of research buildings, a fishery, and a public aquarium.

Lynch cracked his window to listen. More police sirens wailed in the distance. Good.

Two sets of flashers appeared on the road ahead.

The Escalade abruptly turned off the road and swerved around the circular driveway in front of the Birch Aquarium. Lynch and the other police cars followed.

Lynch unsnapped his shoulder holster. The pursuit was going to end here, one way or another.

The Escalade left the driveway and crossed a small pedestrian plaza. It passed the ticket booth and charged through the tall window panels that fronted the building.

Smash!

The Escalade shattered the glass and skidded to a stop in the aquarium's main atrium. Lynch jumped from the police car and pulled out his automatic.

He moved inside the building, dodging guillotines of glass still falling from the broken panes. To his surprise, there were no audible alarms, just bubbling water in the large interactive exhibit tanks. He held his gun in front of him and approached the wrecked Escalade.

The driver's side door was open. No one was inside.

"Drop the gun!" The voice came from behind him.

Lynch slowly turned. Four police officers stood just outside the shattered atrium glass, their guns aimed at him.

"We *will* shoot you," another cop yelled.

Shit.

"I'm with the Department of Justice," Lynch called out. "I'll show you my ID. The driver of this Escalade may be a murderer. We need to find him."

Another cop stepped forward. "What we *need* is for you to put your gun down in the next five seconds."

Lynch sighed and placed his gun on the white-tiled floor.

The cops stepped closer to him. "Now drop to your knees and place your hands behind your head."

"You're letting him get away."

"Don't worry about that. We have about fifty cops en route."

"I can use your help. Let me show you my ID."

"On your knees, hands behind your head."

Lynch sighed. He'd run out of options that didn't involve his shooting death or the murder of four innocent campus police officers.

Dammit.

He raised his hands and slowly dropped to his knees.

———◆———

Less than forty-five minutes later, Kendra arrived at the aquarium. The circular driveway was crowded with police cars and an FBI evidence collection van. TV news teams had already arrived on the scene, and they were setting up their cameras and lights in the area just beyond the pedestrian plaza.

Lynch rushed out to the driveway to greet her. "How are you? I couldn't get any information from these cops."

"I'm fine." She patted her hip. "Just a bruise. What about the driver of that Escalade?"

Lynch swore. "No sign of him yet. It looks like he exited from a door on the building's left side. He could be anywhere by now. I wasted almost ten minutes convincing the campus police that I wasn't the bad guy here."

"Well, you did steal one of their cars."

"Any port in a storm. I was walking from the median overlooking the east parking lot when I saw what happened with that Escalade. Good job getting Tricia out of the way. You saved her life."

"I don't know about that."

"I do. Anyway, you looked like you were okay, and there was a campus police car just a few feet from where I was standing." Lynch shrugged. "I removed the officer and borrowed his vehicle."

"You make it sound so civilized," she said dryly.

"I'm afraid it was anything but." He motioned toward the shattered aquarium windows. "Want to take a look at the car that almost killed you?"

They stepped over the broken glass and walked toward the Escalade, which was illuminated by several high-wattage police work lights.

"What do we know about it?" Kendra asked.

"It was stolen from Horton Plaza earlier today. I'm afraid it looks extremely clean. No prints on the wheel or console controls."

Kendra leaned inside. "Because he wore gloves. Grape grip."

"You're sure of that?"

"Yes." She backed away from the vehicle. "Same odor as in Jackie's apartment. And I don't see any of the evidence techs here wearing purple gloves."

Lynch nodded. "I'll make sure they look for the discarded gloves. But there's something else you should see." He motioned toward an evidence collection tech.

"What is it?"

"Something that will interest you."

The tech walked over with a clear plastic bag. Lynch took it and held it up. It was a porcelain figurine of a woman, dressed in a blue-green gown. Its base was adorned with faded gold lettering.

Kendra gasped. "Naiad. The water nymph."

He nodded. "It was standing up on the dashboard."

She squinted at the statue's fine detail. "This has to be the object that was stolen from the Spalman boy's house. It was purposefully left here for us to find…"

"Yes. And whoever did it knows enough about our investigation to realize we'd make the connection." His lips twisted as he added, "And the son of a bitch was damn confident Tricia was going to die tonight. It's my guess he was prepared to ditch the car once he killed her."

Kendra shuddered as that thought hit home. Tricia had come so close to being crushed under those wheels in that moment before Kendra had pushed her out of the way. "We have to do something. She can't stay here on campus."

Lynch's brows rose. "And what do you propose?"

"We'll convince her to stay with me."

"Easier said than done. You don't think the FBI protective detail will be enough?"

"Not here. Look what just happened. They were just a few yards away, and there still wasn't anything they could do about this Escalade bearing down on her. It'll be easier for them to protect her if she's at my place."

Lynch thought about it for a moment. "I'll certainly feel better if I can take over some aspects of her security. Where is she now?"

"In her dorm. There are two agents stationed outside. I'll call her now." Kendra pulled out her phone and called Tricia's cell phone.

She answered on the first ring. "Kendra! Are you okay?"

"I'm fine. I told you it was just a bruise. But I want to discuss something Lynch and I have just been talking about."

"Really?" Tricia asked warily. "Should I be worried?"

"No, not if you let us help you." Kendra told her

about Lynch's pursuit and the statue that had been left behind in the Escalade.

Tricia was silent for a long moment.

Kendra had to push her. "Tricia? You know where this is going?"

"Yeah, and it's scaring me."

"I'd like you to come stay with me. As long as this monster is out there, you'll be safer there. We can have more control over your security."

Silence. "I'm not stopping my training."

"No one is asking you to."

Tricia was silent for another long moment before responding. "Okay."

Kendra drew a relieved breath. "You'll do it? You're not going to make us wait for your answer or jump through hoops?"

"I would never have been that rude." She laughed. "And I have respect for you, even if you hadn't saved me from being crushed like a cockroach. Too much respect to let that son of a bitch go after you. I haven't had to worry about anyone else being hurt because of me until he targeted you. It's a tough thing to live with, knowing I could be the cause of someone being hurt or killed." Her voice lowered. "Besides, I've got too much to do with my life. No one is going to take it from me. Yes, my eyes were opened tonight. I'll do whatever you want, within reason."

"Then you'll come back to my condo tonight?"

"No. Tomorrow night. I'll be ready to leave the dorm at seven and go direct to the pool. After my training session, I'll come to your condo. After all, I have to pack and make 'reasonable' excuses to my roommates. I don't want to worry them."

"Thanks, Tricia. It's really the best plan."

———

NEXT DAY
KENDRA'S CONDO

Lynch delivered Tricia to Kendra at five the next afternoon. It was obvious Tricia was not pleased. "I told him it was too early," she said as she stood in the doorway of the condo. "He wouldn't pay any attention to me. I never leave the pool until at least seven. I'm in training!"

"Too bad," Lynch said. "I didn't like the setup. I'll try to make it more secure starting tomorrow. Until then she's over to you, Kendra. I've got Scanlon and another of Griffin's top men guarding the condo tonight. I'll be here at six in the morning to pick her up and take her back to the university. Now I've got to go back to make that damn pool facility safe for her." He held up his hand as Tricia started to protest. "I don't want to hear it. We'll talk tomorrow. Don't give Kendra a hard time." He pushed her in the door and left the condo.

Kendra immediately followed him into the hall. "Milo? Any report from Griffin?"

"Sorry. I heard from Griffin just before I left the swim center. I was a little occupied with getting Tricia out of there. Like I told you, the Escalade was stolen from the parking garage at Horton Plaza. They've continued searching it for DNA and prints, but they've turned up nothing. They still might get something from security camera recordings in the area. He'll let us know if they discover anything else."

"Which is basically what we expected," Kendra said wryly. "Now we just wait for the next attack? That sucks."

"Agreed." Lynch turned away. "But until we can find a way to turn it around, we just play a defensive game and keep our naiad water goddess in there alive and well. I'll do my part, go in and do yours."

"Don't worry, I will," she said grimly. "Count on it." She opened the door and went back into the condo.

Tricia said to Kendra the instant she saw her, "Lynch wasn't being reasonable. The pool was absolutely safe. It was crowded with people, but no one came near me. He stayed poolside and I was within calling distance. This isn't going to work out, Kendra."

"Yes, it is," Kendra said firmly. "Because we're going to make it work out. Lynch isn't unreasonable. He probably told you exactly what his problems were with the security at the pool. You probably didn't want to hear them. Isn't that right?"

Tricia was silent for a moment. "Perhaps. But no one could have that many possible threats to deal with in such a restricted area. He went overboard."

"Really. Tell me all about them. I'd like to hear what you consider unreasonable."

Tricia hesitated and then looked away. "You're not going to let me off the hook, are you? Okay, here goes. He said there are six unlocked access points to the aquatic center alone. Four more if someone picked or broke the locks. The dining hall is a security nightmare as far as he's concerned. My dorm is a little better, since you need to swipe a badge to get through any of the four main entrances. But Lynch had no problem getting students to hold the doors open for him when he entered behind them. And he thought I'd be particularly vulnerable between there and my classroom buildings." She made a face. "It sounds much worse when you put it like that."

Kendra's brows rose. "You mean the truth?"

Tricia grimaced. "Yeah, something like that. He didn't like it that I argued with him."

"He's not used to it. You don't know how lucky you were to get him to handle your security. I should have told you more about him before I threw the two of you together." She shrugged. "I liked you, I thought you were smart, that doesn't necessarily mean you can read someone as complex as Lynch. It wasn't fair to him. Tell me, what was your impression of him?"

Tricia frowned thoughtfully. "Very intelligent, sophisticated, lots of charisma and personal magnetism, most of the time he appears to have a great sense of humor." She added, "Not today."

"Okay, now I'll fill in the blanks." Kendra took Tricia's arm and led her back toward the door. "We're going to go downstairs and I'm going to introduce you to my friend Olivia and her dog, Harley. We're going to take the stairs because I need the time to tell you about Lynch and by the time you reach her condo, you'll realize that you can't ever accept anyone at face value, particularly a wild card like Lynch. Which will prepare you to meet Olivia."

"I'm beginning to get nervous. Should I?"

"Nah, because you're not stupid. You're actually quite bright. You're just young, ambitious, and a workaholic, and you're seeing what you want to see." They were in the corridor, and she was leading her toward the staircase. "I'll just open your eyes a bit. Lynch is all the things that you've reeled off to me. But if I'd given you his background you would have seen beyond that surface. You didn't know that he was formerly with the FBI, but it wasn't challenging enough for him. He's a master manipulator and he seldom worked with conventional methods. They called him The Puppetmaster."

"Rather melodramatic."

"That's what I thought until I heard the story of how he once went undercover with two different crime families in Philadelphia and New York and pitted them against each other. They crippled each other's operations and murdered many of each other's top men. The Bureau managed to take down both families eventually."

Tricia gave a low whistle. "You said that wasn't challenging enough for him?"

"Too small a canvas. He's now a black ops strategist for U.S. intelligence agencies. He also does extractions and he's the man everyone goes to when everything is falling apart. If he said all those soft spots at the pool were security dangers, then that's what they were. Because he has the experience to identify and neutralize them better than anyone you've ever met. Do you understand?"

"You've made it very clear." She gave her a mischievous smile. "Except your personal relationship with him."

"Which is none of your business. But I will tell you that when we work together, we discover all kinds of new and different ways that we agree and disagree. He's never let me down and he's always been there when I've been in a corner." She'd paused in front of Olivia's door. "And now that I've explained Lynch, it's time you meet my best friend, Olivia."

"And her dog, Harley," Tricia added. "I love dogs."

"Yes, one must never forget Harley. He was destined to be a rescue dog, but he had problems. He's very brave and loving…just unusual." She rang the bell and the barking started. "So is Olivia. Don't make the same mistake about her as you did Lynch. I've already told you what a fantastic person she is on several levels. You should know that Olivia may be blind, but no one can see deeper than she does."

"I won't forget."

The door flew open, and Harley launched himself at Tricia. Kendra thought he was going to knock her down, but Tricia braced herself and her arms went around the dog. "It's all right, Kendra. He won't take me down. I'm very strong." She looked down at Harley and cradled his head in her hands. "I'm very good with dogs. I used to train them every summer at my uncle's kennels outside Seattle." She looked deep in Harley's eyes. "You're a good boy, but that wasn't good. We'll have to have a talk about what's acceptable." She gave him a hug. "But not now." She looked at Olivia. "Hi, I'm Tricia. You're really gorgeous, aren't you? I bet everyone says that to you because you're blind. Does it annoy you? I bet it does. Particularly since Kendra told me that you have so much more on the ball than what's on the surface. Though it's probably because they feel awkward when they want to say something to make you think just because you have one handicap that being beautiful should make up for it. They should realize that someone as sharp as you wouldn't need that kind of reassurance. That's kind of dumb, isn't it?"

"Exceptionally," Olivia said. "But no dumber than you thinking that you can impress me by supposedly understanding me." She smiled. "Besides, I like the idea of being thought gorgeous. I realize I'm much more than a pretty face, but we're all the composite of our physical and mental abilities and we should take advantage of every element we're given. You're supposed to be a magnificent swimmer, but Kendra says you're also a cyber whiz kid or you'd never be able to spend all that time practicing in the pool and still get straight A's in your major. What else are you, Tricia Walton?"

"Well, I'm not gorgeous." Tricia chuckled. "But I guess I'm okay, and I usually get along with people…until today. I got temperamental with Lynch because I didn't know what I was dealing with. Then I overcompensated with you because I wanted to prove to Kendra that I wasn't a total loser. She saved my neck and I owe her. But I shouldn't have tried to pay a debt to her by involving you." She sighed. "So now I have to find a way to make it up to you. How can I do that? Kendra says you're a super businesswoman. Have any use for a cyber whiz kid? I'm at your service while I'm here."

"I'll consider it." Olivia was smiling. "What do you think, Kendra?"

"Up to you," Kendra said. "You might as well take advantage of her. There may be periods when Lynch and I may have to leave the two of you with Griffin's agents. Since she's a workaholic, she'll be bored to death if we can't keep her busy."

"Oh, I can keep her busy," Olivia said. "I don't have any use for a world-class swimmer, but I can use someone to reorganize my computer files and protect me from cyberattacks." She added, "And she said she was good with dog training when she was being assaulted by Harley. I can't decide if that will be first or second on her schedule."

"Don't worry about it," Tricia said breezily. "I'm very good with organizing my time and you won't be disappointed." She wrinkled her nose. "More than you were when I made my grand entrance just now. I'll even make you forget that gigantic faux pas when you see how valuable I'll be to you."

"We'll see. I can be very demanding." Olivia turned and headed for the kitchen. "Do you cook?"

Tricia shook her head. "I'm terrible. But I could learn."

"Don't you dare. No one cooks in my kitchen but me. But you and Kendra can come and watch a true chef at work. I'll let you entertain me by describing what happened when you got temperamental with Lynch. I would have liked to have been there."

"Whatever you say," Tricia said as she followed her. "Unless you'd rather I work with Harley."

"You're overdoing the humility," Olivia said. "Watch it, Tricia."

Tricia laughed. "I'll strike a balance, I always do. And I usually come out on top."

"I imagine you do." Olivia was laughing, too. "But then so do I. This may be interesting..."

———◆———

After dinner Tricia had a training session with Harley, examined Olivia's computer setup, and then curled up on the couch with Harley and promptly drifted off to sleep.

Kendra got both Olivia and herself a glass of wine and then settled on the chaise on the veranda. "What do you think of her?" she asked. "Too much trouble?"

"Fragile. Very fragile. I have a hunch it's always there beneath the brashness." She took a sip of wine.

"And the strength. She might be trouble. But I can't help but root for her."

"Who wouldn't?" Kendra asked. "She's fought off two attempts to murder her since she was fourteen. It's incredible that it didn't destroy her, but she just kept fighting and showing everyone that they couldn't hurt her. But she's my problem, not yours, Olivia. Anytime she's with you I've arranged for you to have mega protection, yet the threat is still there. I know you asked me to let you help if I went after the person who killed those agents. But I've no right to involve you at all."

"It's been my problem, too, ever since the night you came back after visiting Metcalf in the hospital. You were hurting, and you made me hurt. That kind of crap shouldn't be permitted to exist. You bet I'll take my turn watching that kid. Now stop arguing. We'll use my condo as home base, and you'll all come here to dinner every night and we'll discuss problems." She finished her glass of wine. "Take her up to your condo and put her to bed. She'll probably have a twelve-hour day tomorrow if Lynch has done his job right."

"Are you sure?"

"I couldn't be more certain." She lifted her empty glass in a mock toast. "Hey, my dog has a crush on her. What else can I do?"

"Say no. I promise you'll be safe, but I'll understand if you—"

"Hush." Olivia got to her feet. "I'll see you both tomorrow. Tricia said she wanted to double down on Harley's training after dinner tomorrow." She moved inside. "But you'd better call Lynch tonight and explain that Tricia isn't as naive as she might have seemed. He doesn't suffer fools gladly."

She shook her head. "I'll have her call him and apologize. It's between the two of them."

"Even though you acted as peacekeeper. Which one were you protecting?"

She shrugged. "Maybe both."

"Works for me." Harley had lifted a drowsy head from Tricia's arm as he heard Olivia's voice and she snapped her fingers. "Come on, Harley. You're stuck with me. Your new friend has to go home with Kendra…"

8:40 P.M.
NEXT DAY
FIFTH STREET

"Can't we go to the park, Kendra?" Tricia asked. "It's not dark yet and I'd like to familiarize Harley with the other pups in the dog park. That's got to be an important part of his training. Olivia said that she doesn't usually take him there because he gets too excited. But I'd really like to do the training myself so that I can surprise her."

"Maybe." Kendra looked back over her shoulder and immediately spotted the two FBI agents halfway down the block. "But I'd rather you wait until we can prep Griffin's men so they can check out the area before we go into unknown territory."

"Unknown territory," Tricia repeated. "It sounds like I'm going to take a trip into the frozen wastelands of Antarctica. That park is two blocks away and in one of San Diego's most prestigious neighborhoods."

"I know," Kendra said quietly. She left it at that.

"But that doesn't make any difference, does it?" Tricia said tightly. "Because you think he might be able to reach me anywhere."

There was that fragility again that Olivia had mentioned, Kendra thought. It had come out of the blue because it never really left Tricia. She was always on guard, waiting.

"I just believe we should be careful," she said gently. "I'm responsible for you and I don't like to take chances. Could you wait until tomorrow evening? I'll arrange to have Griffin's men go explore the park while you're at practice during the day."

"Of course I can wait." Tricia didn't look at Kendra as she knelt on the pavement and stroked Harley. "We know how lucky we are, don't we, boy? You live in a real cool neighborhood, Kendra. I like all the action going on in the streets. Everyone seems to be full of enthusiasm and doing interesting things. I think maybe I'd like to live in an area like this once I've done all I want to do and I'm ready to settle down."

"Hmm...now, is that after you've started collecting Social Security?"

"Oops, did I do it again?" She shook her head. "Sorry. I guess it's that I'm feeling a little vulnerable. That makes me very sensitive and aware of everything I want to do in case it's taken away." She lifted her chin. "Which it will *not* be. I won't let it." She gave Harley a final pat. "There's no reason why you should feel responsible for me. I do great on my own. You've already saved my life once and that's your quota." She got to her feet. "After all, when Barrett tried to kill me when I was fourteen, no one hung around and worried about me like you're doing. Oh, I'm not saying my parents didn't care. They're wonderful, but they knew the FBI was keeping an eye on me and left it up to them." She paused. "And me. Just as they should have done. They didn't give me a Lynch, or an Olivia, or a Harley." She yanked her thumb at the agents who were still waiting down the street. "Or those guys who are afraid to follow me into the park."

"They'll be ready by tomorrow," Kendra said.

"You're not getting the point. I'm trying to say thank you. I realize I've been a pain in the ass. I just want you to shut me down when I ask too much." Her hands clenched at her sides. "I want the whole world, you know. I want to be the best swimmer in Olympic history, I want to create a foolproof cyber system that will protect this country from hackers, I want to work with chemists and develop a dog food that will keep dogs like Harley here from dying so damn young."

The faintest smile was curving Kendra's lips. "Is that all?"

She shook her head. "It's just a start. I didn't want you to think I was too ambitious."

"I don't. At your age we all think we're immortal and can shape the world to suit ourselves. I was worse than you because I started later since I was blind until I was twenty. But when I broke free, I was a wild child. In some ways I still am."

"That's good to know. Then I won't feel bad when I add to my list?"

"Not even a little. You appear to be on your way to some of your goals right now, and you had Barrett to contend with."

"Who knows? Maybe the thought of that bastard gave me a bit of a boost now and then."

"Perhaps." It would probably be a good idea to ease Tricia away from any memories of Barrett. "It's getting dark, do you think we should take Harley back now?"

Tricia nodded and started back toward the condo. "I did forget to tell you one other thing that I wanted." She added solemnly, "It's very important."

Kendra gave her a skeptical glance. "Then I suppose I'd better hear it."

Tricia's eyes were twinkling with pure mischief. "I want a really sexy lover who looks at me the way Lynch looks at you!" Then she burst into laughter as she saw Kendra's expression and hurried into the building.

———

Why hadn't he taken the shot? Milo wondered.

That moment when Tricia had been kneeling beside the dog would have been perfect. Those FBI goons had been a good distance from her. He would have been able to get out of this building and into his car before they would have even been able to reach the girl and find out she was dead.

And she would have been dead. He was as good at the basic skills as he was at the planning. Barrett had often been more careless because he liked the thrill of the kill. Milo had tolerated it at times because he'd learned that it kept the subject more firmly under his control. But when he staged a finale for himself, he made sure that there was no encore.

So why not this time?

Because he was enjoying toying with Kendra Michaels, savoring how she would feel when he pulled the trigger? He had been terribly angry with Michaels when she'd wounded him with that nail gun and then stolen Tricia from him. He'd been watching her for two days and had become aware of the growing intimacy between the two women. It was clear they were taking comfort from each other's company. He'd decided that it might be even more enjoyable to indulge himself during that splendid explosion that was to come if he let them both believe they were safe. But he'd only counted on hours, perhaps a day. Why had he let it drag on like this?

There was no way he'd admit that he'd made a mistake or allowed himself to soften. He wouldn't have done that—even the thought offended him. It must only be as he'd first thought, that his instinct had been to just enjoy the Walton kill before he permitted himself to rid himself of Kendra Michaels. But now he was back on track…

CHAPTER
11

Lynch was having a drink in Olivia's condo when they brought Harley back. After he fought off Harley's first bout of enthusiasm, he turned to Tricia. "How is Harley doing? I never had much of a problem with him, but Kendra said you're a miracle worker."

Tricia shrugged. "He's intelligent and full of love. The rest is just training and repetition." Her eyes were twinkling as she added, "You probably didn't have problems with him because you're both male and think alike. Women can be much more complicated."

"Ouch." He grimaced. "I can think of at least three insults hidden in that answer."

"Think deeper. You'll find others." Then she threw back her head and laughed. "Stop looking like that, Kendra. I'm kidding. Lynch and I have come to terms. All I had to do was behave with the proper humility."

"Bullshit," Lynch said. "Shut up, brat, or I'll drown you the next time I catch you alone in that pool."

"You wouldn't stand a chance. I'm a far better swimmer than you are. Besides, it would ruin that fancy reputation you've conned everybody into believing."

Kendra was pleasantly surprised. "Break it up." She'd only seen Lynch briefly in the last two days and had missed that light interaction between the two of them. "You're acting like my students at recess."

"Exactly what I was thinking," Olivia said. "Lynch, while I get Harley some water, why don't you tell Kendra and Tricia why you graced me with your presence? That was much more interesting."

"At least more optimistic," Lynch said. "I just dropped in to tell you both that I've finished plugging the security holes at the swimming center. It will only take a brief scan on my computer every morning to check and then it will be safe until it's locked up at night." His voice was suddenly gentle. "That's one other place that we know you'll be safe, Tricia."

"That's three, isn't it," she asked flippantly. "Kendra's, here at Olivia's, the swim center. Pretty soon I won't be able to count them on one hand." Then her tone was suddenly weary. "It's not enough, Lynch."

"I know it isn't," he said quietly. "You should have the entire world. We'll get there."

"I know. I trust you," Tricia said. "But this crap gets old." She turned to Olivia. "I need to get my mind off it. Is it okay if I work on that computer update for a while tonight? I'll sleep sounder."

"Be my guest." Olivia laughed. "Or my slave. Whichever you choose to call it."

"Mistress of your fate," Tricia said. "That sounds better." She turned to Kendra. "Go on back to your condo. I'll have the guard escort me when I'm ready. Or I might curl up on Olivia's couch."

Kendra frowned. "Let me know."

"I know the rules. All of them." She patted Harley on the head. "Come on, buddy. Let's get to work." She glanced over her shoulder at Lynch. "Make sure her condo's safe. Do you hear me?"

"I hear you," he said dryly. "I believe I can take care of that. Good night, Olivia. Tricia."

———◆———

As soon as the door closed behind Lynch and Kendra, Olivia turned away and moved over to her office area in the corner of the living room where Tricia was adjusting the computer. "You did that very well. I was impressed."

Tricia was silent. "I don't know what you mean."

Olivia laughed. "Then perhaps I should ask if you're really going to have trouble sleeping tonight, or if I should get you a cup of strong coffee to keep you awake."

Another silence. "You thought I was lying?"

"I thought you were using your weakness and turning it into a strength."

"You're very perceptive. Kendra was right. You do see more than the rest of us." She paused. "It was only half a lie."

"But you really wanted to give Lynch and Kendra an opportunity to go to bed together."

She nodded. "I think they're lovers. Naturally I'm in their way."

"They have a complicated relationship. But they're both clever. They'd find a way if the time was right."

"I couldn't take a chance on cheating them. I'm not good about knowing stuff like that...I've never had sex yet."

"Why not? These days kids seem to start early." She paused. "That rape attempt when you were fourteen?"

"Maybe. I don't know. I don't like to think it would be. That would mean I was afraid. I *won't* be afraid. It could be that I'm so busy, I believe it would get in the way."

"That could be true. And I don't think you're afraid. You reach out for everything. That's a good thing. You don't want to miss out on that particular experience."

"Evidently *you* didn't." She hesitated. "I don't want to offend you, but I'm...curious. Do you think it's less...or more since you're blind?"

"It's probably a mixed bag. But if I had to choose, I'd go for touch instead of vision on that score. It's electric and the heat and mystery is so intense that..." Olivia broke off. "However, it's different every time. You'll have to tell me yourself if you decide to experiment later. I'll be interested to hear about it."

"Hmm. I guess it's only fair. But I don't know when that will be, Olivia."

"When you want it to be. You're only twenty. You have plenty of time." She smiled. "But there's one thing I have to know before I settle down with Harley to listen to my John Williams concert."

"What's that?"

"Are you going to need that cup of strong coffee?" Tricia chuckled. "Yes, please."

Lynch only stopped in the hall outside Olivia's condo to talk to Sam Eber, the night guard, for a brief moment before he joined Kendra at the elevator. "I just wanted to make sure that Sam would be on the alert no matter which way Tricia jumped." He pressed the button. "She seemed to be a bit off kilter back there. How was she when you were walking Harley?"

"Do you mean did I think she was going to thumb her nose at us and run back to her dorm?" Kendra shook her head. "She was a little upset when I asked her to delay going to the dog park until tomorrow, but she bounced back after a few minutes. And who could blame her for being fed up when her life must seem to be one big negative? I believe she's being very patient considering what she's been put through." She stepped on the elevator and pressed the button for her floor. "You must think so, too, or you wouldn't have been joking with her. We can't expect her to be full of sunshine and rainbows all the time. That would be ridiculous."

"And you're being very defensive," Lynch said quietly. "I'm not attacking her. I admire her, but I realize that anyone who has gone through what she has might be prone to emotional difficulties that could cause her to consider going to hide in the nearest cave."

Kendra shook her head. "Not Tricia. She's stronger than that."

"You might be right. I just want to be sure we don't expect too much from her. She's doing that all on her own. She's trying to be a combination of Wonder Woman and a female Einstein." He glanced at her. "And perhaps a little of Kendra Michaels. We don't want her to get lost along the way. She's too valuable a human being."

"My, how you've changed, Lynch," she murmured.

"Not really. I've just been watching her try to break her own records at that pool. She has a passion to win. I'm very fond of passion."

"I've noticed. That's what makes you—" Her phone was ringing, and she glanced at the ID. "Blocked." She frowned and pressed the SPEAKER button. "Can't be Griffin. What the hell?" She answered, "Kendra Michaels."

"How delighted I am to talk to you again, Kendra. I decided tonight that just seeing that lovely face wasn't giving me the satisfaction I needed to feel that rush that was so exciting before. Have you missed me?"

She tensed. She recognized that voice. "How could I? I don't know who the hell you are."

"Yes, you do. You're much too smart to forget me. I'm willing to wager you've figured out several interesting things about me just from hearing me speak in that construction site. Isn't that true?"

"It might be. If I cared to think about you."

"Oh, you'd care. I don't believe you can care about much of anything else at the moment. That's what domination is all about. Didn't Jackie explain that to you?"

"She didn't have time to explain anything before you killed her."

"But I did allow her enough time to see you. I wanted you to know that I was stronger than Jackie even at the end. She was never a worthy Alpha. Pure delusions of grandeur. Did she tell you anything of interest?"

"That your name is Milo. I'm tracking you down now."

He chuckled. "Lies. And more delusions of grandeur. How do you know I didn't lie to her and give her a false name? And how do you know that I don't have another Beta in the FBI feeding me information? Don't you believe that would be the crowning achievement for an Alpha? Imagine the power that would give me. How else would I have been able to subdue Barrett so easily? How else would I know he was going to betray me?" He paused. "How else would I have been able to research plans that would allow me to kill the maximum number of agents in that explosion?"

"And you could be lying to me now, trying to make a fool of me."

He laughed. "Yes, I could. But you don't know if I am. Am I willing to serve up a valuable FBI informant to try to fool you? I rather think I am." He was no longer laughing. "You've been getting in my way, Kendra. I can't tell you how angry I was when I was removing the nails from my flesh after our first encounter. And Jackie was almost willing to betray me when she ran into you. She knew what I could do to her, and yet she risked it. Now you're considering taking away another death that would be very exciting for me? How can I allow that, Kendra?"

"You're not going to have a choice," she said hoarsely. "Not from the day you blew up those detectives in that crater, you bastard."

He was chuckling again. "That's what I wanted. I needed to get you aroused enough for you to be an intriguing adversary. I believe you've reached that point now. I'll start picking off the people around you that you care about. Is Lynch listening?"

"Yes."

"He'll be included, of course. I'm looking forward to him. He's the perfect example of the Omega. Do you realize I've found that an Omega is really a totally independent Alpha who cannot be controlled? And Tricia, the divine swimmer…I almost killed her when I was pointing my rifle at her as she knelt beside that dog tonight. But you were getting into my head even then. Next time I'll kill her *and* that mutt."

Another stunning, terrifying revelation. Don't let him know how it had affected her. "You're not going to get the chance."

"Watch me," he whispered.

He cut the connection.

Kendra drew a shaky breath. "Son of a *bitch*."

"Yes," Lynch said grimly as he pulled her out of the elevator on her floor and nudged her toward her condo door. "But I need to get you inside before I start adding any more obscene words to that chant." He was unlocking the door. "And I have a couple of phone calls to make first."

She pulled away from him. "I'll get myself inside. Who are you calling?"

"Griffin. I want more guards at the condos." He was talking on the phone a moment later.

She stopped listening and wandered across the room to the window and looked down at the street below.

Next time I'll kill her and that mutt.

"Stop thinking about it. Griffin is sending two more agents to guard the condos." Lynch was standing behind her, his hands on her shoulders. "I've alerted Sam at Olivia's of the possible immediate threat. Everyone will be safe."

"Will they?" She was still looking down at the street. "I thought we were safe on that walk this evening. I thought I was being so careful not letting her go to the dog park." She shuddered. "And he was out there, sighting down at us with a rifle. I have to know where he was, Lynch."

"We'll find out," Lynch said gently. "First thing tomorrow."

"No." She whirled to face him. "*Now.* I want to go down there right now and find out. I don't want to be that vulnerable again. I remember the exact position where Tricia and Harley were standing when he was aiming that gun. We were down the block near the business section. You'll be able to tell me where he was standing, won't you?"

"Probably. Almost certainly."

"Of course you will. You're an expert." She turned and headed for the door. "Let's go."

———◆———

Milo stared at his phone a good five minutes after his call with Kendra Michaels ended. He felt a tingling, a charge, that left him wanting more. It felt good to be on the front lines again, rather than pulling strings in the background.

But that approach had its own rewards, and he'd been cultivating three new front men—and one front *woman*—for his next wave of killings. Two of the men were in Europe, one was in New York, and the woman was in Mexico. He hadn't decided which one he'd trust with such responsibility, but he had high hopes for each of them.

But he'd also had high hopes for James Michael Barrett. The man had carried out his assignments well, skillfully executing the targets they had chosen together. Too bad he had eventually become so sloppy and gotten caught. Even then he kept his mouth shut for the better part of two years, telling the authorities nothing about their lethal partnership. But when Barrett struck a deal with the DA to reveal the location of Dayna Voyles' corpse, the writing was on the wall. Milo knew he had to terminate Barrett before the idiot could expose everything.

That fool. Barrett started to get sloppy around the time he was researching Tricia Walton for the last of their planned kills. He'd fixated on her and become obsessed. Milo grimaced at the thought. He'd given Barrett the girl's swim goggles as a reward for staying silent, but he knew he'd eventually have to kill him.

Milo smiled. He believed in meticulous planning, but that trigger bomb he planted in Dayna Voyles' grave was a master stroke of improvisation. Still, in the end, it would go down as just an exciting diversion. After another few days, he'd return to his life's work.

All in good time.

Why look to the future when he had such delicious loose ends to occupy him here?

———

A strong wind was blowing when Kendra and Lynch left her condo and reached the cross street. That was the only difference Kendra noticed from the time she'd been with Tricia a few hours before. No chill, no feeling of menace. Shouldn't she feel something? She would have thought that the darkness would have made the closed office buildings appear more starkly barren and threatening. Yet all she could think about was how the sunlight must have looked shining on that rifle when she'd thought they were safe.

"I was standing here." Kendra moved two yards away. "Tricia was kneeling beside Harley right on this spot. We were talking. Should I stand here until you get a fix on the position?"

Lynch shook his head. "I think it had to be the Acme Mortgage Building." He was standing in front of her, gazing at the building. "I'll go see if I can get the security guards to show me the roof. I don't need you. Go stand in the vestibule until I get back."

"Why should I do that?" Then she slowly nodded. "You think he might still be here? You think that he could be trying to trick me?"

"I don't believe it's likely. He doesn't know that you don't react or think like anyone else. Who else would run out here to verify exactly where he would have positioned himself?"

"But you're still being careful." She was trying to work it out. "And it's because he's so clever. You're wondering if he could have researched and guessed what I'd do."

"It's not likely," he repeated. "But why take chances? Just wait for me here."

"There could be a threat to you, too. What if he's still there?"

"I hope he is," Lynch said grimly. "I want him very badly."

"So do I." She fell into step with him. "Let's just see how well he knows me..."

Fifteen minutes later they were standing on the roof of the Acme building looking down at the street twenty floors below.

Kendra took a step closer to the edge. "Here." She squatted down; her eyes narrowed. "It would have been here, wouldn't it?"

Lynch nodded. "He would have had a perfect shot." The beam of his flashlight was raking the area. "And I'll bet he didn't leave anything behind. He probably avoided all security cameras. I'll bring a forensics team up tomorrow to verify, but he wouldn't have given you even a hint if he'd been worried about it. Can we go back to the condo now? That security guard standing over there is getting a little nervous. He didn't want to bring us up here."

"But you persuaded him." She slowly stood up. "I wasn't worried. You're always able to persuade anyone to do what you want."

"I haven't had too much luck with you tonight."

"Because you knew it was important to me." She took one last look down at the street. "He would have seen the two of us and Harley. He even would have been able to see the two detectives down the block. Was he afraid of them? Why didn't he take that shot?"

"Maybe his cup was overflowing, and he couldn't make up his mind."

Her gaze flew to his face. "Do you mean what I think you do?"

"I wish I didn't. But I'm only stating the obvious. You were the one he chose to call and taunt tonight. You've seen that he has reason to hate you. These days he might be using Tricia to get to you."

"It's something to think about." Then she shook her head. "Even if I was a desirable target, it wouldn't stop him from going after Tricia. Though I suppose I should be grateful that it caused confusion."

"Yes, by all means, let's be grateful." Lynch's tone was ironic. "Now may I take you back to your condo? Milo brought up a couple of new items in that conversation that had nothing to do with his sniper abilities. I have a few things to explore before I take Tricia to the swim center in the morning."

She was already heading for the roof exit door. "I just couldn't get my mind off the thought of Tricia and Harley lying dead in the street. I still can't. That bastard was damn good at making me—" She broke off and drew a deep breath. "We'll go back and have coffee and talk about what was truth and what was lies. Okay?"

"Very much okay," Lynch said quietly. "I realize what's important to you. That's why we're here on this rooftop. You didn't make a mistake. I told Griffin to make certain the exterior area around the condos was safe, but I left it up to him. I should have done it myself. Any mistake was mine."

"Bullshit." She glanced back at him. "Griffin. You. Me. We're all to blame. We just can't let it happen again."

"And it won't." He was following her toward the elevator shaft. "Coffee and an analytical in-depth conversation about how to take down that psychopath seems to be just what we need to prevent it."

———————

FORTY-FIVE MINUTES LATER
KENDRA'S CONDO

Kendra poured coffee into Lynch's cup. "It was Milo's references to the FBI that you were disturbed about."

She sat down on the couch beside him. "I was stunned at the time, but then I thought that perhaps he was only trying to upset me and show me how powerful he could be."

"And that could have been his aim, but if his megalomania is strong enough, he might have been bragging about a true accomplishment. It must be frustrating to have to hide how clever he is to everyone around him when he's so proud of himself. Keeping that power secret is a weapon in itself." His lips twisted. "And he's clearly fond of weapons and being able to strike from ambush. Everything he said about the advantages he might have had by recruiting an FBI informant was absolutely correct. The more I consider it, the more I believe that there's no reason why he wouldn't want to make a habit of acquiring Betas to worship at his temple whenever he could."

"That's a terrifying idea," Kendra said. "I don't like the thought of some psycho running around the planet being able to manipulate people just because they don't have the will to resist him. It's hard to believe that could happen."

"Because you can't imagine it happening to you." He shrugged. "I agree with you on all counts. I can't imagine it either. But Jackie Gabert not only imagined, she participated as an Alpha. She must have run across any number of people she was able to dominate enough to satisfy her."

She made a face. "Betas?"

"Whatever. That's what she called David Spalman. I don't think either one of us will deny that kid exhibited all the signs of weakness and submission that she claimed a subject had to possess. I don't know what would constitute a character that could fall under domination like that, but if it exists then there could be a problem." He was frowning thoughtfully. "Then there was Dusenberry. He was a completely different case and circumstance, but he was dominated and compelled to do what Milo wanted about the goggles."

"And Barrett?" Kendra took a sip of her coffee. "You're accepting all of this a little too easily, Lynch."

"Maybe I am." Lynch smiled. "But then Milo said I was the perfect example of an Omega. I'm finding most of this fairly reasonable. If you accept that Barrett could be dominated, then you have to accept that a powerful Alpha like Milo could do it." He paused. "Even to the point that Milo ordered most of the killings committed by Barrett."

"Most of them? That's scary."

"But you're not scared. You were heading in that direction anyway." He added, "And you have to keep on going if you're going to get to what Milo said about FBI informants. Are you there yet?"

She slowly nodded. "I believe it's possible considering the size of his ego. Since we're supposed to be victims, he would feel safer that he could preen a bit to us." She frowned. "And that possibility is very dangerous. The FBI knows what we're doing at any given moment. They have to know in order for us to keep Tricia safe." Her gaze flew up to his face. "Griffin is sending extra guards. How do we know if they can be trusted?"

"Griffin isn't going to take chances with anyone who isn't trustworthy. Besides, I asked Sam to call me when they got here. I'll go down and check them out."

She relaxed. "It's all crazy, isn't it? If the FBI can't be trusted, who can be?"

He shook his head. "We trust ourselves just as we've always done. Beyond that, we have friends at the Bureau, and we'll know who is rock-solid."

She wrinkled her nose. "I won't."

"Then you'll leave it to me." He brushed his lips on the top of her head. "And perhaps Milo is full of bullshit, and it will all be for nothing. That's not bad, either. It will be—" His phone rang and he glanced down at the ID. "Sam." He put his coffee cup on the end table and got to his feet. "Stay put. I'll lock you in. I shouldn't be long, but I need to check credentials. I'll be back to tell you who Griffin chose on this short notice."

She nodded as she watched him walk to the door. "You'd better," she said dryly. "After you've completely riddled my faith in the Bureau, I could use a little reassurance." She smiled. "On a number of subjects. Milo was a little too enthusiastic about future contact with you. I think I'll spend a little time until you get back looking up the definition and complete description of an Omega man."

———◆———

"Move over…"

Lynch's voice, Kendra realized drowsily, soft, deep, infinitely male. She scooted over on the couch and slipped into his arms. This was right. This is what she had wanted. Why had it taken so long?

"Too long…"

"Not my fault. This is what I've been wanting all along." He cuddled her cheek into the hollow of his shoulder where she liked it. "Hush. You're still not ready and I'm good with that. You're getting closer all the time. Go back to sleep. You're exhausted. It's been one hell of an evening for you. I just want to hold you for a little while before I have to shower and get Tricia to the center."

She wanted to hold him, too. It seemed very important at this moment. "Tricia...safe?"

"Yes, though it took forever to check those FBI credentials. I'm sure far longer than it did for you to check mine as an Omega wannabe."

"No. You'll be surprised, you come...very close. I'll tell you...later."

"You do that." He pulled her closer. "I can hardly wait to hear what else that bastard was right about."

"You should be glad. It was good that he was right about you this time." She snuggled closer. "Omega...I like it..."

CHAPTER

12

"Time to wake up." Lynch was kneeling beside her, and Kendra was vaguely aware he smelled of soap and shampoo and spicy aftershave. "I've got to go. I was thinking about letting you sleep but that's not going to work. I blew that about two in the morning."

"What are you talking about?" Kendra yawned. "Blew what?"

"My chance for a graceful exit. I've got to scoot Tricia out of Olivia's condo, and I doubt if I can keep Olivia from calling you and asking for explanations the minute Tricia's out of the building. I had problems with her during the night."

"Problems?" Kendra was suddenly wide awake. She went stiff and sat upright. "What problems? Why didn't you tell me? Problems with Olivia?"

"Well, more trouble with Harley. You know how sensitive that dog can be. He heard Sam talking to me in the hall, and then the two men Griffin sent arrived. He started to make a typical Harley uproar. Olivia heard it and came out to check with Sam."

"What did you tell her?"

"That there had been trouble, but it had been taken care of. That you'd talk to her in the morning about it and we'd prefer not to mention it to Tricia until she'd finished her training for the day."

"And Olivia accepted that? I can't believe it."

"Neither could I, but she said Tricia was already settled in the guest room and there was no use disturbing her." His lips tightened grimly. "But I'll bet Olivia will give you the third degree the minute she sees you, so be prepared."

"No bet. She ordinarily would have marched up and demanded to know what was happening."

"She isn't shy about doing that with me," Lynch said. "I was expecting it. I did say you were tired and might be sleeping."

"Who knows why?" Kendra asked. "All I know is that it's going to be a very difficult conversation with both of them."

"And I didn't help."

"You did all you could. What could you say? Just take care of Tricia today."

"I will. At least I made sure the aquatic center is safe." He paused. "I've told Sam he's to assign one of those men Griffin sent him to you today. Don't argue, Kendra."

"Don't be ridiculous. I will argue. It's Tricia we have to concentrate on. Milo might hate me, but he seemed to prefer going after anyone close to me. Like you, Lynch. Or he might not know about my mother yet, but he could find out. Then there's Olivia. How many guards are you going to have to assign to keep everyone around me safe?"

"As many as necessary. But I'll settle for you at the moment. I tend to be selfish that way." He headed for the door. "Though I'll give Griffin a call and tell him I want surveillance on your mother and Olivia, too. It won't be too difficult. All I have to do is pull the strings. He wants me to owe him. I'll see you this evening and we'll discuss anyone else on your list. Lock the door behind me."

Kendra's hands clenched as she watched the door shut behind him. She'd never seen Lynch this determined. He'd always listened to her. He could be madly annoying at times and managed to get his own way more often than not. But it always ended with both of them working together until they found a strategy to merge and succeed.

Merge.

And the merging had often been physical as well as mental. Passion as well as laughter. It was when she'd realized she was growing to *need* him that she'd panicked, because she didn't want to be that dependent on anyone. She'd thought she was safe with a man as independent and self-sufficient as Lynch, but what if that wasn't the truth? She'd taken a step back, but she always seemed to move toward him again.

Or Lynch moved toward her.

As he had this time.

He'd been careful and moved with slow deliberation. But she knew how powerful he could be when he decided to go for something he wanted. Now he wanted to protect her, and he would pull out all the stops until he got his way.

Her phone rang.

It was Olivia. "Lynch just took Tricia," she said curtly. "Are you coming here, or should I come to you?"

"I'll come to you. I'll shower and be down in thirty minutes."

"Good." She ended the call.

Kendra flinched and immediately headed for the bathroom. Olivia's tone had been definitely cool, and she had a right to be irritated. Kendra should have found a way to contact her and tell her what had happened last night. She'd been upset but Olivia was her friend, and she was as concerned about Tricia as Kendra. It didn't matter that she hadn't wanted to worry Olivia by telling her that Milo had turned his venom toward her. She deserved honesty, not an apology.

But when Olivia opened the door to her knock, after greeting Harley, she found herself quickly apologizing. "You have a right to be pissed off. I don't know why you were so kind to Lynch last night, but you deserved to hear the truth from both of us. He was trying to organize a defensive action and he knew I was upset. I didn't know about it until this morning when he woke me."

"You were asleep? He said you were, but I thought he was lying."

"He was." She ran her hand through her hair. "Or maybe he wasn't. I fell asleep after he left the condo. He might have wanted to ask me to discuss it with you after he came back."

"Lynch seldom hesitates to give me either good or bad news. Why are you defending him?"

She sighed. "I don't know. I'm really irritated with him at the moment. It was just a really bad night for both of us and I felt as if I shouldn't let him take the entire blame."

"Bad night?" Olivia grimaced. "That will be a disappointment to Tricia. Though I suspected when Harley and I interrupted Lynch's meeting in the hall that I was going to have to give her bad news of some sort." She gestured to the couch. "Sit down and tell me why you're making excuses for Lynch, and if I should prepare to go after him with guns blazing."

———◆———

"Holy shit," Olivia said as Kendra finished. "I can see why you didn't want to tell Tricia any of this before she finished with her training. Not exactly the thing she'd want to have to think about all day."

"Or any part of her day," Kendra said. "That was why Griffin's sending extra agents here to help out Sam. I wanted to reassure her that Lynch said that the Acme building security will be covered and the other buildings are being checked out to make certain they'd be sniper-proof. Lynch is doing everything he can to keep her safe." She added wryly, "As well as any other potential victims in Milo's sights. Lynch is going overboard as usual. But in the case of you or my mother, I wouldn't think of reining him in."

"Neither would I. I have no objection to him taking a little trouble to keep me alive," Olivia said. "You probably mean yourself by him going overboard. You feel that because you've taken all those lessons in self-defense, you should be able to take care of yourself." She smiled. "I've taken a few myself, but I don't mind being taken care of by a big, strong detective. We all have our strengths."

"Yes, we do. I believe that's what you told Tricia when you first met her. You've gotten to know her much better since then. She's been your shadow except when she's at school."

"She likes to work, so do I." She added, "And she loves my dog." She was suddenly no longer smiling. "Which makes me furious when I think how that bastard threatened to kill Harley as well as Tricia. Kill a helpless animal because she was good to him? We've got to find a way to castrate that son of a bitch."

"I'll bet Tricia would be glad to research ways and means to do that." Kendra bent down to stroke Harley's head. "She'd have a lot of company, boy."

He looked up at her with his blue and brown eyes as if he understood. Maybe he did, Kendra thought.

"What do you intend to do today?" Olivia asked. "I'd think you'd want to have a little talk with Griffin about what Milo said about having a cohort at FBI headquarters. I didn't like that at all."

"Neither did I," Kendra said. "But Lynch has mega influence with Griffin, and that means he has a free pass into every department. He'd be able to go forth and conquer."

She nodded. "I can see Lynch in that role. But I can't see you letting him do it. I thought that you said you were annoyed at him at the moment." She frowned. "Which reminds me, didn't you tell me you'd had a bad night with Lynch? I was going to ask you about that."

"You've just heard it." She narrowed her eyes. "What did you think I meant?" She remembered something else. "You even said Tricia would be disappointed. What was that about?"

"Probably better to skip it," Olivia said. "We were

on two different tracks. Your story was much more important and to the point." She changed the subject. "Why don't I fix us breakfast? Then we'll talk about how we're going to break it to Tricia about what happened to you last night."

"Olivia."

She shrugged. "I didn't think you'd fall for that. I thought I'd try. Okay. Reverse. While I fix breakfast, I'll tell you why Tricia decided to spend the night with me."

"She was upset and depressed."

"Would you like an omelet or pancakes?"

"Omelet." She followed her and sat down at the bar. "She wasn't upset?"

"She was, but that's her life these days. It doesn't stop her from thinking about other people. She likes you very much, Kendra. She wants the best for you. She realizes she owes you a good deal and she's determined to pay you."

"Where is all this going?"

"She's very bright and she's figured out that Lynch is your lover. She approves."

"What?"

"But she also thought she might be in your way, so she's trying to be diplomatic."

"She told you all this?"

"The subject came up. Naturally I didn't encourage her."

"But you didn't discourage her."

"That wasn't my place. I stay out of your affairs. She's old enough to make her own decisions."

"You didn't offer an opinion?"

"Only that your relationship was complicated, which is absolutely true. Why are we discussing this?

There was clearly a misunderstanding and I'm sure the two of you can straighten it out later."

"I'm sure we can, too. But it would have helped if you hadn't decided to aid and abet."

"You didn't listen to me. I'm Madam Neutral where you're concerned."

Kendra made a rude noise.

Olivia was smiling faintly. "Until I decide you're really being unreasonable. Then as a friend it's my duty to weigh in with my opinion. But I figured you were happy to have Lynch around to give you affection and support. I hope he was satisfactory?"

Kendra had the briefest vision of Lynch holding her, tucking her head on his shoulder, the sound of his voice giving her that sense that everything was as it should be. "As I said, it was a bad night. Lynch is usually a help when you need someone in your corner."

"Yes. That's why I like the idea that he usually comes flying to your corner when you have problems." Olivia was dishing the omelet onto a plate. "Even when you find it annoying. However, independence is a wonderful thing and I'm usually the first one to applaud it."

"Usually? Eternally." Kendra picked up her fork. "You wrote the book."

"We wrote it together," Olivia said quietly. "From the day we met at the academy. But you have a tendency lately to strike out on your own. While I've become a bit more mellow."

"I didn't notice. You're as tough as ever."

"I didn't say I wasn't. I'm just not constantly on the defense these days."

She stiffened. "You think I am?"

"Not entirely. I think that you deal with people like Milo so much that you sometimes automatically look for weakness in yourself and relationships so that you can crush it."

Kendra's eyes widened. "That would be terrible. Not with you. Never with you."

"No, I'm an exception. I hope I always will be."

Kendra reached out and covered Olivia's hand with her own. "You will. No question."

"I'm just saying that you should be careful not to throw out the baby with the bathwater. Don't let the Milos of the world take anything away from you."

Kendra suddenly chuckled. "Did I ever tell you how I hate that saying? The mere idea of throwing out a baby horrifies me."

"Good, then you'll remember it." Olivia poured herself a cup of coffee. "Now finish your omelet and then tell me what you're going to do today so that we can tell Tricia something positive. She's going to need it when we unload that story you just told me."

"I've got an idea how I can take a few baby steps. But it's not going to be easy, I may get blown out of the water." She reached for her phone. "And there's a call I have to make."

———

"Are you crazy, Kendra?" Metcalf interrupted her before she even finished explaining. "You'd actually believe a murdering son of a bitch like that Milo?" He swore long and vehemently. "There's no way any of our agents would cooperate in a scheme to kill a fellow officer. I know most of those guys in our office."

"But not all of them," Kendra said. "And I do

know that it sounds crazy. I wouldn't have even called you if it wasn't a life-or-death case. Just look on it as an exercise to eliminate a possibility."

"A possibility to railroad my friends who risk their lives every day to catch the bad guys. Some of them have been assigned to keep you and that young swimmer alive."

"And I'll do my best to clear them of any wrongful charges. You know that, Metcalf. You know *me*. As I said, I only want to eliminate. We're both aware that there are crooked cops out there. We'll have to go to Griffin eventually, but that means a full-scale investigation. I'd rather have someone I trust who has keen eyes and great instincts and might have run across anything that didn't seem quite…right on a case. All I want you to do is point me in the right direction about personality, attitude, and a willingness to ignore the Bureau's stringent rules of conduct. I'm not trying to pin a crime on anyone. Do you believe you can think about it today and then text me with what you come up with? It will save us time when we have to pore over the stuff Griffin will give us."

He was silent. Then he finally growled, "He'll tell you the same thing I did."

"We'll be ready for it. I hope you're both right. I hope Milo was lying through his teeth." She paused. "I didn't want to ask you to do this. Are you going to help me?"

"I'll do it. I trust you. If it was anyone else, I'd tell them to go to hell. But you'll be fair and careful and not try to frame anyone." He added curtly, "But you owe me, Kendra."

"Yes, I do. I'll be waiting for your text. Thanks, Metcalf."

She ended the call.

Then she called Lynch at the swim center. "Metcalf will give me his list by the end of the day. You should realize he really didn't like it or me by the end of the call. I don't blame him. If the situation wasn't so difficult, I'd never have reached out to him. I've done my part, now you'd better come through with help from Griffin."

"You sound very grim," Lynch said. "I've already called Griffin and made an appointment for us with him for this evening. I'll drop off Tricia with Olivia after she finishes and pick you up." He added, "And I'll be the one to tell Tricia about Milo and his damn rifle before I turn her over to Olivia."

"I can do that. It's my job."

"Our job. I'm doing it. Be ready to go."

He cut the connection.

8:15 P.M.
SPECIAL AGENT GRIFFIN'S OFFICE

"You can't expect me to go along with this, Lynch," Griffin said harshly. "It's all crap. You can't believe that asshole could persuade any of my agents to turn rogue. Hell, you were an agent yourself before you turned black ops. And what if there was a leak to the media that I was investigating my own men?"

"There wouldn't be a leak," Lynch said. "You're too careful to allow that to happen. So, scratch that threat. And it will only be me and Kendra who examine the files we're given. We'll be quick, but thorough. We'll be in and out before you know it."

"Oh, I'd know it," Griffin said flatly. "I'd keep my

eye on you twenty-four seven, *if* I was stupid enough to let you have a look at my personnel records." He turned to Kendra. "You're going along with this? I thought you had more sense."

"I want to call Milo's bluff," Kendra said. "He was trying to panic me. I don't believe we're going to find anything, but we have to explore every path. We need you to help us, Griffin. You know we'll be careful. You don't owe me anything, but Lynch appears to think you might be willing to strike a deal with him."

"Really? I've already been more than cooperative with you, Lynch." He turned back to Lynch. "What have you got to offer me?"

"What do you want?"

Griffin leaned back in his chair. "Let's talk about it."

"Let's not. One favor, at your discretion. No more," Lynch said. "I'm not playing games. You wouldn't get that bribe if I didn't think you were a decent agent beneath all that bullshit."

Griffin's face flushed. "You're the one who came to me."

"Yes or no? You know I'm good for it. Give me what I want, or we'll walk out of here and I'll find some other way. But you'll have to prepare yourself for that way being much more intrusive. And it might involve other government agencies."

"Arrogant bastard."

"Right. Yes or no?"

Griffin was frowning. "You're not going to find anything." He paused. "And if you find something suspect, you bring it to me."

"No problem."

"I'll need a couple of days to pull together those files. I have to be discreet about it."

"You won't need to worry about that. Fifteen minutes from now, I'll have the personnel files of everyone in your office downloaded into my iPad."

Griffin swore. "Courtesy of your sources in the DOJ?"

"My sources prefer to remain anonymous."

Griffin swore again. "Then why did you even ask me?"

"Professional courtesy. Thanks for your help. We appreciate it."

"You're welcome," Griffin said ironically. "Anytime." He glanced at Kendra. "It seems every time you turn around, you're attracting more attention from Milo. You might prove even more valuable than I thought possible. Perhaps we should discuss it."

"Back off," Lynch said coldly.

"I was speaking to Kendra," Griffin said. "You and I have had our discussion. She's always been much more reasonable." He smiled. "We'll talk later, Kendra."

He strolled out of the office.

"Bastard," Lynch muttered as he nudged Kendra toward the elevator.

"What did you expect?" Kendra asked. "His pride was wounded, and he felt the need to lash out. You were controlling the situation from the moment we walked into the office. He didn't like it."

"Too bad. He was obviously trying to negotiate. I wanted to avoid that at all costs. His hurt feelings shouldn't have involved you," Lynch said.

"I agree. I'll make my own decisions." She shot him a glance as she stepped on the elevator. "And after last night Griffin's idea is becoming more appealing. Unless we can come up with another solution soon, Griffin may get what he wants."

"We'll come up with another solution. It might not be as soon as you'd like, but it will be better than any alternative Griffin can offer you." He was suddenly smiling. "Hey, give me a break. I know I was a little too overbearing and it pissed you off. But it's not as if we're standing still."

"Overbearing? Not accurate. I was thinking domineering."

"Ouch." Lynch grimaced. "Maybe I was. I was scared, and I had to be sure you'd listen to me."

"Scared? I believe you said that before. You don't get scared. And you did exactly the wrong thing if you wanted me to pay attention to anything you said."

"Which should tell you how scared I was. I would have been fired from any of the agencies and companies I work for if I'd conducted their affairs the way I've handled you since I came back."

"Handled?" Kendra repeated.

"See?" He shook his head. "I did it again." His smile deepened and became rueful and yet almost endearing. "There can be only one explanation. You're intimidating me."

"Bullshit." But she found herself smiling at the sheer ridiculousness of the idea. "How many world dictators have you faced down?"

"That's different, I'm not vulnerable to any of those assholes." His voice lowered to velvet softness as he coaxed, "I just need a little more time. We're already making progress. Tomorrow might be a breakthrough."

"And it might not." She looked away from him so that she could ignore the magnetism and wouldn't see how damnably charismatic he was being. "Olivia told me that I need something to tell Tricia that's positive.

She's right, all I have right now are 'mights' and 'maybes.'"

"Then I'll work on positive," Lynch said. "Just don't let Griffin drop in tomorrow while you're checking over those records and talk you into anything."

She still didn't look at him. "Don't worry about that. I just hope Tricia will be feeling better about things by then."

He was silent for a long moment. "Maybe she'll be more resilient than you think. We'll see when we get back to the condo." Lynch looked down at his phone. "Before we get on the road, I need to make a call or two to make sure I get those employee files as soon as I think I can."

"Fine. I'll meet you at the car."

"What are you going to do?"

"Pay a visit to the one other person I know who will probably still be here."

***

Kendra took the elevator to the third floor, where she stepped toward a conference room with Trey Suber's name now on a plaque next to the door. She looked around the spacious quarters and turned to Trey. "They gave you this entire room?"

"Nice, huh?"

Kendra looked at the row of bulletin boards lining one side of the room and six large monitors affixed to the other. "You must have something on Griffin. Almost everyone else in this place is working out of little cubicles."

"I always consult on several cases at once. He thought it would help me to be able to spread out.

When the financial crimes team moved downtown, I got this room for myself."

"He probably wants to keep you happy, so you don't leave for Washington."

Kendra looked at a tripod-mounted telescope sitting in the corner of the room. "Hmm. I didn't figure you for a Peeping Tom."

Trey smiled. "I'm not *only* into serial killers. I'm kind of an amateur astronomer."

Kendra leaned over and looked through the eyepiece. "It's hard to see anything in the city, isn't it?"

"It's better than you might think. But for serious stargazing, I go to Julian or the desert. You know, it's possible to see the entire Milky Way from only one percent of the U.S. One of those spots happens to be less than ninety minutes from here."

"Wow." She straightened and turned toward one of the monitors, which was cycling gory crime scene photos of Jackie Gabert. The one beside it displayed several shots of Stewart Dusenberry at the construction scene.

Kendra blanched at the sight. "I'm surprised you don't have shots of the bomb victims."

"They're all here." Suber waved to a dark monitor. "They're all loaded on screen three. I usually leave that one off unless I need to take a look. People around here don't appreciate seeing pictures of their dismembered friends and colleagues."

"Imagine that."

He looked down. "To tell you the truth, I'm not crazy about those shots, either."

Kendra looked at him in surprise. "Squeamish? That doesn't sound like the Trey Suber I know."

He shrugged. "I've worked hundreds of serial

killer cases and studied thousands more. But this is the first time one of them murdered someone I knew. It's different."

"Yes, it is."

"I liked Cynthia Strode. She was always nice to me. Some people around here, they look at my website and trading cards and treat me like some kind of weirdo."

Kendra tried to remember if she'd ever treated Trey that way. She hoped not.

He paced across the room. "Cynthia was a good person. I want to catch this guy."

"Me too." She stepped toward him. "That's why I came down here."

"What do you mean?"

"This may not be anything, but I want you to look at this case in a different light." She lowered her voice. "I've already spoken to Griffin about this, but there's been some indication that the killer may be in law enforcement. Someone who may even work in this very building."

He gave her a skeptical look. "And where did this indication come from? The killer?"

"I'm just asking you to consider it. You know the people here, and you know more about serial killers than anyone."

"That's why I'm having a hard time believing it. Serial killers in law enforcement are a rare phenomenon. *Really* rare. Not unheard of, as you well know. But I think you're wasting your time. And if you want to pull me down that rabbit hole, you'd be wasting my time."

Trey seemed angry, almost combative. But as he'd said, it was a personal case for him. She needed to cut him some slack. It hadn't been her intention to alienate him.

"Okay, for the moment, put aside the possibility that a law-enforcement officer may be involved."

"Thank you."

"What do you think of our case?"

"Well, I've been thinking about the psychological dynamics of the case."

"That makes two of us."

Trey spoke quickly, as he often did when discussing one of their investigations. "There hasn't been a lot of research done with dominance hierarchies as it relates to serial killer teams, probably because teams like this are so rare."

"This seems more like a cult."

"Exactly!" Trey wrinkled his brow. "In my experience, as much as participants like to dress up their behavior with terminology and concepts from other disciplines like psychology or even physics, at its root it's just classic cult-like behavior. A charismatic leader who needs to control, preying on followers who need to *be* controlled. But not every wannabe leader, or so-called Alpha, has the skills to find, influence, and control followers. Jackie Gabert seemed particularly ham-fisted in her attempts. Which may be one reason she's in a drawer in the morgue right now."

"Well, I can personally testify to her ham-fistedness."

"A little bit of knowledge can be a dangerous thing. That seems especially true when you're dealing with a serial killer."

Trey picked up a palm-size remote and used it to cycle through scores of photos taken at Jackie's murder scene. "There's a ritualistic aspect to our killer, one that seems to involve deliberation and planning. But he's also a skilled improvisor. He's shown a willingness to kill to cover his tracks, especially when our investigation identifies someone who might be able to point the way toward him."

Kendra turned from the photos. "Again, a law-enforcement agent or someone else intimately familiar with our investigation would know who those people are."

Trey shook his head. "I'm still not buying it."

She backed toward the door. "Just...think about it. Okay?"

"No, it's not okay. Good night, Kendra," he said coldly.

Give it up. She left his office.

———

Tricia wasn't with Olivia when they got back to her condo.

Olivia shrugged. "Don't blame me. I was ready to help any way I could. But I struck out. She stayed with me for about twenty minutes, but she didn't say more than a few words. Then she said she was going to your place to rest. I didn't try to stop her. It was evident that she was upset, but I wasn't the one she wanted to talk to." She turned to Lynch. "What was her reaction when you first told her?"

"Shocked, angry, then she closed up and I couldn't tell what she was feeling. I tried to reassure her, but she just politely said she knew I'd do everything possible, and she was quiet for the rest of the drive back here. I was hoping she'd confide in you, Olivia."

"Well, she obviously didn't," Kendra said. "And I was too busy trying to help bulldoze Griffin to be here when she needed me. Hell, I should have been the one to tell her in the first place." She turned toward the door. "I'll see you both later. I'm going to go up and see if I can do anything."

Lynch took a step forward. "Do you want me to—"

"No, you've had your turn." She said over her shoulder, "And I'm sure you were your usual persuasive self. It's nothing you did wrong; she's just gone through too much. She probably won't listen to me, either."

But she had to try, Kendra thought, as she took the elevator up to her condo. She had to find out if there was something she could do to help Tricia get over the fear she must be feeling. If she could keep her from closing down as she had when Lynch had first told her about Milo and his rifle.

Then she was unlocking her front door and going into the foyer. "Tricia?" she called as she slammed the door. "I'm home. Is there anything that I can—"

"What are you shouting about?" Tricia came out of the kitchen sipping her favorite green vegetable drink. "Have you eaten yet? I could make us grilled cheese sandwiches."

"Are you okay?" But Kendra could see that the question was unnecessary. Tricia was in her tie-dyed lime-green PJs and matching furry slippers, and the trauma and edginess Kendra had expected was entirely missing from her expression. She looked almost serene. "We were worried about you."

"You're always worried about me," Tricia said flippantly. "So is Olivia, but she hides it better. You don't even try."

"Because it's my job to worry about you," Kendra said lightly. "I've got the right to probe and be a pain in the ass. But you don't have the right to make fun of me this time. It was reasonable for me to think you might be upset. Lynch said you were shocked and angry and then you shut down."

"All very true," she said as she sat down on the couch and tucked her feet beneath her. "Lynch was incredibly perceptive and understanding, but I'm sure those razor-sharp eyes noticed every emotion I was trying so desperately to hide. The only way I could protect myself until I could pull myself together was to withdraw inside." She took another sip of her drink. "You should understand that maneuver, I've seen you do it yourself when you wanted to avoid confronting something unpleasant."

"Really?"

She nodded. "Not very often. Usually you meet everything head-on, you only withdraw when you're trying to keep from telling someone to go to hell."

Kendra chuckled. "I didn't realize I was that obvious. I know I'm not very good at it."

Tricia grinned back at her. "Takes one to know one. I've been hiding for a long time." Her smile ebbed and then was gone. "I needed to use it this time. It was a bad moment for me. It wasn't only that I knew he was planning on killing me, but he would have shot Harley, too, just for the hell of it. You actually talked to that son of a bitch. That's not good. He's reaching out to you." She shivered. "It brought back that time when he ran you down in that car and I thought he'd killed you. I hoped nothing like that would ever happen to you again. But it sounds as if what you did is causing him to zero in on you. Perhaps if I'd leave you, he'd forget about you."

"I don't think that's going to happen," Kendra said

dryly. "He has a long memory. We have to hold on until we can catch him and put him away. In the meantime, we just have to keep you safe. Lynch told you that we've taken steps to make certain that Milo can't get that close to you again."

She nodded. "And I believe that you're doing everything possible." Her voice lowered until it was almost a whisper. "But I don't know how long I can take knowing that he's out there waiting. It's been too long. One way or another I've been his victim since I was a kid in high school. I need to *do* something."

Kendra reached out and took her hand. "You have been doing something. You didn't let him beat you, and you've become a remarkable human being. You've never been his victim. I don't know anyone who could do more."

"All I've been doing lately is marking time and relying on you and Lynch and Olivia. It's not enough." She held up her hand. "But I'm not going to turn rebel right now. I have an important swim meet at Long Beach next Saturday, and I have to clear my mind of everything but that until it's over. Besides, I don't want to get in your way when you're going full-scale after Milo. So just tell me what progress you've made. Lynch said that Metcalf gave you a couple of names of agents who might have helped Milo. That sounded promising."

Kendra nodded. "It was promising that he even let me bulldoze him into doing it. He wasn't being too cooperative. He wouldn't say a word about character flaws that might be suspicious. The most he'd do was give me two names of agents who had been on duty at crime scenes of murders we now attribute to Milo. At first, he said he was going to give me three names, but he backed out on revealing the third agent. He said he wasn't going to dirty the other agent's reputation when he knew he could have nothing to do with that filth." She shrugged. "But I was considering Metcalf as a backup anyway in case Lynch couldn't get Griffin to let us examine the other personnel records. I should have known that Lynch would come through. I'll be at the Bureau first thing tomorrow scanning them." She released Tricia's hand and got to her feet. "So that's my job while Lynch is with you at the center. I'll probably work all morning on them and then break for a while. I don't want to get so numb that I miss something. I have some other research I want to do while I'm at the FBI office that could be just as important." She changed the subject as she headed for the kitchen. "Do you know, I *am* hungry. That grilled cheese sandwich sounded good. Do you want one?"

"I'll fix it." Tricia jumped to her feet and followed her. "But you can't leave me hanging like that. What's just as important?"

"Something that Griffin evidently struck out on and then just dropped. We've been so busy with being on the defensive that I didn't pick up on it and see what I could do. There are times I can see more than what's on the surface. I believe I'll take a stab at it." She smiled at Tricia as she opened the refrigerator. "I'm tired of just calling that bastard Milo. I want a last name." She pulled out the cheese. "Dammit, I want a history!"

———◆———

She called Lynch after Tricia had gone to bed. "I just wanted to let you know that Tricia is okay. Yes, she was upset, but she bounced back, and she was nearly normal by the time I came up to the condo expecting to comfort her. Whatever is normal for her. It's hard to judge sometimes. All I know is she's one tough cookie."

"No wonder you get along so well. I'll let Olivia know. She'll be relieved."

"Are you still there?"

"Yep, she made dinner and we sat and drank and waited to know if Tricia was all right. She seems to dominate our lives these days, doesn't she?"

"Just as Milo dominates hers. It's got to end. She knows it, Lynch."

"And so do we. Go to bed. Maybe you'll get lucky checking those records."

"That's what I have in mind. If I find out anything interesting, I'll call and let you know right away." She paused. "Did you know Tricia has a swim meet this Saturday at Long Beach? Is that going to prove a security nightmare for you?"

"Maybe. Hopefully only a challenge. I've already started checking out the area. Whatever we find, we'll have to deal with it. We'd never be able to persuade her to skip it. It's getting too close to the time the athletes are going to be chosen for the Olympics." He added ruefully, "It would help if we could get a better handle on what to expect from Milo. It's like working in the dark."

"Now, *that's* something I have some experience with. Twenty years' worth. Good night, Lynch."

CHAPTER

13

The plaque on the wall of the cubicle read SPE-CIAL AGENT GARY WENDELL.

Kendra poked her head in the cubicle and saw a short, sandy-haired young man wearing horn-rimmed glasses sitting before a computer. "Hi, I'm Kendra Michaels. I don't believe we've met. I don't want to bother you, but I wonder if you can help me."

"It's no bother." Wendell straightened in his chair. "Everyone knows who you are, and no one is going to complain whatever you do. We have orders to co-operate fully with you." He took several clipboards off the visitor's chair. "Sit down. But you should know, I'm not in regular personnel. They usually tap me for specialty jobs."

"That's what I've been told." She sat down and took out her laptop computer. "And that you were the one who did the background check on Jackie Gabert. Do you still have your file on her?"

"I have my own copy," he said warily. "I turned in the original just as I was told to do." He added quickly, "And it was a good, solid investigation. I did it quickly, because those were my orders, but I was thorough. There wasn't anything in the report that was shoddy."

"I didn't think there was," she said quietly. "I'm sure you were very efficient, and all the facts are correct. I'm not trying to hang you out to dry, Wendell." She made a face. "All your fellow agents I encountered today have been staring at me as if I was a spy for internal investigations. Which is perfectly natural considering what they know I'm doing. No one wants their personnel records gone through even if they're super agents. I can only assure you that I don't think you did anything wrong. I'm looking at anything you might have missed. Could I see the Gabert files?"

"Sure." He was rifling through his file drawer and pulled out a folder and handed it to her. "It's as clean as a whistle. Ask me any questions you like."

"I intend to do that." She looked at the photos of Jackie on the first page. The first was a publicity photo of Jackie in business attire looking attractive and vibrantly alive; the second was a photo of Jackie as the bloody corpse Kendra had seen at her apartment. She flinched as she gazed at it, remembering that night.

"You were there, weren't you?" Wendell asked. His eyes were fixed intently on her face. "I heard that from some of the guys. I was wondering if I should get a final interview from you, but Griffin said that his interview with you was enough."

She found herself grateful that Griffin hadn't exposed her to this young agent. "I'm certain it was more than enough. That night was chaos."

"But you got to work with Lynch." Wendell's voice was suddenly eager. "I've heard he's fantastic. I'd give anything to work one case with him. Is he as good as they tell me?"

"He's good." She dropped the subject. She really didn't need to listen to this guy's hero worship of Lynch. She looked down at the report. "It appears to be complete in every detail. So many details... You might say I had a personal relationship with Jackie, but otherwise I knew nothing about her background. I'm certain they filled you in on the principal things we're looking for in that background."

He nodded. "Milo." He went on, "And some weird cult that both he and Jackie Gabert might belong to."

"You've got it."

"No, I haven't," he said flatly. "I didn't run across either one when I was questioning everyone in Gabert's life. No Milo. None of her acquaintances knew anything about a Milo she might have had a relationship with. This domination cult might exist, but no one identifies it as a cult, and they don't talk about it if you ask them."

"How far back did you go?"

"Reagan High School. I thought grade school would be a bit ridiculous." He added sarcastically, "Do you want me to go back to kindergarten? Say the word."

"We'll discuss it later. But you must have gotten to know Jackie pretty well while you were compiling this tome. Neither of us wants to sit here while I read over this complete report. Why don't you tell me in your own words about Jackie Gabert?"

"Starting at what point?"

"Since you don't have kindergarten, start at high school."

He grimaced. "That was a fairly smart-ass remark. Sorry."

"I'll forgive you. If you start talking, Wendell."

He grinned. "Actually, Jackie was an interesting subject in a lot of ways. Her mother was a corporate lawyer and her father a college professor, neither of whom evidently had much use for a child. She spent most of her younger years at boarding schools. Her parents divorced when she was fifteen and her mother received custody. Evidently money was tight then and she put Jackie in public school. She was smart and her grades were excellent, but she became something of a rebel and experimented with drugs, sex, and whatever else she could find that intrigued her."

"Cult activity?"

"No, but she did display a dislike for restraint and was picked up by the police on several minor infractions."

"Domination tendencies?"

He nodded. "Jackie was something of a bully. She wasn't well liked by the other students. But whenever she got into trouble with her peers, she managed to finesse her way out. Like I said, she was smart. She also kept her grades up and was able to get a scholarship to UCLA. She'd evidently matured a little by then and shed some of her more annoying faults. She joined several clubs, began to take communication classes, and got a job waiting tables so that she could back-pack all over Europe. By the time she graduated from the university she had a 3.9 GPA and had already had eight freelance articles accepted in major magazines. She's had several love affairs that we could track over the years." He met Kendra's eyes. "Yes, they seemed entirely normal and intelligent and didn't have any bad feelings toward Jackie. They laughed when I mentioned a possible cult."

"But that could be a natural reaction if she managed to end up as the Alpha figure. She might retain the control."

"You're reaching."

"I'm looking for answers." She looked down at the report. "And I'm getting frustrated. No Milo. Nothing else that appears abnormal until she encountered Barrett. Where did she meet Milo? That wasn't a casual relationship she had with Milo. He had an effect on her."

"Then you're wrong," Wendell said. "No long-term or short-term relationship with anyone other than the men I interviewed."

"There *had* to be one." She was still going over the report.

"If what you say is true, it wasn't one of her college lovers or one of the men she met later. Yet it was definitely a man she spent time with, who was an important Alpha in her life."

"You're wasting your time," Wendell said flatly. "I did a good job. You can see that by the reports."

"Yes," she said absently, "you built the scenario year by year. Anyone can follow it and see the people in her life and the changes as she moved from stage to stage." She stiffened as something hit home. "The changes!" She took out her phone and quickly started copying texts from the report.

Wendell was frowning. "What the hell!"

"It's okay," Kendra said. "I may have found what I need." She jumped to her feet. "I've got to go follow up. You've been very helpful. Thank you."

She was calling Lynch as she walked down the hall

to the office they'd given her. "Lynch, you know all kinds of hotshot detectives with Interpol, I want you to choose one and tell him he has to help me with information when I call him this afternoon."

"Interpol? What are you up to?"

"I'm trying to find Milo. I checked Jackie's history on the FBI record and the detective can't determine any Milo in Jackie's life here in the U.S. I was getting very frustrated until I went through the report, and I noticed that during her college years she'd gone backpacking in Europe several times. I have dates, locations, length of stay. And after each visit when she returned there were subtle changes in her actions and behavior." She paused. "Almost as if she'd been groomed...tutored. So maybe Milo isn't American. Or if he is, he was in Europe at the same time as Jackie. Probably by design. And if he had that much influence on her, I'd bet he was her Alpha. Perhaps the first one who introduced her to the domination game."

Lynch was silent. Then he gave a low whistle. "Could be. You'd know better than I. It's obvious you've been studying the possibilities." He suddenly chuckled. "Did you get around to scanning those FBI personnel records?"

"Of course. But finding Milo seemed more important. I'll get back to it later."

"Right. Sooner, if your chosen task doesn't pan out."

"Can you give me a name at Interpol?"

"Yes, Pierre Dumont. He's a good man. I was able to help him out on a project in India. I'll call him now and ask him to contact you right away."

"Good. What's right away?"

"I'll put a priority on it. You are in a hurry."

"Damn right. I'm not only curious, I realize this

could be another blind alley and I desperately don't want it to be. Besides, I think I might actually have a chance of getting something done at last. That's more than we've been able to do so far."

"True. But you're obviously trying to make up for it. Give me a progress report when you get a chance."

"I will. Thanks, Lynch."

"My pleasure. I like to see you this eager. I know how frustrated you've been. I think you'll be happy with Dumont."

———◆———

Kendra received a phone call an hour and fifteen minutes later.

"Pierre Dumont, Mademoiselle Michaels. I understand we're going to work together. My friend Lynch was most determined that we should locate this mystery man. You have nothing to worry about. I'm really superb as you'll see by examining my credentials. I'm texting them to you now."

His enthusiasm, coupled with that charming French accent, startled her. "That's not necessary. If you've been recommended by Lynch, I'm sure you're very competent."

"More than competent. And I believe trust is essential in a relationship. I've taken the trouble to access your dossier and I think we'll be a magnificent team. You appear to be not only unique but completely engaging. I'm a lucky man."

That was even more peculiar than his first words to her. She pulled up his text. Good God, he looked like a movie star or maybe that French president. How had he become a policeman with Interpol? Ignore everything but that Lynch had said he was good at his job. He wouldn't have steered her wrong. "I'll feel lucky myself if you can help me track down any of Jackie Gabert's companions while she was visiting Europe. We believe the man we're looking for has the first name Milo and we have no other info about him. We have no nationality and have no idea in what country they might have met. Lynch got his DHS contacts to send us the itinerary for the first two trips Jackie took abroad. Pretty common destinations for a college kid. London, Paris, Berlin, Rome, Madrid, Athens, Amsterdam. Berlin and Amsterdam were the only two cities she visited during both trips. However, she took three other trips before she graduated college. I haven't examined those tours yet, so I won't vouch for the repetition factor. I thought we should concentrate first on her trips to the countries where she made repetitive visits. In case the man she was meeting was a foreign national or worked in a particular country."

"Good place to start. By all means, send me everything," Pierre said. "We'll begin with hotels and youth hostels and go on to tour groups. I'll text you not only the contacts of the places she supposedly stayed, but also comparable hotels in case she changed her mind after she reached a city. I'll get on it right away." He hesitated. "How much can you help?"

"You mean how many languages do I speak?" She hated to admit it. "I can only do London, Madrid, and Rome. But anything else you need me to check on, I'll find a way."

"No problem. I really prefer to have my local contacts do the initial work anyway. Just leave it in my hands and I'll bring you in at the end for analysis.

That's what Lynch said was your strong point. While my strong point is digging and probing. If I dig up all the facts and you put them together, then we'll still do a splendid job."

She wasn't happy about that. "As I said, if you need me, I'll find a way."

"I'm sure you will. But let me get started with weeding out the unimportant. You do Rome and Madrid. I should be able to get back to you by tomorrow sometime with the rest. Satisfactory?"

"I have an idea any work you do will be more than satisfactory."

"I have the same idea. Wonderful being on the same page, isn't it? I'll be in touch."

He ended the call.

She sat there a moment, scowling down at her phone. Then she dialed Lynch. "I just hung up from Pierre Dumont and he's everything you said he was. He said we might wrap this up by tomorrow sometime."

"That sounds reasonable. Then why do you sound unhappy?"

"Because I can only help with Madrid and Rome and I'm feeling useless. I should speak more languages."

"I'm afraid it's a little late for that at the moment."

"I should have learned them before this."

"You would have, if they were absolutely necessary."

"They're necessary now. I was counting on being totally involved in finding Milo." She was silent a moment. "How many languages do you speak?"

"Nine. And several dialects." He added quickly, "But that's only because I need them in my job."

"But you can never tell when you might need them," she said curtly. "I need them *now*. I'm not going to be caught like this again."

"Admit it, you've just become accustomed to being the smartest person in the room. I believe you keep busy enough without becoming a language expert," Lynch said. "But you're not listening, are you?"

"I'm listening. You're just wrong. If you need a skill, you have to acquire it. I'll have to make time for it." She added, "Though I'll have to be satisfied with Rome and Madrid now. I'll begin working on them this afternoon. But thank heavens you gave me Dumont."

"I could help, you know."

"No, you're busy with Tricia. Dumont likes his own contacts anyway. If he doesn't come through for me tomorrow, I might ask you."

"I'm at your disposal."

"Yeah, I know," she said sourly. "Along with all nine languages and several dialects."

———

Tricia and Lynch were both already at Olivia's condo when Kendra arrived that evening. "You're an hour late," Olivia said as she handed her a glass of wine. "I wasn't about to let my dinner spoil, so you'll have to do with salad and leftovers."

"That's fine. Sorry. Time got away from me." She turned to Tricia. "Did Lynch tell you I was on Milo's trail?"

"No details." Tricia grinned. "He was too busy telling me about your struggle with linguistics. He made that sound much more amusing."

Kendra gave Lynch a baleful glance. "Traitor."

"After a hard day's work, I thought Tricia needed a smile." He was smiling himself. "Besides, you didn't call me back, so I didn't have any more details. How did it go?"

"I didn't come up with anything in Rome and Madrid. Pierre must have been too busy to fill me in on the rest of the cities. I'll know more tomorrow." Her gaze shifted back to Tricia. "I wanted you to know that we're not just spinning our wheels. I've got a hunch this is going to pay off."

"I'll second that," Lynch said. "It's got a damn good chance, Tricia. I just couldn't resist teasing Kendra a bit. She's always too fun to resist."

"Don't worry, I'll return the favor." Kendra started to eat the salad Olivia had set before her. "Anyway, it's a really good start, Tricia."

"I know it will be," Tricia said quietly. "You wouldn't fill me with false hope. Thanks for all your hard work."

Kendra grimaced. "I wish you hadn't said that. It was very touching, but I'll immediately start to worry about disappointing you."

Tricia chuckled. "You're right, Lynch. She *is* fun."

"Double-crosser." She sighed. "I'm surrounded." She took another bite of salad before she said to Lynch, "I'm tempted not to tell you about what I found when I was going through those FBI personnel records."

Lynch's eyes narrowed. "You got around to looking at them? I didn't think you had the time."

"I was feeling a little guilty. I took the time." She winked at Olivia. "That's why I get leftovers."

"What did you find?" Lynch asked.

"Nothing," Kendra said. "Even the two names that Metcalf gave me didn't look that promising. I was frustrated."

"You should have been," Olivia murmured. "It was an excellent dinner."

"It always is," Kendra said. "That's why being so frustrated led me to take another step."

"And that was?"

"Remember when I told you Metcalf had given me the names of two detectives who could possibly have something to do with the murders? He was basing them on the fact that both detectives had been on duty and present at the murder scenes. He said there was a third man, but he refused to give me the name because there was no way he could have anything to do with the murders." She shrugged. "I wanted to clear the decks, so I called Metcalf back and I kept at him until I got him to give me the name."

"And?" Lynch asked.

She made a face. "Metcalf was right. No way. It was Trey Suber. But at least it will put a period to Milo's big lie about FBI involvement."

Lynch's brows rose. "And keep you from having to look at any more personnel records when you want to dive in and go after Milo?"

"Basically, that's correct. I had to be sure." She met his gaze. "And we both realize that Suber would have an excellent reason for being at that crime scene."

"Without doubt." Lynch grinned. "And Metcalf would tar and feather us if we dared look askance at his hero."

"You should have heard him this afternoon when I was insisting he tell me who that third man was." She shook her head mournfully. "Even his mother likes me better than he does now."

Lance exploded in laughter. "Lord, that must be the final condemnation."

"It's not funny. He was my friend."

"And he will be again." Lynch tried to stop

laughing. "He's being torn between loyalties. He'd never seen you when you were being a hard-ass. Give him a week or two."

"I wasn't being a hard-ass; I was being reasonable. He couldn't see that I—" She stopped. He was still laughing. Even Olivia's lips were quirking. "Never mind. I'll find a way to make it okay with him."

"Yes, you will." Lynch was no longer smiling, and his voice was gentle. "You always do." He turned to Olivia. "I think this would be a good time to give her those excellent leftovers so she can go get some rest. One way and another she's had a tiring day."

"I was about to do that," Olivia said. "I don't need you to order me about, Lynch." She disappeared into the kitchen.

Lynch shrugged. "I believe that's my exit line. Olivia can occasionally be protective of you, Kendra. Maybe she thinks I've been a trifle disrespectful."

Kendra gazed at him in surprise. "She'd let you know."

"I think she just did." He was heading for the door. "It's difficult to tell sometimes. Your friend can be as mysterious as a Greek oracle."

"Tell her that," Kendra said. "She'd enjoy the comparison. She might even forgive you for giving her orders."

"It was a suggestion, not an—" He held up his hands in surrender. "Call me tomorrow when Dumont does his final revelation. I'll be waiting. Good night, ladies." He gave Harley a final pat and was gone.

CHAPTER

14

Kendra's hands were shaking after she hung up the phone.

She was soaring with relief and excitement, and she took a deep breath. *Calm down*, she told herself. It was great news, but it was only the beginning. There was so much work to do, and it must be done right. She looked down at her pad and started to clean up the notes she'd made hurriedly as Pierre had reeled off the info. Then she stopped. Later. She could do this later. She wasn't going to forget one word or name. Right now, she had to share this with Lynch. She steadied her hands and dialed his number.

"It's about time," Lynch said when he picked up. "I was thinking Dumont wasn't as good as—"

"Milo Fletcher," she interrupted. "His name is Milo Fletcher."

Lynch was silent for an instant. "Dumont located him? He's sure?"

"He located where he was when he hooked up with Jackie years ago. He doesn't know where he is now. But he has to be somewhere in San Diego, doesn't he? That's where he killed Jackie and all those FBI agents. That's where he was pointing that damn rifle at us."

"Not necessarily. We can't take anything for granted. Not even that Dumont is correct. You have a right to be excited, but go slow, take it easy. Give me the details. Where did Jackie meet Milo Fletcher?"

"Amsterdam." She tried to follow his advice and be slow and precise. "Pierre went down the list of countries and he didn't find anything of interest until Jackie traveled to Amsterdam and stayed at a small bed-and-breakfast in the center of the city. His contact questioned the owner who said that she was constantly in the company of an older man after the first few days. He was tall, good looking, and she seemed to be totally besotted with him. She did everything he suggested. At first, they spent time at the museums, but toward the end of her tour they spent the majority of their time in the Red Light District of the city."

"Where Milo was presumably introducing her to a variety of carnal pleasures," Lynch said.

"Jackie was no innocent," Kendra said. "But she could have been learning a few new games she hadn't thought of playing. At any rate, whenever she went back to Europe in the next few years, she returned to Amsterdam…and Milo Fletcher."

"And what did Dumont find out about our Milo?" Lynch asked.

"That by the end of her third tour he had Jackie turning tricks in the Red Light District for him. He evidently completely dominated her." She paused. "And she wasn't the first one. Pierre said he had a

contact who knew the Red Light District very well
and he got him answers from the proprietors. Milo
Fletcher had brought three or four girls to service
customers in the past. He often hit the hostels and
bed-and-breakfasts and occasionally chose a girl to
seduce to his way of thinking. It started as two lovers
playing a domination game, but it ended with him
totally in control. He was a professor of psychology,
and he was very good at what he did. But Jackie
clearly decided, though she liked the power game, she
didn't like being under his thumb, and left him to try
a little domination on her own."

"What else do we know about Milo Fletcher?"

"That he disappeared from Amsterdam about a
year later, coincidentally about the same time as one
of the new girls he'd been bringing to the Red Light
District ended up drowning in a canal."

"Is he a U.S. citizen?"

"Yes, born in Philadelphia, got his degree from
Princeton, spent at least ten years touring Europe."

"Relatives? Friends?"

She shook her head. "I've no idea yet."

"But brilliant, well educated, and has no moral
compass."

"That about covers it. Apparently also has a gigantic ego, and he was able to move around the world by
using his abilities and people to his advantage. Murder
seemed to be on his agenda even all those years ago,
but Pierre said he'd checked, and Fletcher had no
Interpol record. He's in the process of trying to find
out anything more, but said he doubts if the FBI is
going to be able turn up anything on him, either."

"We'll have to see, won't we?" Lynch said grimly.
"It appears he's excellent at cleaning up after himself,

but he's not a ghost and something will show up somewhere. Thanks to your dogged determination we now have a name, and we have a history. Let me work a bit and call a few people and I'll bet we'll find the bastard."

"Sounds easy. It won't be."

"Sure it will. You've done all the hard stuff. We'll do the rest together. It's always easier when we're together. Now close up there at the FBI office and I'll see you at the condo. I know you're going to want to tell Tricia about the progress."

"You're right. At last we have something to tell her. Bye, Lynch."

She ended the call and leaned back in her chair. Some of the excitement was gone but she felt lighter, more motivated just discussing it with Lynch. He was also right about everything being easier when they were together. Everything and anything seemed possible at this moment.

She started to gather her notes to put them in her briefcase to take them home and share with him.

———————

She got the call after she pulled into her spot at the condo parking garage.

NUMBER BLOCKED.

She tensed.

Shit!

Not now. Not when she was experiencing this surge of hope.

Take the call. Find something in it to screw the son of a bitch.

She punched the access. "Too bad you don't have

anyone else to harass, Milo. You're beginning to bore me."

Silence. "Then I'll have to make our encounters more interesting." His voice was silky smooth and filled with malice. "Believe me I have enough experience to assure that you'll find our future meetings unforgettable."

"I doubt that. I haven't found you to be at all unusual compared with the other creeps I've caught or removed from this earthly realm." She added, "Did you have a reason to call me? I don't want to be late for dinner."

"Bitch." His voice was suddenly low and filled with venom. "You don't know who you're talking to. I'll remember every word you say, and I'll punish you in very special, painful ways for each one."

"I know who I'm talking to. A braggart and a bully. We've kept you from touching your target and you're feeling helpless and want to feel like a big man. Unless you have something intriguing to say, I'm going to hang up now."

"I could have taken you out at any time," he said harshly. "Do you think a few extra guards would keep me away? I could tell you stories that would make you shake. I was just giving you time to build yourself up so that I could knock you down again. You've been spending a lot of time at the FBI, haven't you? You think you're going to find the mole at the heart of my arrangement with Griffin's detectives? It won't happen. He's too clever. And every time you believe you're safe, he'll be setting you up for me. He's just another weakling I can bend to my will. It didn't take me long at all to bring him down." His voice went lower still. "But you've made me angry this time. I warned you, didn't I? You didn't pay attention to me. I'm going to choose a target that will hurt you very, very much, Kendra. And the most enjoyable aspect for me will be I know you'll be looking around at all the people you care about and wondering...which one?"

Kendra felt a bolt of panic. "Why don't you just try to go after me? Are you afraid that you wouldn't be able to take me down?"

"No, it's because I want to see your pain."

He cut the connection.

***

Kendra sat there in the car for another five minutes to try to recover from the ugliness and shock of the conversation with Milo. She probably shouldn't have gotten so angry and taunted him, but she hadn't been able to resist. She had been so frustrated that they hadn't been able to score off the bastard. And, yes, there had been that little bit of exhilaration that she had made a small breakthrough during the last couple of days. She hadn't been able to tell him of that success, but it had made her heady enough to try to strike sparks.

But she hadn't wanted to turn that malice on anyone but herself. Face it, the threat had already been in place, her defiance had just reinforced it. Her mother and Olivia had security and Lynch was always on guard. Just sit here for another moment and then go up and pretend that she hadn't received that ugly reminder that Milo was always with them. He hadn't really told her anything new and there wasn't any reason to upset anyone else.

After dinner Lynch watched Olivia come toward him across the room with a feeling of foreboding. Her face was without expression, but he could tell she was pissed off. She thrust the glass of tequila she was carrying at him. "Here. Drink it. Smile. Pretend to be sociable." She lifted her own brandy to her lips. "What happened? When you came into the condo tonight you told me everything was okay." She gestured to where Kendra was sitting on the couch beside Tricia laughing and talking. "What the hell did you do to her, Lynch?"

He wasn't about to question or deny the charge. Olivia was too sharp, and he'd been wondering the same thing since Kendra had shown up an hour ago. "Nothing. When I talked to her on the phone, she was excited and eager to start hunting that bastard down. I thought she was still okay when she came in and was filling Tricia in on the progress she and Dumont had made."

"I didn't," Olivia said flatly. "She was phony, and Kendra is never phony. She's talking too fast and laughing too much. She was even doing that with me. Tricia's not noticing because she doesn't know her as well as we do. Something's wrong. Find out what it is."

"I had every intention of doing that," Lynch said. "I don't need you to push me, Olivia. Whatever is wrong, I'm not responsible, but that doesn't mean anything. I won't have her upset if I can make it right. Now find a way to keep Tricia down here and send Kendra up to her condo. I'll meet her there and talk privately to her. Agreed?"

Olivia nodded. "As long as you let me know what's wrong. I *hate* this, Lynch."

Of course she did, Lynch thought. She and Kendra

had been closer than sisters growing up in that school for the physically challenged, and they still were. "I know you do. We'll get it taken care of."

"Is that supposed to comfort me?" Olivia was smiling crookedly. "That almost works, Lynch. Except no one takes care of me but me."

"And occasionally Kendra. She reaches out to you as much as you reach out to her." He grinned. "And woe to anyone who gets between you. I tremble at the thought."

"Bullshit." She turned away. "Slip out of here and go up to her condo and I'll handle everything else. But you'd better get the job done."

"Absolutely. Whatever you say." He put his tequila down on the end table. "Run along and do your duty. I'll report directly to you when I know the scoop and how to fix it. Trust me."

———◆———

"Lynch!" Kendra threw open her door and saw him sitting on the couch in the living room casually thumbing through an issue of *National Geographic*. "What are you doing here? Olivia said there was some kind of emergency, and I should come up and check on you. You don't look like it's an emergency."

"I hadn't read the latest copy of *Geo*." He tossed the magazine on the coffee table. "That might be described as a minor emergency."

"Not in my world," she said. "And not in yours. What's going on, Lynch?"

"That's what Olivia and I were wondering," he said quietly. "I was planning on asking you a little later as befits my rather problematic status, but Olivia also noticed what she designated as phony behavior on your part and accused me of causing it. She told me I had to go fix it." He spread his hands. "Here I am. Tell me how I go about it."

Her hands clenched into fists at her sides. "It's not as if I was acting weird. Tricia didn't think so."

"No, you just weren't being genuine. We're used to genuine. It's like a red flag when we don't see it. You might keep that in mind in the future."

"I will. You can bet on it."

"And remember that Olivia appears to be an expert on all the many facets of phony. It makes her very nervous." He was walking toward her. "Me too. Are you going to tell me what changed between the time I spoke to you on the phone and when you walked into Olivia's condo?"

"I don't seem to have a choice," she said. "It was no big deal. I didn't see why anyone else should be upset. It's not as if it would help anyone to know about it. Part of it was my fault anyway. I was angry."

"What part of what?"

She reached in her handbag and pulled out her phone. "See for yourself." She handed it to him. "I'm not going to listen to it again. I'm going to take my shower and, if you're still here after I come out, we might talk about it." She was heading for her shower. "And then again, we might not."

She slammed the bathroom door behind her.

━━━━◆━━━━

Kendra came out of the shower forty minutes later and Lynch was sitting on the couch again drinking a cup of coffee. He got to his feet and gestured to the couch. "Sit down. I'll get you a coffee. Because I do think we need to talk about that call and why you didn't tell me about it."

"I've said all I wanted to say." She wearily rubbed the back of her neck. "And I've told you why I didn't tell anyone. It was ugly and I didn't want anyone else to have to dip into Milo's foul mind. He would have enjoyed the attention too much."

"I'm not anyone." He handed her the coffee, then dropped down on the couch beside her. "And I wouldn't mind dipping into Milo's mind. I've been storing up all the ugly things he's been doing and spewing out of that gutter mouth. I figured there would be a time I could return it all in triplicate." He reached out and took her hand. "Along with a few additional torments I could invent and carry out on the bastard myself."

"That's not a bad idea." Kendra shuddered. "When I remember what he did to Jackie."

"And we have no idea what he's done to other victims." His hand tightened on hers. "Now tell me why you didn't tell anybody about this damn call."

Her voice was stilted. "It was something Milo said about how I'd be looking at all those people I cared about and wondering which one he'd choose to kill next. When I walked into Olivia's condo, all of a sudden, I found I was doing it." She closed her eyes for an instant. "Maybe it was foolish, but I couldn't stop." She looked him in the eye. "Even you, Lynch. I kept telling myself that you were always too on guard to let it happen to you. But then I remembered what happened at that construction site. He almost killed you then. No one is really safe from him."

His lips tightened. "And that was the purpose of

his call. He deals in terror, it's a form of power. He wanted to keep the tension high, because he hadn't been able to make a move on either you or Tricia since the rifle episode."

"I could tell myself that, but it didn't stop my mind from remembering how I felt when I thought you were dead." She looked down into the coffee in her cup. "He was so smart to go down that path. Memories are such an important part of how we feel about the people we care about. Everything always comes streaming back to us when they're threatened." Her voice was trembling. "And we can't stop it. I have so many memories connected with you. Repeat cases. And Milo wants to destroy those memories." Her hand turned white as it clenched the cup. "He wants to destroy *you*."

"And he won't." Lynch took the cup from her hand and put it on the coffee table. Then he grasped her two hands and held tight. "Stop insulting me. Because somewhere in those memories you know that it took a hell of a lot for anyone to get even close to killing me. Milo isn't that good."

"Stop joking. He's damn good. I *can't* let him kill you."

"Joking?" He was looking down into her eyes as he added roughly, "Don't you dare cry, Kendra. I've been so blasted controlled and civilized and now you're going to blow it."

"I'm not going to cry. I'm just telling you that I—"

He was kissing her, hard. He lifted his head. "I know what you're telling me," he said thickly. "You're saying that I'm not stable and you'd prefer to have someone around who is steadier and normal and won't go off to Johannesburg at the drop of a hat. But you're also telling me that I have a chance of convincing you that what we have is Fourth of July explosive and worth keeping me around. I've known that all along. You're not stringing me along. What you feel for me is about more than just sex." He kissed her again. "I'm willing to go the distance. I just have to make sure, whatever we turn out to be together, that you see that it's worth your while."

He felt so *good*. She pressed closer so that she could feel the hardness, the muscles, the *heat* of him. It had been too long. She was on fire. "You're talking too much," she whispered. "I don't want talk. I don't want explanations. I'm tired of being careful and reasonable. There are only two things I want from you now." She rubbed back and forth on his body as she untied her robe. "I want you naked." She shrugged out of the robe and lay back and opened her legs. "And then I want you to do what you promised and go the distance."

———

Kendra tried to catch her breath as Lynch lifted her off him onto the bed, then lost it again as his teeth began to pull at her nipple. She bit down on her lower lip to keep from groaning at what his fingers were now doing inside her.

He lifted his head. "I should really call Olivia," he said as his tongue moved teasingly on her breast. "I promised I'd call her after I talked to you."

"Don't you dare. Besides, that had to be over three hours ago. She'll realize you're—" She threw her head back to keep from screaming as he went still deeper. "—occupied."

"But it's you who are occupied," he murmured. "Beautifully occupied. But maybe not quite enough…" He moved over her. "Let's see how much more you can take."

"You've already explored that—" But he was doing it again and going still deeper. *Fantastic…Don't stop. Don't stop.*

He wasn't stopping, and every word increased the depth and rhythm. "Why would Olivia…think…we were occupied?"

"Olivia might be blind, but she knows we were lovers. Tricia thinks…the same thing."

"*Are* lovers," he corrected. "Present tense. No doubt. Very present and so tense. Say it." He was going faster, deeper, so deep, and he was incredibly intense, looking down at her. "Say it."

Her head went back as that tension built. Heat. Fullness. Lynch. "Are lovers," she gasped. "Are lovers, dammit. Satisfied?"

"No, not nearly. But close, Kendra. Very close. Now let's take it all the way…"

———◆———

6:15 A.M.
NEXT DAY

"I've got to go." Lynch's lips moved across the hollow of her throat. "Time to get Tricia to the center." He pulled down the cover and kissed Kendra's breasts. "And probably have to put up with a few smirks and sly glances judging from what you told me."

"No, you won't. She's cool." Kendra yawned. "And Olivia said she approved of you."

"I'm honored," he said ironically. "All I care about is if you approve."

How could he ask that when her body was still smooth and heavy with lust and every muscle lax and full of the carnal memory of what he had done to her? Even now her body was beginning to tingle and ready just looking at him. "You might say that." She rolled away from him. "I'm going back to the FBI office this morning. I'll call you if I find out anything more."

"Do that." He headed for the door. "But there's no hurry. You could rest for a couple more hours."

"No, I couldn't." She sat up in bed. "There's no going back after last night, and I'm not sure I'd want to. You know what you did to me. What we did to each other. I'll have to think about it. But I know damn well I'm going to keep going forward on every other front."

"I never thought anything else." He smiled. "I'll step back and not push for a little while. It's pretty clear that you'll let me know when the time is right." He nodded. "Thank you for a lovely evening and I hope and plan that there may be many more."

Then he was gone.

And Kendra was on her feet and heading for the shower.

An hour later she was showered and dressed and knocking on Olivia's door.

"Come in and have some oatmeal and orange juice." Olivia pulled Harley away from her and headed toward the breakfast bar. "You don't need to make explanations. Lynch did that when he picked up Tricia." She poured her a cup of coffee. "About that bastard's call, nothing else. He left the rest to my imagination." Her lips tightened. "You should have told me about it. It made me mad as hell. Not only that he was threatening you, but that he was using people you care about to do it." She touched her chest. "And I know damn well I was one of those people. You've done all you can to protect me and your mom and Tricia and even Lynch. But from now on that isn't your business. We can look after ourselves. I promise you I can. Okay, I'll be extra careful. Don't insult me by treating me as if I'm helpless. Now will you back off?"

"If that's what you want."

Olivia sighed. "You're lying, aren't you?"

"Yes."

"I should have known. Finish your coffee while I get your oatmeal." She disappeared into the kitchen.

Another party heard from, Kendra thought wryly. Who would have guessed that her decision to keep Milo's ugliness to herself would have sent out this spiraling whirlpool that had already caused an emotional upheaval? All the more reason to forget about her own to focus on bringing Milo down. Even when she was trying desperately to keep the search going, he seemed to be in the shadows waiting to pounce.

Harley was whimpering and laying his big head on her knee. "Hey, boy." She reached down and stroked his throat. "Are you upset with me because Olivia is? I'm right, you know. That asshole wanted to hurt you, too. We've got to keep him away from everyone we care about. And I don't know how long we'll have to do it…"

<hr />

NEXT DAY
KENDRA'S CONDO

It was just past 10:00 P.M. when Kendra's phone vibrated on her bedside table. She checked the caller

ID screen and saw it was Metcalf. She answered it. "Listen, you're supposed to be getting rest. Stop worrying. I told you that I'd see that everything was going to be okay, and you'd have nothing to feel guilty about. I'll call you tomorrow and—"

"It's too late. Then you haven't heard?"

"Heard what?"

"The Bureau has been rounding up traffic and security camera footage around the murder scenes of our cases. Lynch has been pushing them."

"I know. It was a good move. Last I heard, they hadn't come up with anything."

"That changed a little while ago. They have footage of an MG that was present at both murder scenes just before each event. Same car, same plate."

Kendra sat up straight. "Do we have a name?"

"We do." He was muttering a curse beneath his breath. "It's Trey Suber."

Her breath left her. "Trey?"

"I haven't seen the footage, but the car and plate are a clear match. And apparently his cell phone was pinging towers in those areas, too. It was *him*."

"I can't believe it. There has to be an explanation."

"That's what I thought. Well, if there is, Suber isn't giving it to anyone. He's missing."

"What?"

"He's disappeared. Someone may have tipped him off. Griffin and the team got a warrant to search his house. They're there now."

Kendra shook her head, trying to process what she'd just been told. "I can't believe it."

"Believe it. Do you think I'm not sick about it? I worked with him. I respected him. I was mad as hell that you'd made me even tell you that there might be the slightest reason to question him. But maybe you were right, and I was wrong."

"Lynch and I weren't sure you were wrong. We trusted Suber, too."

"Then he might have duped all of us. God, I hope not. At any rate, I knew you'd want to know right away."

"Thanks, Metcalf."

"What are you going to do?"

"What do you think? I'm going to Suber's house. Right now."

"I thought you'd say that. I wish I could go with you."

"Just stay home and rest. I'll let you know what I find out."

Kendra ended the call.

She sat for a long moment, still trying to make sense of it all. Trey Suber? It was ridiculous to even contemplate. But to some, it would be too easy. His lifelong fascination with serial killers would make him immediate fodder for news stations and true crime shows.

Her phone vibrated in her hand. Lynch. She answered it. "Hi, Lynch."

"You're not going to believe this," he began. "I just heard from Griffin that—"

"Trey Suber?" she interrupted.

"Yes. Looks like I'm not the only one with sources."

"Metcalf just called."

"Then you know they're tearing apart his house. I can pick you up in fifteen minutes."

"I can meet you there quicker than that. I'm looking at his address on my phone right now."

"Kendra, just sit tight and I'll—"

"See you there." She cut the connection.

CHAPTER

15

Twelve minutes later, Kendra rolled up in front of Trey Suber's one-story mid-century home in a hip, walkable neighborhood that straddled North Park and University Heights. Street parking was likely in short supply at any time but was nonexistent with the seven or eight FBI cars and vans now crowded in front of the home. Kendra found a spot around the corner and walked back to the busy scene. Lynch was there waiting for her.

"Nice house," Lynch said. "How in the hell does Suber afford a place like this? I just checked, and he paid 3.7 million when he moved here last year."

"Family money?" Kendra ventured. "Or maybe those serial killer trading cards sell a lot better than we ever guessed."

"Family money," a familiar voice called out. Griffin walked down the driveway. "His parents are major shareholders in a chain of senior communities in the Southeast."

"I never knew that," Kendra said.

"He never talks about it. I only know because it turned up on his background check." Griffin looked between Kendra and Lynch. "I felt it only fair that I let you know what we found out about Suber since you've been pushing us to check video, Lynch. But I don't recall asking you to join us here."

"An oversight, I'm sure." Lynch smiled. "No offense taken."

Kendra watched as four crime scene techs approached the open front door. "Any sign of Trey?"

Griffin shook his head. "No, he isn't answering his phone. We've just started gathering information here."

"Have you really put his car at those crime scenes?"

Griffin lowered his voice. "Yes. And there in the days before each one. Suber would be the first to tell you that serial killers commonly stalk their victims in the days or weeks prior to their murders. We never imagined that he might have firsthand knowledge."

"And do the traffic and surveillance cams show us his face?" Lynch asked.

"Not definitively. But we're gathering video from other feeds, and some are from better-lit areas. And his cell phone pings line up with each location on the videos."

"Still no sign of him?" Lynch asked.

"He's vanished. And it looks like his phone has been turned off. It appears he doesn't want to be found."

Kendra nodded. Exactly as Metcalf told her. She gestured toward the open front door. "May we?"

"Sure. But I'm warning you, it's not going to make you feel better about him."

"What does *that* mean?"

"Take a look. If anything in there speaks to you, let me know."

Kendra and Lynch walked up the driveway to Suber's house. At first it appeared that the interior lights were off, but as they entered, she realized the walls were charcoal gray and absorbed what little light emanated from the art-deco-styled wall sconces. The walls were decorated with framed black-and-white posters and photographs, each illuminated with a ceiling-mounted spotlight.

"What are these?" Kendra asked.

"One guess," Lynch said.

"Serial killers."

He nodded. "I recognized Jeffrey Dahmer as we walked through the foyer, and if I'm not mistaken, that's Son of Sam over by the kitchen."

"Wow. I wonder what kind of reaction he gets when he brings his dates back here."

"Probably not unlike what we're seeing from his colleagues right now."

Kendra glanced around to see the grimaces and outright disgust on the faces of Suber's fellow agents as they searched the house. "This is what Griffin was talking about."

An FBI photographer moved around the room, snapping shots of the various serial killer prints.

Lynch shook his head. "Just wait until Discovery ID and *Dateline* get hold of those shots."

Kendra stepped around the living room coffee table, which was covered on all sides with Suber's serial killer trading cards and coated with clear lacquer.

From there they moved to the bedrooms, which were the only rooms remotely resembling normal decorating taste. Even there, the charcoal-gray wall color gave the appearance of a cave. "At least he doesn't sleep with killers' faces looking down on him," she said.

Kendra opened the master bedroom closet, glanced inside, then moved to the bathroom. After a quick look, she turned back to Lynch. "He left in a hurry. He took six shirts and four pairs of pants. He took a razor and toothbrush with him, but he didn't plan to be gone more than a few days."

"How do you get all that?"

Two FBI investigators stopped to listen. They obviously wanted to know, too.

She pointed across the room. "The closet is packed tight, but his clothes are neatly organized and hung. There are six empty hangers sticking up and out among the shirts, which would be the case if you grabbed each article of clothing and quickly pulled it out. Four other hangers are sticking out among his slacks. There's an impression in the closet's carpeted floor of a small rolling suitcase, which there's no sign of around here. He obviously took it with him."

"Good." Lynch flashed his movie-star smile, obviously enjoying this. "Keep going."

She pointed to the bathroom. "There are empty charging docks next to the sink, one for an electric razor and one for a power toothbrush. He took the razor and toothbrush, but not the charging docks. He probably thought he'd be back before the power ran out in each."

"A valid assumption."

She glanced around. "But there's nothing to suggest he actually might have committed murder."

One of the FBI agents waved his arms around. "Except this whole creepy place."

"It doesn't mean he's guilty," Kendra said. "The

FBI knew who he was when they recruited him. You might even say it was *why* they recruited him."

The agents gave each other a doubtful look. It was no use talking to them, Kendra realized. They'd already made up their minds about Trey.

As she walked back toward the front door, she paused next to a telescope aimed out a living room window.

"It's a nice one," Lynch said. "A Celestron."

"Yeah, Trey's something of an amateur astronomer." Kendra pulled out her phone and snapped a photo of the telescope.

She turned to see Griffin behind her. "Okay," he said. "You mean you can't tell us exactly where Trey Suber went?"

"Jeez, Griffin. Give me a little time."

"It's okay. We'll find him." Griffin's eyes came to rest on the trading card coffee table. "The guys are right. Creepy. But not as creepy as the auction catalog of serial killer memorabilia in the bookshelf. You had one thing right, though: We knew who he was when we recruited him."

Griffin moved toward the kitchen.

Kendra and Lynch left the house and walked down the driveway. As they made their way to the street, even more FBI agents arrived.

"Looks like this is turning into a tourist attraction," Lynch said. "Word must be getting around the office."

"I'm sure it is," Kendra said. "I don't know what to make of this. I talked to Trey the other day, and he was genuinely upset over Cynthia's death."

"He could just be a brilliant actor."

Kendra nodded. "It's possible. It wouldn't be the first time we've all been fooled by a psychopath." She grimaced. "I admit that I couldn't keep from shuddering when we were looking at Trey's decorating choices."

His gaze shifted to her face. "You hid it well. You always do. Do you want company?"

Her first instinct was to say no. To protect her independence and not let him know how much she needed him. Wasted effort—he already knew that as far as sex was concerned, she thought ruefully. And no one could say that passionate need wasn't mutual. Why keep pulling away in a half-assed attempt to put some safe distance between them so that she wouldn't feel too much? Her feelings about Lynch were always complicated, but they didn't have to be tonight. She could wrestle with it later.

"Sure." She smiled. "Meet back at my place?"

"Can't wait. See you there."

He turned and strolled down the street.

She watched him for a moment, memories searing back to her. She couldn't wait, either.

Kendra walked around the corner to her car. Maybe she was making a mistake, but what the hell. She needed to drown out the thought of Milo and those hideous photos in Suber's apartment. She raised her phone and downloaded an app. In less than a minute, she'd installed it and began to use it.

"Hello, Kendra."

She froze as a figure stepped from the shadows near her car.

It was Trey Suber.

She instinctively straightened into a defensive posture. She slid her fingers over her keys, preparing to jab at the slightest sign of aggression. "Trey...What are you doing?"

"Don't be afraid."

"Easier said than done."

"I'm not here to hurt you. I wouldn't hurt anyone."

"Your coworkers aren't so sure. They didn't appreciate your photo collection."

"I'm being set up."

"I believe you."

He reacted in surprise. "You *do*?"

"Yes."

"Pardon me for asking, but... why?"

She held up her phone and showed him the screen. "The Celestron SkyPortal app."

He still looked confused. "Yeah?"

"The telescope in your living room was still positioned in the same coordinates that you set the last time you used it."

He thought for a moment. "That was the night of the five-planet convergence."

Kendra smiled. "Of course it was. The only reason I knew about it is because the TV meteorologists wouldn't shut up about it for the entire week before. I used this app to find out what coordinates your telescope would have been set for to view it. It matched the numbers on your telescope's LCD screen."

"Clever. But how does that clear me of murder charges?"

"That was the night Jackie Gabert was killed. This app says the apex of the alignment, when these telescope coordinates would have been applied, was within twenty minutes of her murder. You couldn't have done it. You were here geeking out on the cosmos."

Trey nodded. "Wow."

She motioned for him to follow her. "Let's go back to your house and tell Griffin."

"No."

"Come on, Trey…"

"Sorry." He adjusted his glasses. "Kendra…I was nowhere near any of those places."

"Somehow, they have video, Trey. Traffic cams and private security cameras. Help us sort this out."

"It wasn't me. It wasn't my car."

"Did you know they can read the license plate?"

"I heard. But I'm telling you, it wasn't me."

"Why was your phone pinging the cell towers nearby?"

"I'm still trying to figure that out."

"You work for an organization whose *job* it is to figure it out. Go talk to them. They're crawling all over your house."

"I know. But someone is setting me up and I need to figure out what's going on. My options would be extremely limited if I'm stuck in a jail cell."

"No one's talking about jail."

"Yet. But you were just with them all. Tell me, was anyone shocked at the thought I might be involved? Or did my house confirm every dark and twisted thing they ever thought of me?"

"Mmm…Probably the dark and twisted thing."

"Just what I thought."

"Trey, you're just making yourself look more guilty by dropping out of sight."

"I know. And I promise I'll go in when I think the time is right. But first I need your help."

"Why me?"

"Because you're smart. Brilliant, really."

"So are your FBI colleagues."

"I don't want to ask them to destroy their careers for me. Even when and if I can set things straight, anyone who has helped me will still be fired. They can't fire you. And if they never ask you to consult on a case again, you'll probably send me a big box of chocolates."

She smiled. "I might."

"So will you help me?"

"I'm not giving you a place to stay."

"I don't want that." He reached into his jacket and slowly pulled out a folded sheet of paper. "This is everywhere I remember going in the days before each murder. Get them to pull camera feeds. They'll see I was nowhere near those crime scenes, unless I've suddenly acquired the ability to be in two places at once."

"That would be a good trick."

"Wouldn't it?" He extended this paper toward her. Seeing her reluctance to move closer, he placed it on the roof of her car.

"How do I get in touch with you?"

"You don't. This way if it comes out that you've been in contact with me, you won't have to lie if Griffin asks you to help track me down. I'll call you from a burner phone. Every time I call you, it'll be from a 678 area code. That's how you'll know it's me."

"Got it."

Trey backed away until he was once again lost in the shadows. "Thanks, Kendra. I've told you the truth. I'll be in touch…"

———

FORTY MINUTES LATER
KENDRA'S CONDO

"Let me get this straight." Lynch stretched his legs out before the couch. "It didn't occur to you to run back to the house where there were zillions of FBI personnel and tell them Suber was wandering around the neighborhood?"

Kendra shook her head. "I figured he'd be gone by the time I could bring anyone back." She paused. "And he'd given me that list, and I didn't think it would hurt to check it out. It might save him from being arrested. He does need proof of some kind."

"Hmm. Those telescope coordinates you noticed go a long way toward giving him a decent alibi."

"It isn't enough. You saw how all those agents were leaning toward putting him in a cell and throwing away the key. Hell, I was feeling the same way. Trey is bizarre, and I can't understand how he could be intrigued by all those sickening serial killers. But I thought we agreed that what he was doing with that interest helped law enforcement to catch the bad guys."

"We did." He shook his head. "But you went into the aiding-and-abetting category tonight. Griffin wouldn't understand."

"And Trey tried to save me from having anyone think that I was helping him."

"Which you were doing." He tilted his head. "And are still doing. Right?"

"Maybe." She thought about it. "Probably. "But while I was driving home tonight, I was playing *What If*. What if Trey was right about being set up? Who would do it? Why would anyone pick on Trey?"

"And you decided?"

"It was Milo who told me he had a conspirator working with the FBI. That could have been the start of the setup. He wanted to make me mistrust the agents who might help us. Why would anyone choose

Trey to set up? You'd think that anyone as clever as Trey would be difficult to frame, that they'd prefer someone easier, with a lower profile." She added, "Unless they were looking for a challenge."

"Like Milo."

"Like Milo," she repeated. "And we know Milo has a vicious streak. He might have been aiming at a target he wanted to destroy."

"And that was Trey Suber."

She nodded. "He received a lot of publicity when he was hired by the FBI for their serial killer investigations. It featured his background and how many serial killers he'd helped catch during his career. But he hadn't caught Milo nor any of the people he'd subjugated. Though he probably came close and made them uncomfortable. No doubt he was a constant threat to Milo and the cult he created, and he must have wanted to take him down."

"So, he started to put together a plan to frame Suber," Lynch said. "That makes sense." He reached over and gently touched her cheek. "And you evidently put together a plan to get Suber's ass out of trouble."

"Not yet. I'm busy hunting down Milo. I believe I've located a Robert Benjamin who was his roommate for two terms at Princeton. It wasn't easy, Milo had acolytes and didn't bother with friendships." She changed the subject back to Suber. "But we should help Suber get out on his own." She smiled. "If you decide to help him. I wouldn't want you to do anything against your conscience."

"My conscience has amazing limits." He pulled her head down in the hollow of his shoulder. "Haven't you noticed? While you're not tracking Milo, we can see what we can do for Suber. But you know that Milo will probably be following and keeping his eye on us? It might be an opportunity."

"That sounds like bait. Aren't you the one who told me not to do that?"

"I still don't like the idea, but it's not so bad if I'm in the mix. We'll see, it might not happen."

She had to laugh. "But you're already anticipating how to trap the bastard and hang him out to dry."

"One has to always take advantage of fortuitous circumstances. In this case we might make our own. I didn't like how upset you got when that son of a bitch called you. I don't want it to happen again. I need to wrap this up."

"However, you might call that a fortuitous circumstance because of what came after."

"That's true." His lips brushed her temple. "That was indeed fortuitous, every time, every way. You might even call it many-splendored."

"I might." She nestled closer to him. "If I wanted to be verbose. I prefer simplicity."

"You didn't prefer it last time. You embraced the hard and complicated." He rubbed his lips on the hollow of her throat. "But tonight could be different. This is good, too. Just relax and we'll see what comes. Maybe nothing, maybe something world shaking. It doesn't matter, does it?"

"No, you're right…this is good, too." She sighed and said reluctantly, "But I should call Griffin first."

"If you must."

Kendra looked at the paper Trey had given her. "I'm impressed at his level of detail. He knows where he was and what he was doing probably every moment those security cameras and cell towers say he was somewhere else."

Lynch raised his phone and snapped a photo of the paper. "While Griffin runs this down, I'll reach out to some of my sources. It might be faster than going through Griffin's official channels."

"It usually is." Kendra lifted her phone, punched Griffin's number, and put the call on speaker. He answered on the first ring. "Are you still at Suber's place?"

"No, I'm almost home. The evidence team will be working most of the night."

"Well, I've got some more evidence for you guys. I was parked around the corner, and Suber left a note on my car. He claims that wasn't him or his car in the videos."

Griffin cursed. "Why doesn't he come in and tell us himself?"

"Maybe he's afraid he won't get a fair hearing. And judging from the attitude of your people at his house tonight, I can see why he might think that. Anyway, he wrote out all the places he claims to have really been while your traffic cams and cell towers are telling you otherwise. Maybe he'll come in after you confirm it."

He didn't speak for a moment. "You believe him, don't you?"

"Yes. Don't you?"

"I want to. He's been valuable to the Bureau." He sighed. "Okay, send me a scan. We'll follow up on it. Put the note in a baggie, and I'll have someone come by and pick it up in the morning."

"I'll bring it to you. I was planning to come there anyway. I'm still working on tracking Milo. I think I've found a lead to his roommate at Princeton."

"Good." Griffin paused. "And if you talk to Suber,

tell him he'd do himself a big favor by getting his ass into the office."

"Will do. In the meantime, make sure your team takes a good look at his living room telescope."

"What?"

She cut the connection.

Lynch chuckled. "I think he knows you've spoken with Trey."

"I didn't lie. Trey did put this note on my car. I just happened to be there at the time." She put her phone down on the coffee table and nestled her head back in the exact place on his shoulder. "Now where were we...?"

CHAPTER

16

Kendra ran along the Embarcadero, taking in the spectacular sight of the Jacobs Park concert shell beside the bay. She'd been neglecting her daily exercise regimen, and it felt good to be doing something normal again. Tricia was training at the aquatic center, and Lynch was tied up in a lengthy conference call with the deputy attorney general.

A perfect time to steal an hour or two for herself. She *needed* this.

The San Diego Symphony was rehearsing in the concert shell, an event the public was always invited to attend free of charge. She often ate breakfast while watching the orchestra prepare for its evening performances. She enjoyed the rehearsals more than the actual shows; it was fascinating to see the various ways that world-class conductors coaxed such breathtaking performances from their musicians.

Kendra smiled as she ran past. The orchestra was

playing Jupiter from Holst's *The Planets*, and she felt her spirit soar with the music. Maybe she'd tack on an extra mile or two to today's—

Her fitness watch vibrated.

She turned her wrist to see that she was getting a call from Griffin.

Damn. She tapped her Bluetooth headset. "Griffin, this better be good. You're interrupting an *amazing* performance of—"

"Kendra, I need to see you at my office right now." He had an edge in his voice. More than usual.

She stopped running once she had moved farther from the concert shell. "What's going on?"

"Can you come to my office immediately?"

"Uh, sure. But can you tell me what—"

"I'll tell you when you get here. I'll be waiting."

Griffin hung up the phone.

———◆———

It took an hour for Kendra to run back to her condo, shower, and drive to the FBI building. She had barely stepped into the fifth-floor reception area when Griffin appeared and motioned for her to join him in his office.

He closed the door behind them and walked around behind his desk. "Kendra...do I need to place you under twenty-four-hour surveillance?"

"What?"

He sat and motioned for her to take a seat in front of his desk. "Do I need to have you surveilled twenty-four seven, have your house bugged and phones tapped?"

"Why would you do that?"

He stared at her a long moment before replying. "Trey Suber."

Oh, shit. This might be a problem. Kendra put on her best poker face. "What about him?"

"I suspect you've been in contact with our friend Trey. That was very cute with you saying you found his note on your car, but I'm no longer amused. The time has come for him to come in."

She leaned forward in her chair. "Why? What's changed since last night?"

"We took his computers and gave them the full forensics workup. He's too smart to leave anything incriminating on them, but we just got the report of his online activity from his ISP."

Oh, God. This wasn't going to be good.

Griffin let out a long breath. "He visited several websites that give step-by-step instructions on making homemade bombs."

"After what happened last week, I'm sure most of the people in this building have done that."

"Except Suber did it in the two days *before* the explosion."

And there it was. Kendra felt her poker face crumbling. "Shit."

"Yeah. But don't feel bad. I'm the asshole who hired him."

She shook her head. "I can't believe it."

"You're the one who led the charge to look at our own agents as possible suspects."

"Trust me, I'm thinking about that right now. It was the smart thing to do, based on the information we had. Maybe it was all part of the same plan."

Griffin leaned forward. "I know I resisted the idea of looking in-house for suspects, but it did make sense.

We have a very limited pool of individuals who could have done this. Only so many people knew where Dayna Voyles was buried. There was less than forty-eight hours between the time that Barrett drew that map for the DA's office and when that bomb went off. In that time, maybe thirty people saw the map, and almost all of them were law-enforcement officers. Suber was one of them."

"You're forgetting someone else who knew where that body was buried."

"Barrett?"

"Yes. We know he was communicating with people on the outside."

He nodded. "We've all been running that angle down, and it's gotten us nowhere so far."

"But wouldn't framing Suber be the best way to make us *stop* looking for someone else? If we believed that one of our own agents was responsible? An agent half the office thinks is kind of nuts anyway?"

"More than half, to be honest. Especially since we got a peek at what his home looks like."

"In his note, Suber told us where he really was when those security and traffic cams spotted his car. Have you even tried to verify his locations?"

"Of course, but it takes time. Time to get security camera footage, time to pore through all that night-time video until we find something that gives us a clear picture of what we're looking for. Look, I *really* want to believe what you're saying. But if Suber is innocent, he needs to come in and work with us. He's not doing himself any favors with his disappearing act."

She hated it when Griffin made so much sense. She nodded reluctantly. "I agree."

"So will you help us bring him in?"

"Griffin…I was being honest when I said I didn't have any way of contacting him."

"Fine. If that's true…"

"It is."

"Then I'm guessing that means he may reach out to *you*."

"He…may. It's possible."

"If that happens, perhaps you'll convince him to come in and allow us all to help him."

"*If* that happens."

"Otherwise, that brings us back to the beginning of our conversation."

"Spying on me, tapping my phones, bugging my home?"

"Yeah, that part. If you were in my position and wanted to find a suspect in a mass murder, and you had a reasonable expectation he might try to contact someone you knew, could you think of a better and more expedient way to catch him?"

Again, Griffin was making perfect sense. Damn. "No. It's probably what I would suggest."

"I'm glad you agree. Because, one way or another, we're bringing him in."

Lynch called Kendra on her drive back to the condo. After she filled him in on her meeting with Griffin, he was quiet for a long moment.

"What are you thinking?" she said.

"A couple of things. As much as I'm not crazy about you being the target of a surveillance state, Griffin makes a good point. He needs to find Suber and bring him in."

"Yes."

"And, at the moment, I rather like the idea of armed government agents always nearby, watching your every move. There's a killer out there who has you in his crosshairs. If Griffin decides to do this now, I'm all for it."

"I thought you might think that."

"Of course, you could just do as Griffin asks and convince Suber to go in."

"If and when I hear from him."

"You'll hear from him soon, I'm sure. Just have your pitch ready. In the meantime, what are we doing today?"

"I'm going to track down the physician who may have known Milo Fletcher. You?"

"More conference calls, I'm afraid. It's starting to get contentious in Johannesburg, and a heat wave is showing just how negligent some of their corrupt politicians have been in maintaining the energy grid. There could be a riot if we're not careful."

"Good luck. I'll keep you posted on what I find out."

— ◆ —

It took Kendra most of the afternoon to find Robert Benjamin, a physician who worked with the U.N. in Nigeria, and even then he tried to politely brush her off. "Look, Dr. Michaels, you're wasting your time. I have no idea where he is. I haven't even spoken to Milo in years. Which was the best thing for both of us. We never did get along. He was always a domineering asshole and weird as hell. The only reason we roomed together was that we were both there on scholarships and we didn't have a choice. The minute I was able to get a job I moved out and left him to his weirdo friends."

"You're my only hope unless you can give me any other names," Kendra said urgently. "He's something of a mystery man. Trust me, I have access to some incredible government resources. I don't have anything close to a current U.S. address for Milo. Or even a former one, for that matter. Or family members and known associates."

"Except me," Benjamin said sourly.

"Except you. I didn't even know how he managed to deal with the usual college entry forms, much less scholarship requests. Do you know?"

"Chicanery, bribery, lies. Anything that would get him where he wanted to go. He was very clever in his way, and he tried to manipulate me, too. But we were too different, he didn't have anything I wanted. I heard later that he quit the university and was living in Europe. I'm sure that he was able to function very well there."

She was getting nowhere. "When and why did he get in touch with you?"

"Two years ago. I was in L.A. at a seminar, and he popped in and asked me to do him a favor. He had a young kid with him who had overdosed and asked me to treat him. I refused and told him to check him into a hospital. He said that was inconvenient and if I didn't help, he'd have to let the boy die. He was totally cold, the usual Milo. I knew he'd probably do it. I gave the kid emergency treatment and sent them on their way. But I got the boy's ID, and I notified the drug hotline together with Milo's name as contact."

"Milo Fletcher?"

"No, he was going under a different name then.

Milo…" He had to think a moment. "Milo King. I thought it was like him to adopt a royal name for himself. He always had delusions of grandeur."

"What was the boy's name?"

"David Spalman. I tried to check with the hotline, but they had no record. I was wondering if he made it that night."

"That time maybe, but he ended up driving off a cliff recently. Probably thanks to Milo."

He muttered a curse. "Damn bastard."

"Can you tell me anything else about Milo?"

"Only that he was driving a fancy blue Bugatti Chiron with California plates." He paused. "And he was the same beast I knew all those years ago. It made me glad that most of the time I live in the jungles of Nigeria and nowhere near him. Good luck, Dr. Michaels."

"Thank you." She ended the call and phoned Lynch.

She quickly told him what she'd learned. "Very sketchy. But at least we know he's a San Diego resident."

"Maybe. Though there's a good chance that he followed Jackie Gabert here after he thought Amsterdam might be getting a little too hot for him. You said Dumont told you he was a user."

"If he did, it seems Jackie was too wary to help him. He was the head honcho in Amsterdam and he prostituted her. She probably wanted to be the one in charge once she broke with him." Her lips curled. "But Milo obviously had no trouble establishing himself as premier Alpha with other people in Jackie's cult circle. He even went behind her back and continued to pursue Barrett."

"In his own little world," Lynch said thoughtfully.

"He liked the power he managed to develop here so much that when things began to go wrong, he tried to work it out instead of leaving the area as he had Amsterdam. And it's good to know he has delusions of grandeur. We might be able to use it, if we see an opening."

"How?"

"I have no idea yet. But we're beginning to see breaks in the façade. Check any info about a Milo King you can find. I doubt if you'll have any luck. That was two years ago, and I bet he regularly changes his identity."

"And what are you going to do?"

"I'm going after the King's chariot."

"What?"

"He drove a fancy blue Bugatti Chiron then. Again, he probably changed his car regularly, since it's a status symbol. Not only for identity purposes but for the grandeur complex. A new car would be a necessity with that kind of mindset. I'll check used-car lots for the Bugatti Chiron to tap info and then go after the newest and flashiest cars on the market."

"That should be easy enough for you," she said dryly. "You're an expert in that category."

"Well, they'll definitely realize I appreciate a good automobile."

"In the three-hundred-thousand-dollar ballpark?"

"Or higher. He chose to call himself King, re-member?"

"How can I forget? The sheer arrogance of it makes me ill. I'm content with hunting for any reference to the King himself and leave the chariot to you."

LATE AFTERNOON
OLIVIA'S CONDO

"A citizen of our fair city?" Olivia repeated to Kendra. "Well, there was always that chance since all Milo's devilry has lately been centered here."

"But it's verification and we needed that." Kendra was gazing at Olivia appraisingly. "And you're looking particularly gorgeous today. That's the designer suit you bought in New York last year. What's the occasion?"

"Does there have to be an occasion? I felt like I needed a lift."

"Really? Tricia is practicing heats with her swim team tonight." Kendra's eyes were narrowed on her face. "Want to have dinner with me and Lynch?"

"I'd love to, but I can't."

"Gotcha," Kendra said. "Do you have a date? What's the occasion?"

"Can't you let me get by with anything?"

"Not when you're looking that gorgeous. You've got to be up to something interesting."

She sighed. "I'm being interviewed for an Australian TV show."

Kendra smiled. "My world-famous friend. Are they doing it at your place?"

"No. Atlas Studios near Balboa Park. TV shows from other places use it when they want to do studio interviews here in town. I've done quite a few there."

"Want me to go with you?"

"Nah, you'll be bored out of your mind. How many times can you sit and listen to me talk about myself?"

"Your story never gets old, Olivia. I love hearing

about how you've taken your little website to a media empire."

"Not quite an empire. I'm just glad people like what I do."

"Come on, you're a star."

"Bullshit."

Kendra abruptly stopped smiling. "Seriously, I'd feel better if you let me go with you. I don't like the idea of you going anywhere alone."

"I'm not going to be alone. I have a driver, and that nice FBI agent Dan Pembrook who works night shift and practically lives on my doorstep is following at a discreet distance. It's already been arranged."

"That may not be good enough. What about when you get to the studio?"

"I know that entire studio like the back of my hand. The techs and hosts are all expecting me."

"And will your agent be there waiting until you finish?"

"He'll be outside in his car." She held up her hand. "That's as far as I'll go," she said flatly. "One of the reasons I'm such a draw is that they get feedback from the audience that they didn't realize I was blind until the host announces it at the end of the interview. Until that time, I'm just an interesting subject that has entertained them." Her voice was intense and dead serious. "One of the reasons I do these interviews is that it gives the public a new and healthier viewpoint on the blind."

"Very clever and I can see why you might prefer it like that. But I don't like it."

"Too bad," Olivia said. "Dan won't release me to the dreaded TV people until he's certain I'll be safe. So have your dinner with Lynch and I'll see you when I get home."

She added as she headed for the door, "And I know you're frowning at me so stop it."

"You deserve it," Kendra said. "I'm not going to leave it like this."

"Yes, you are. Because you know I'm just as independent as you." She tossed her a smile over her shoulder. "And I'll throw you out and make you cook your own dinners if you give me any trouble."

She shut the door behind her.

Olivia leaned forward in the town car as they approached the broadcast studio. Her usual car service's best driver, Todd, was behind the wheel, and he'd gotten her there in less than ten minutes.

"How long do you think it'll be, Ms. Moore?"

"Probably less than an hour. It's a Sydney afternoon news and talk show, and I'll only be on for one segment."

"Looks like the parking lot is gated shut, so I'll find somewhere nearby to park. Call me when you're finished, and I'll meet you right in front."

"Sure thing."

"Uh, there's something you should know." She heard the rustle of fabric as Todd turned in his seat. "It looks like we've been followed all the way from your building."

"Black Ford Explorer SUV?"

"Yes."

"It's an FBI agent. Dan's my shadow for the week."

"Wow. I guess you must have a good story there."

"I'll tell it to you sometime."

He pulled to the curb and unlocked her door. "See you in a bit. Good luck, Ms. Moore."

"Thanks, Todd." She pressed a button to extend her collapsible white cane and climbed out of the car. Her drivers were always good about placing her directly across from the buildings' main entrances and telling her if there were any obstacles she needed to address. She'd barely moved a few feet when she heard the building's door open and then caught a faint whiff of air-conditioning.

"Olivia Moore?" There were hurried, eager footsteps and an Australian-accented male voice she recognized from the phone a few days before.

She smiled. "Edward Shrum?"

"That's me. We're very happy to have you on the show. Right this way."

He spoke with a pleasant lilt that couldn't quite mask the undercurrent of nervousness she often heard from those who worked in live television.

"Hold on one moment," she said. "I believe my agent will be joining us."

"Your agent?"

She heard another set of hurried footsteps, then another familiar voice. "Sorry, I had to park. Pretend I'm not even here."

Olivia recognized the voice as belonging to Special Agent Dan Pembrook, who often took the night shift in serving as her shadow. She turned back toward Shrum. "My agent, Dan Pembrook. Edward Shrum. Shall we go inside?"

"Uh, sure."

They entered the chilly studio. The complex was quiet, as it often was whenever she did evening interviews there. Shrum clearly wasn't accustomed to dealing with a blind person as he awkwardly tried to lead her down the corridor. "Would you like me to—" He stopped. "I'm not sure what the best way to do this is..."

"Relax," she said. "You lead, I'll follow. I'll hear you, and I have my cane, so I won't walk into a wall or something."

"Perfect." He sounded relieved. "We'll start in makeup. Connie should be here any second now."

"Sounds like a plan."

She followed him to the makeup room, where their footsteps clicked more loudly on the tile floor. She heard a slight high-pitched ringing on the right side of the room, which she knew was the sound of light-bulbs over the makeup mirrors. One of the buzzing bulbs was obviously about to burn out. She felt for the long counter beneath the lights and put down her clutch purse.

Shrum patted the back of a makeup chair. "Have a seat. There's a bottle of water on the counter if you'd like to wet your whistle." He flipped on a radio. "I'll be back when Connie gets here."

He left the room.

Agent Pembrook, who had been waiting in the hallway, stepped inside and spoke quietly. "So, I'm your agent now?"

Olivia smiled. "You are, aren't you? Just not the kind of agent he thinks."

"I guess you have a point." He chuckled. "I'll go give the place the once-over."

"Fine."

He stepped out of the room.

Olivia reached forward to pull the phone from her purse, but she felt only the smooth granite countertop where she knew the purse had been. She ran both hands over the cool surface.

Nothing.

Had it fallen to the floor?

Surely she would have heard that, but the radio was making it hard to hear anything else. She dropped to her knees and felt the tile floor.

No purse.

What the hell?

She *knew* she had brought it in with her.

Had Agent Pembrook picked it up?

No, he'd never taken it upon himself to carry her things for her. Like almost all other FBI agents, especially those in protective mode, he liked to keep his hands free.

That left only Shrum. But why in the hell would he—?

"Olivia…!"

The yell came from down the hallway, around the corner.

It was Pembrook!

She ran for the door. Even with the blaring radio, she could hear there was a scuffle under way.

Quick steps.

Dragging heels.

Pained grunts.

Her first instinct was to help, but that's not why Pembrook had cried out. He'd been *warning* her.

The best way to help him was to get the hell out of there. She ran down the hallway, away from the sounds.

Behind her, she could hear choking and gurgling.

She ran with her hands outstretched, retracing the path she'd taken inside. A right turn, another right, a quick left…

She ran smack into a closed door.

No…!

She pulled and pushed on the door handle. Locked. She still had at least one corridor to go until she would reach the sidewalk.

She froze. Behind her, the sounds of the struggle had ended.

There was only the sound of footsteps, and they were coming toward her. Hard leather soles clicked on the tile floor.

Click-click.

Click-click.

She cocked her head. The footsteps weren't Pembrook, who slightly favored his right leg.

They belonged to Shrum. If that was even really his name.

Of course it wasn't his name.

It was Milo.

Her heart started beating harder.

That's who it had to be.

A trap.

She'd heard those shoes when he escorted her inside, accompanied by the tapping of steel-tipped laces.

Click-click.

Tap-tap.

The footsteps stopped.

She could tell from the echo that he'd stopped at one of the hallway intersections, trying to figure out where she'd gone. It wouldn't take a genius to figure out she was trying to make her way back to the main entrance.

She backed away from the locked door. How in the hell were they alone here? Had this maniac rented it just to lure her to a place she felt comfortable?

Click-click.

Tap-tap.

She had to get the hell away from here. To somewhere, anywhere other than this locked door.

She peeled off to the right.

Click-click.

Tap-tap.

She sprinted down the corridor, slowing only to kick off her shoes to quiet her movements. But she wasn't invisible. Fluorescent lights still buzzed overhead, and she assumed there could also be windows casting lights from the city.

She needed to get someplace where she could hide.

Of course…

The studio. If she could get there.

She tried to remember the layout from her previous visits. It was a large grid, with offices, makeup, and green rooms making up one half, and three studios on the other. To get to the studio side, she needed to run back in the direction she'd just come.

While, of course, avoiding the man chasing her.

She put a hand on the wall and followed it to the next juncture, then turned and ran up a corridor she hoped would take her back to one of the studios.

After what seemed like thirty yards or so, she froze.

Click-click.

Tap-tap.

He was in one of the corridors parallel to hers, still moving away from the studios.

Click-click.

Tap-tap.

She waited until she was sure he'd passed her, then she ran toward the end of the hallway. With her hands still outstretched, she finally hit a tall studio door.

She knew Studio A was the first one she'd come to.

There it was! She felt for the handle and pulled.

Locked.

She turned and bolted for the studio next door. She ran only a few feet when she slid on a puddle and lost her footing. She collapsed in a heap on top of something.

Or *someone*.

She recoiled, but it took her only seconds to realize that it wasn't Shrum. This figure was still, terribly still.

Oh, God.

It had to be Agent Pembrook. She was sure of it.

She felt his chest, which was sopping wet.

Drenched in blood. Like the floor all around her.

She felt his face. He still wore his glasses, which he'd constantly taken off and wiped with his jacket. She felt down to his neck, which was sliced open and still oozing blood.

He was dead.

And the last thing he'd done with his life was yell a warning to her.

She felt for his shoulder holster. Empty. She didn't have time to feel around for a gun. Shrum probably took it after he killed him.

Olivia stood, struggling to keep her balance on the bloody floor. She put her hands on the wall and moved toward the next studio. She found the door handle and pulled.

It opened.

She stepped inside. It was cooler, and she could no longer hear the buzzing of lights. She was fairly certain it was dark.

Good. Here, at least, she had a chance.

She moved through the studio, feeling her way past a stack of chairs and a microphone stand.

Now if she could only find the stage console. Because once she found that, she had a chance of—

There. There it was. She felt the panel's smooth side surface.

She moved around and crouched behind it. She'd heard directors making calls while seated here. Somewhere there had to be a phone. She felt the console's rear side.

Contact! She gripped the phone handset and raised it to her ear.

Nothing.

Mustn't panic. Just keep punching buttons until she got a dial tone. The first one triggered a feedback whine that sounded over the ceiling speakers.

Damn.

She'd activated the P.A. system, probably for the entire building. She punched another button.

Dial tone.

She felt for the keypad and dialed 911.

The operator answered immediately. "Emergency services."

Olivia whispered into the phone. "I'm locked in Atlas Studios with a maniac. He's already killed a man, and now he's coming after me. Please send someone. Send everyone."

"Ma'am, I need you to speak louder."

"I can't."

"Ma'am, if you don't speak louder, there's no way I can—"

"Atlas Studios." Olivia raised her voice slightly. "Now! I'm trapped in here with a killer."

The studio door swung open.

Shit.

She put down the phone.

"I know you're in here, Olivia."

It was the same voice she'd heard before, but without the Australian accent, and the tone was mocking.

Click-click.

Tap-tap.

He was unsteady, uncertain in his gait.

It *was* dark. And if he wanted to turn on the studio lights, it would be more difficult than flipping a wall switch.

"You led me right to you," he said. "Want to know how?"

She didn't answer. She didn't move.

"Your friend's blood. Your footprints tracked his blood right to this door, Olivia. It was clearly meant to be. Thank you."

A sound came from the console in front of her.

It was the telephone, she realized. The operator's voice squawked from the handset still dangling off the hook.

Olivia backed away still farther.

"You found a phone." The man clicked his tongue. "That means I'll just have to work faster."

He stepped closer.

Her hands closed around a boom microphone stand…

Click-click.

Tap-tap.

She jumped to her feet and swung the mic stand in front of her.

Contact!

He staggered backward.

Before he could recover, she struck him again. And again.

He grunted in pain.

She threw the stand in his direction and ran. There

was an almost inaudible buzz in the rear of the studio, one she often heard in institutional buildings.

An illuminated exit sign.

She knew there was a rear door that led to a stairwell, but she had no idea where it went. Tech workers came and went from there during her interviews.

She pushed open the door and felt the rough concrete walls of the stairwell. As the door closed behind her, she heard her pursuer staggering toward her.

She ran and half fell, half stumbled down the concrete stairs.

Her ankle twisted, and she felt pain in her wrist as she caught herself on the landing. She crawled toward the next set of stairs.

Except there were none.

End of the line.

No…!

She'd felt something on the way down. She stood and brushed her hands over the wall and felt a smooth glass case.

A firehose?

She struck the glass with her elbow. As it shattered over and around her, she gripped a large, jagged piece in her right hand.

She crouched on the stairs, barely feeling the glass slicing into her fingers.

The door swung open above her.

Could he see her? Or was it dark in here, too?

He didn't move for a long moment.

"Olivia…There's nowhere left to run."

She held her breath.

He stepped forward, then back on the landing.

He couldn't see her. It was dark in here, too! He didn't know if she'd gone up or down…

"Sorry you found yourself in this position, Olivia...It's your friend Kendra's fault, not yours."

She squeezed the glass piece harder, and blood dripped from her fingers.

"I can't promise you won't suffer, Olivia...I've gone through a lot of trouble to make this happen, and I need something for *me*."

Sick son of a bitch.

Her ankle throbbed, and the ache from her wrist was growing more intense by the second.

"I'm impressed, Olivia...If I wasn't so angry about the trouble you've given me, I might even be easier on you. You put up a good fight. But I'm afraid—

He stopped short. He was reacting to some commotion behind him.

Glass breaking. Shouting men.

He chuckled. "Too bad. Another time, Olivia..."

He bolted from the stairwell.

CHAPTER
17

"Olivia!"

Kendra ran toward the paramedic unit as she and Lynch spotted her. They were on the sidewalk in front of Atlas Studios in the middle of what had become a busy taped-off crime scene populated by police and FBI agents. Television news crews were setting up just yards away.

Olivia turned from the paramedic who was bandaging her ankle. "Kendra?"

Kendra pushed through the crowded sidewalk and squeezed her tight. "Griffin told me you weren't hurt badly the minute he got the report, but I was afraid to believe it." She couldn't say anything else for a long moment. "It's true?"

"I'm okay," Olivia finally said. She was trying to be strong, but her voice quavered. "I'm okay."

Kendra pulled back and looked at her blood-soaked clothes. "You don't look okay."

"The blood isn't mine. It's the FBI agent's. He's dead."

"Pembrook," Lynch said. "My source at the Bureau told me he was taken down. I'm sorry, Olivia."

Olivia nodded. "Milo was here. It had to be a trap. I guess I couldn't believe I'd be that important to him, but I was wrong. The son of a bitch wanted me bad enough to kill Pembrook."

Kendra took Olivia's hands in her own. "Tell me what happened. As much as you can, okay?"

Olivia told her about her entire encounter, from her arrival at the studio to the moment police broke in after her 911 call. After she finished, she was having trouble holding it together. "I thought that we were doing everything right. I had security. I'd been notified by the studio. Yet that psychopath is still out there...and now a man is dead."

"Two men." Griffin approached from the building's front doors. He lowered his voice. "We just found the night supervisor's body in an upstairs bathroom."

Kendra looked up in disbelief. "How in the hell did this happen?"

"We're still putting it together, but it seems that Milo represented himself as the producer of a Sydney TV talk show. He contracted with this facility for a satellite uplink, then at the last minute announced a two-hour delay. There were three members of the studio's tech team who went out for dinner. They were supposed to be back at nine thirty."

Lynch nodded. "The supervisor was the only one left here, so Milo killed him and waited for Olivia to arrive."

"Yes." Griffin's lips tightened. "Agent Pembrook was a good man. He must have been caught by surprise."

"He was," Olivia said. "We had no idea anything

was wrong. It was business as usual for a TV interview."

Behind Kendra and Lynch, something was causing a minor commotion on the sidewalk. The sea of cops and FBI agents parted to make way for a solitary figure limping toward them.

It was Metcalf.

He wore sweatpants and a warm-up jacket, and his bruised and battered face was intensely focused on each obviously painful step.

Kendra stepped toward him. "Metcalf... You should be home."

He continued his slow walk toward them. "No. When I heard what happened to Olivia, there was no way I could stay there. We've all been through too much together. I grabbed an Uber."

Olivia raised her head in surprise. She'd been able to control herself so far, but this brought a single tear running down her cheek. "Metcalf..."

He leaned down and hugged her. "I'm sorry, Olivia. Damn bastard. This should never have happened to you."

She squeezed him tight. "You're a complete idiot."

"Tell me something I don't know."

She finally let him go. "Thank you for coming. But now you need to go home and rest."

"Not until I know you're okay."

She nodded impatiently. "I'm okay. Can't you see?"

"Yeah?"

"Yeah."

"I'll stick around to just be certain. I'm going to talk to some of the investigators here at the scene, and after that—"

"No," Griffin said. "You're going home. Right now."

"I can't do that."

"You can. And you will. I'll take you there myself."

Metcalf looked at Kendra and Lynch.

Kendra shrugged. "This is one time I'm on Griffin's side. Go home."

"We need you back at a hundred percent," Griffin said gruffly. "You can hardly stand up straight. You need help back to my car?"

Metcalf hesitated before speaking. "Probably. But there's no way in hell I'm going to let these guys see me leaning on you all the way out of here."

Griffin smiled. "You survived a bomb blast. You're a total badass as far as any of us are concerned. But I totally understand. Let's go. I'm parked nearby."

Metcalf was still looking back at Olivia. "You're sure you're fine?"

"No, not fine. But I'm better than you are. After I get the paramedics to take me to somewhere I can get a change of clothes and a shower, I'll be even better. Get out of here, Metcalf."

"I'll call you later," he called over his shoulder.

"Do that." Olivia turned to Kendra. "Now will you please get me the hell away from here? I can't take much more. I want to go home."

LATER THAT EVENING
OLIVIA'S CONDO

"Is she all right?" Tricia brushed Harley aside and practically whisked Olivia inside the condo. "They said he pushed her down a flight of stairs." Her gaze was raking Olivia's face. "I don't see any facial bruising. But she's limping and her wrist is bandaged. You should have taken her to the ER and had her checked."

"No, they shouldn't," Olivia said firmly. "I'd know if I was badly hurt, and there wasn't an injury. I'm a little stiff and sore but I'll be fine."

"You can't be sure," Tricia said. "And we can't let that asshole think he can take you down. Sit and I'll get you something to drink."

"Let her alone, Tricia," Kendra said quietly. "She knows her own body and she'd tell us if there was any serious injury."

"Let her alone?" Tricia asked fiercely. "How can I do that? She got hurt because of me. She might have been killed and it would have been my fault."

"Don't be ridiculous," Olivia said coldly. "No one is responsible for me, but me. I made the choice to go for that interview. If you want to feel bad about something, Dan Pembrook, a fine FBI agent, lost his life because Milo set that trap for me. He has a wife, and I'll have to call her and let her tell me I'm not worth a shit and certainly not her husband's life."

"Agents' wives know that's always a possibility," Lynch said quietly. "And he took every precaution he could."

"That doesn't change anything," Olivia said. "I'm the one he was protecting. I'll call his supervisor and find out when I can make the call."

"Well, it won't be tonight," Kendra said. "Sit down and have a cup of tea. Then we'll get you to bed. You've had a rough evening."

"I'll get the tea." Tricia headed for the kitchen.

"I can get myself to bed," Olivia said as she sat down at the bar. "Stop hovering, Kendra."

"Let me hover," Kendra said. "I wasn't certain I was going to ever get the chance again. I was scared, Olivia."

"So was I." Olivia added after a moment, "It was those damn steps. I'd never gone down that staircase before. I didn't know where I was going, and I didn't know who was going to be there at the bottom waiting for me."

"But you made it through," Kendra said. "And we only just missed getting Milo."

"Which seems to be the common result where Milo is concerned," Olivia said. "And then we start another page and hope no one gets killed."

"None of it was your fault," Tricia said as she came out of the kitchen carrying the cup of tea. "You were just conducting your life as you'd ordinarily do." She set the cup in front of Olivia. "We all know who bears the blame for putting you through this."

"Yeah, Milo," Kendra said quickly. "And that's the only blame instigated by this entire nightmare."

"I don't agree," Tricia said. "None of this would have happened if I hadn't involved her in my affairs."

"Hardly *your* affairs," Olivia said. "Last I heard, the initial attack on you wasn't with your consent. You were an innocent victim. Everything else that followed started from there. I don't want to hear about it, Tricia."

Tricia opened her lips to speak and then closed them again. "I don't want to upset you any more than you are. I just had to have my say." She turned to Kendra. "I'm going up to your condo to go to bed. Will you walk me to the elevator?"

Kendra nodded as she followed her to the door. "Olivia doesn't need any more conflict. I know what you're feeling, but it's over and she's safe." She glanced back at Olivia. "Drink your tea. I'll be right back."

Olivia nodded mockingly. "Yes, ma'am."

Kendra made a face as she shut the door behind her. "She must be more upset than I thought. Her reply should have been much more biting when I gave her that order. She was almost...tame."

"Can you blame her?" Tricia punched the elevator button. "She looked like she'd been through a tornado."

"No, she didn't. She was tough. I was proud of her."

"So was I," Tricia said. "But she was drained, and I don't like to see her like that. She's so strong, and it hurts me."

"Go ahead, say it," Kendra said quietly. "You had a reason for getting me alone. Why?"

"Everyone was shutting me down and I had to get it out." She drew a deep breath. "You've been good to me, Kendra. No one has ever been better to me. And you gave me Lynch and Olivia and they've been wonderful, too. But what happened to Olivia tonight mustn't ever happen again. Something has to change."

"We're increasing security. We're doing everything we can, Tricia."

"I know you are." Her voice was suddenly full of pain. "That's part of what's wrong. You're all doing everything, and I'm not doing anything. And I had to stand on the sidelines tonight and watch a woman who's good, and funny, and brighter than almost anyone I've ever met, almost get killed. Do you realize what that did to me?"

"I have an idea," Kendra said. "But you'll have to accept it as your part in what we're all doing to catch Milo."

"I don't know if I can." She tensed her jaw. "Do you remember how, the first time I met you, I told you everything I did after the attack to make myself stronger and smarter so that I'd be able to fight off anyone who came after me again? When Barrett was caught and killed, I thought I was safe. I had no idea that there would be a Milo in the wings. But I remember everything I taught myself. Maybe it's time I did a little refresher."

"No, it's *not*," Kendra said sharply. "Don't even think about it."

"For the time being that's all I'm doing…thinking about it. I have that swim meet at Long Beach day after tomorrow and I have to be ready. But I felt I had to tell you how I feel. I can't let anyone else take a risk meant for me. Something has to change." She got on the elevator and punched the button. "We'll discuss it after I win that meet Saturday."

"You're so sure that you'll win?"

"I'm very, very fast." The elevator door was closing. "Right now, that competition is the least of my worries."

Kendra turned and headed back to Olivia's condo. She was feeling the same way. Tricia had been balanced too long on that dangerous edge. It was going to be difficult to persuade her to stand down when one of her favorite people had been targeted. Kendra was only grateful that discussion was going to be postponed until after the swim meet Saturday. Perhaps by that time they would have found ammunition to convince Tricia to be more patient.

11:00 A.M.
NEXT DAY
KENDRA'S CONDO

Lynch spent the night with Kendra, but he was awake and on the computer hours before she stirred.

He'd arranged a wonderful breakfast to be delivered from her favorite downtown brunch spot, and as they finished consuming it, Kendra's phone vibrated in her pocket. She pulled it out and looked at the caller ID screen.

"Who is it?" Lynch said.

"Unknown caller, but it's a 678 area code. That's what Trey Suber told me to watch for. It's probably him."

She pressed the TALK switch. "Trey?"

"Yeah. Hi, Kendra."

She didn't like the tone of his voice. His high-energy demeanor had been replaced with one of total defeat. "You sound tired."

"I'm running out of ideas."

"That doesn't sound like you, Trey. Have you thought about what I said? About going in and talking to your colleagues? They want to help you."

"I'm not so sure about that."

"I am. Just…keep it in mind, okay?"

"Sure. Thanks, Kendra. Listen, I'm calling to see if you'd made any progress on that photo of Milo."

"As a matter of fact, I have. I'd like to show it to you and see if it triggers anything in that mental serial killer database of yours."

"Text me a copy of it."

"I'd feel better if I could just show it to you in person. I'm fairly close by. You're on G Street, walking east from the bay?"

Trey was silent for a long moment before speaking. "Has Lynch found a way to track me on this phone? Or…" He chuckled. "I forgot who I'm talking to."

"Obviously."

"What gave me away?"

"Approach and departure horns for the harbor cruise boats. Very distinctive. You were near Navy Pier. A minute or so later, I could hear the bell for the trolley. You're clearly walking east. But even that sound has started to recede. Are you at State Street yet?"

He chuckled again. "Almost."

"Lynch and I will meet you at Pantoja Park in ten minutes. On the G Street side. Okay?"

After another pause, he replied, "Okay. See you there."

Kendra ended the call and immediately made another. "Griffin... Trey is meeting me at Pantoja Park in ten minutes."

"How did you swing that?" Griffin asked.

"He trusts me," she said quietly. "He'll be there."

She cut the connection.

"Wow," Lynch said. "Trey may not forgive you."

"Something had to be done. We'll work it out. I talked to Griffin a little while ago. It'll be okay."

"Okay for who?"

She checked her watch. "Let's go."

***

It was a short car ride to Pantoja Park, a rectangle of grass and mature trees in a densely developed area of downtown San Diego. At the moment, it was home to dog walkers, resting tourists, and office workers eating their lunches.

Plus Trey Suber. He nodded to Kendra and Lynch as they parked on the street alongside the park.

"He really has no idea," Lynch said.

"It's better this way."

They climbed out of the car and walked toward him. Even though Kendra knew he had his razor and several changes of clothes, he was unshaven and slightly unkempt. He wore sunglasses and a blue flat cap in an obvious attempt to mask his appearance. The stress of the past few days was clearly showing on his face and posture.

Kendra smiled as she and Lynch approached. "This is a good look for you, Trey. You might consider permanently adding it into your fashion rotation."

"You're too kind. It's a little too hipsterish for my taste."

Lynch shook his hand. "You pull it off."

"I don't know about that. But it'll work for now." He turned to Kendra. "Let me look at that photo."

Before Kendra could reply, two black SUVs squealed to a stop on the street beside them. Griffin and three other dark-suited FBI agents jumped from the vehicles and converged on them.

Trey backed away in panic. "What the hell?"

"Just relax," Kendra said. "It's okay."

Trey glared at her. "*You* did this?"

Griffin held up his hands in a way that was meant to be reassuring. "Suber, it's fine. We know you were being set up."

Trey froze. "You do?"

"Yes," Kendra said. "Everyone knows it."

Trey waved his arms at the approaching agents. "Then what the hell is all this about?"

Griffin and the agents stopped on the sidewalk in front of him. "We weren't sure you would believe us," Griffin said. "We were afraid you'd think you were walking into a trap. We couldn't be sure that you wouldn't resist and get yourself killed. Now don't be an idiot. We have proof that someone was trying to frame you."

Trey looked at Kendra, who nodded.

"Griffin told me this morning," she said. "They've been working overtime to clear you, Trey. You were just a little too obvious a candidate to be true."

Trey let out a long breath, as if finally letting the tension escape from his body. "I know I'm not the most popular agent in the Bureau. So how in the hell did they do it?"

"We'll show you everything back at the office," Griffin said. "But someone obviously created a fake license plate with a graphics program on their computer. It could have been printed on a large glossy label and stuck over the plates on a vehicle that's an exact match for yours."

"That I'd already figured," Trey said.

"Well, as we studied the video footage, it became apparent under some lighting conditions that the phony license plate wasn't backed by the same reflective film that real plates are."

"Did you check out my locations I provided Kendra?"

"We did. We have a Home Depot security camera that puts you and your car on the other side of town at the exact same time as some of these other camera sightings. We've always been impressed with you, Suber, but even you would have trouble being in two places at once."

Trey smiled. "Hey, don't underestimate me. But what about my phone?"

"Spoofed. That's a bit more sophisticated, but we run across hackers every day who'd be willing to do it for a thousand bucks. Someone spoofed your service account and the MAC address of your phone. Again, your phone account was hitting towers at the same time in two different parts of town."

Trey nodded. "And I guess someone cracked my home Wi-Fi and made those bomb-making Internet searches in the days before the explosion."

"Yes," Griffin said. "You should button that down. They probably parked in front of your place and did it on a laptop. Lucky for you, you like to work ridiculous hours. Our building security cameras show that you were in your office while most of those searches were being done, mostly between ten P.M. and midnight. You're in the clear, Suber."

Trey nodded. "Great." He was looking a little lost. "I guess I get to go home again?"

"Disappointed?" Kendra asked.

"Well, it was kind of exciting while it lasted. I've never been a man of mystery before. Not that I'm not grateful."

"You'll have to be content with going back to work," Kendra said. "We need you more than ever."

"Yeah." Trey pulled off his hat and sunglasses. "And I *really* want to get this guy."

<hr/>

LONG BEACH SWIM CENTER
SOUTHERN CALIFORNIA REGIONAL
SWIM MEET

"This place is already mobbed." Kendra's gaze skimmed over the crowded, noisy sports center before turning to Tricia. "Lynch isn't going to like this."

Tricia shrugged. "Between the media and the

audience, it's always like this on meet days. It's a university, the swimmers would be disappointed if they didn't have their hour in the sun. You told me Lynch has been here since dawn checking security. He's not going to let anything happen to me." She shook her head as she studied Kendra's face. "Stop worrying. For Pete's sake, I want you to enjoy watching me be a star. All the time we've been together you've done nothing but take care of me and give me support as if I were a half-wit kid. That wasn't really me." She added ruefully, "The star isn't, either, but maybe you'll be able to find something you can respect in between."

"I've always respected you, Tricia," Kendra said. "Respected and liked you and considered you my friend." She suddenly grinned. "And I always knew the star was hiding somewhere beneath, but it was kind of her not to try to intimidate me. I promise I'll be properly full of respect and adulation if the star peeks out today."

"'If'?" Tricia repeated. "A little confidence, please." She gave Kendra a quick hug. "Now go find a front-row seat and watch me show off for you." She broke away from her and ran toward her coach standing by the locker room door.

Kendra hesitated, watching Tricia with her teammates and coach all looking alike in their blue swimsuits, slim bodies, and glowing health and vitality. Yet even at this distance she could tell that Tricia was distinctive, the way she moved, her grace…

Then Tricia was suddenly looking across the center at Kendra. She took a step away from her teammates, lifted her thumb, and jerked it toward the audience seats.

Kendra broke into laughter. Yes, definitely

distinctive, she thought, as she moved toward the front row of the seats where Tricia had told her to sit. Evidently, she was designated audience and not guardian or caregiver today and Tricia was making sure that she knew it.

———————

TWO HOURS LATER

"Having a good time?" Lynch asked as he stopped by Kendra's chair. "I was keeping an eye on you, and I saw you on your feet a couple times."

"More than a couple," Kendra said. "And I wasn't alone. Tricia had everyone on their feet cheering during that last heat. Were you watching?"

"I admit I couldn't resist after she broke that record," Lynch said. "That should make the evening news. I was proud of her."

"Me too." Kendra could still feel that coursing excitement. "She said she was going to show off for me. She certainly did. I had no idea she was that fast. You've been watching her every day. I guess you knew how good she was."

"I talked to her coach, and she said Tricia was going to set more than one record at the Olympics this year. I guess today was a preview."

"If she gets the opportunity. I told you how upset she was the other evening."

"Maybe after she got this chance of being in the limelight, she might be willing to devote herself to her practice and forget about Milo for a while."

"I don't think so."

He shrugged. "Neither do I. But I'm looking for a

bright side." He grinned. "And I believe we have one on the horizon. I just heard from Ripley, one of my contacts I've had combing the used-car lots in the city, and he thinks he's located a Cadillac Milo turned in for a new model." He added, "And the Walmart store across the highway that managed to get a photo when he turned the car over to the dealer."

Kendra tensed. "You're saying we have a photo of Milo?"

"Three." He held up his fingers. "Or so Ripley tells me. He's something of an overachiever. He promises to text them to me within the next hour or so."

"Good," Kendra said. "Because the minute we get our hands on his photo we'll broadcast it to the entire world. It's what we've been waiting for."

"And as soon as he realizes we have it, he might disappear into the hands of the best plastic surgeon available," Lynch said. "We'd better make hay while the sun shines and find him before he returns to anonymity."

Kendra checked her watch. "This can't last much longer. There's one more heat and then the medal awards."

He shook his head. "You said she's showing off for you. We can wait for Ripley." He started down the aisle. "I'd better get back to the locker room and make certain everything is going as scheduled. I'll see you later."

She watched him leave. This had been good news all around today, she thought. Tricia acing it over the other swimmers. And then the news about the photos. It was incredible how important that ID was going to be to them. She glanced around the center. Milo could be here right now, and they would never know. Her probing gaze went from face to face. She was as blind as Olivia had been when Milo had caught her at that studio. It had been a long time since Kendra had felt so helpless.

But that danger was going to vanish after today.

Yes, it was going to be a good day.

———◆———

Music.

Sports reporters everywhere.

Noise.

The aisles were jammed with people.

And Kendra didn't stand a chance of making it to the locker room to get to Tricia.

She tried to call Lynch, but he didn't answer. He was probably running interference between Tricia and the media and anyone else who was getting too near to her.

But now she could see the media surrounding the brilliant blue caps of the swimmers. That had to be where Tricia could be found. Just go for it. Kendra dove into the crowd and started to fight her way toward the bright lights.

But she didn't spot Tricia until she reached almost the center of the crowd. Then she caught sight of her blue swim cap with her name in white letters emblazoned across the front. "Tricia!" Kendra called out. "Congratulations! I thought I'd come back and tell you how much—"

But it wasn't Tricia. The girl who had turned around was a freckle-faced, young team member that Kendra vaguely remembered Tricia had called Babs. Her height and build resembled Tricia's, and she wore aviator sunglasses that further obscured her features. The girl was giggling as she saw Kendra's shocked surprise. "Hi, not Tricia." She tapped the name on her cap. "This was Tricia's idea. She's been hounded by the media lately, and she asked if I'd wear this to give her a chance to slip away."

Kendra cursed under her breath and looked around. "When did this happen?"

"After the meet, a minute or so after the final scores were posted. It worked. The reporters saw the cap and followed me and the rest of the team outside while she hid out in the locker room."

"I can see that," Kendra said. "The locker room, you said?"

"That's right, she said if I ran into you to tell you she'd meet you after she was dressed." She turned back to the TV cameraman. "Yes, I've been training with Tricia since she was accepted on the team, and we all knew that she was special…"

Yes, she was special, Kendra thought as she whirled away and started to push toward the locker room. But that didn't mean that she could turn Lynch's plans upside down because she wanted to be kind to a teammate. Lynch might have followed that cap lead, too, and that meant Tricia could be left unprotected.

"Kendra!" It was Lynch, grabbing her arm and pushing her out of the mob around the media reporters. "I just heard what she said about the locker room. Let's get the hell over there." He added grimly, "And I might do bodily damage to Tricia when we locate her." He was pushing them both through the crowds. "I can understand losing her in this media free-for-all. No one could guess that she'd break two world records today. But up to that time I had her under surveillance. There was no way she should have added to the confusion by this crazy trick."

"I'm not arguing," Kendra said. "I can see how this would be the perfect opportunity for Milo to step in and take advantage of all the uproar." She shook her head. "But I can understand how Tricia might be giddy and want to spread the joy. How often does something like this happen to a young swimmer? It must seem like a miracle."

"You'll forgive me if I lack your understanding. I just want to keep her alive. Stay behind me." They'd reached the locker room and he went in ahead of her.

It was empty.

"Babs said she'd see me after she was dressed." Kendra went to the lockers, found Tricia's name, and opened it. "Only her swimsuit. All of her regular clothes are gone. She must have dressed and left the locker room."

Lynch was swearing softly beneath his breath. "Then she's out in that mob outside?"

"Maybe not." Kendra was looking at the swimsuit hanging in locker. "There's a plastic envelope dangling on the hanger." She took the envelope off the hanger. "It's addressed to me."

"You'd just better hope it's not from Milo."

"Don't even think that." But as she was opening the envelope her hands were trembling. "She's probably telling me where we can meet her."

She scanned the letter.

"Oh, shit."

"Not good?"

She thrust the letter at him. "Not disaster. Not at all good."

She watched his face as he read.

Kendra,

I told you that it couldn't continue this way. I have to stop it before someone else gets hurt. I can't rely on anyone else to do it for me. First,

I want you to know that Milo had nothing to do with me leaving today. It's all my plan and I've been thinking about it for a long time. This seemed the perfect time if I could pull off breaking at least one record. I'll try not to involve you at all, but if I find it necessary to make sure he's gone forever, I might let you help. Don't expect it. I've been waiting a long time for this. I want to do it alone.

I'll call you soon so that you'll see I'm well, and let you yell at me and tell me what an idiot I am. Thank you for everything.

Love,
Tricia

"So much for her being giddy and wanting to share the joy," Lynch said dryly. "She was calculating every possibility to skip out on us and go after Milo. Even down to using her athletic skill as a swimmer to accomplish it."

"She probably was a little giddy," Kendra said. "We always knew she was complicated. She told us once she wanted the whole world. Well, right now she's going after Milo. She's probably considering it his time." She paused. "What's next? Griffin?"

He nodded. "We warn him to put his agents on alert for anyone of her description. Then we talk to her coach and ask if she has any hint of where she'd go. After that, we discreetly conduct our own investigation."

"And one more thing," Kendra said. "We call your contact Ripley and get hold of that photo of Milo. It seems to be the only weapon we might have to work with. If Tricia's going after him, we want her to know what the bastard looks like."

CHAPTER
18

Let me get this straight," Lynch said slowly and precisely to Griffin on the phone. "You refuse to commit FBI resources to track down Tricia? When you know that Milo will be after her?"

"It was her choice to leave your protection and the agents we've assigned to watch over her," Griffin said brusquely. "I refuse to risk the lives of any more of my people over someone who refuses to cooperate with us. If she shows herself, and I'm convinced that she'll draw out our killer, I'll consider putting agents back on a protective detail. But I'm done with dealing with a college kid who doesn't know what she wants. For all I know, she might just be hungry for more headlines like she got on NBC today."

"Bullshit." Kendra took the phone from Lynch. "The only thing Tricia is hungry for is Milo's head on a platter, Griffin. You'd be smart to keep an eye on her, because she'll try to draw him to her. You want the killer who butchered those agents who ended up in that crater? So does Tricia, and she'll do anything to get him. Help her."

"If you get any credible evidence on Milo, let me know, Kendra. I'll maintain the surveillance on you and Olivia since you appear to still be targets." He cut the connection.

She muttered a curse as she handed Lynch back his phone. "He won't listen. Why?"

"You know why," Lynch said. "Griffin has priorities, and they're all about his agents. You just don't want to hear them. Neither do I. We could have used his help tracking Tricia, but he's clearly annoyed." He shrugged. "I've reached out to my sources." He showed Kendra his phone. "Her signal isn't hitting any towers, so either she's turned her phone off or she's using a burner. If she reaches out, we can try tracking her."

"So we just sit around and wait?"

"Of course not. We do it the old-fashioned way. Let's go over to Tricia's dorm and talk to a few of her roommates and see if she confided in any of them. I'm sure the beer is flowing and they're celebrating big time by now. They might be ready to talk about how they helped out their old buddy."

Kendra nodded. "I went over all the names that Tricia's mentioned to me since she's been staying here. One of them is Babs Murphy who is on the team and traded swim caps with her. She might know something more." She was already heading for the front door. "And she has at least four other friends that she—"

"Hold it." Lynch's phone was pinging. "This must be those photos from Riley."

She instantly turned back and crossed the room toward Lynch. "Took long enough."

"You wanted the best possible three reproductions." He handed her his phone again. "What do you think of him?"

Milo Fletcher.

Kendra didn't know what she had expected. His image had grown out of all proportion in her mind. This was the monster, the Alpha, the man who could turn vulnerable teenage boys and tough women like Jackie into shadows of themselves and then destroy them.

Milo was somewhere in his middle to late thirties. Slim, well dressed, and smiling at the used-car dealer with charm and intensity. Good looking, dark hair and eyes. The second photo was more of a close-up and revealed the tightness around his lips, the flicker of impatience in his eyes. The third photo showed the strength of shoulders and arms and a hand that was gesturing and very expressive.

It also showed a tattoo on the man's collarbone.

"This is it," Kendra said. "The circle-triangle tattoo that the dog walker saw down the street from Jackie's apartment!"

Lynch nodded. "It's only visible on this third picture. The collar covers it on the others. This is our man."

"I remember how he completely fooled Olivia at that studio. I think he's deceptive, and capable of anything, including the murders we know he committed." She turned around and headed for the door again. "And I want to keep him as far away from Tricia as we can manage."

"Am I in trouble?"

Barbara "Babs" Murphy stood in the doorway of the dorm room she shared with Tricia Walton looking like she was about to jump out of her skin. She was much more guarded than she had been at the swim meet.

"No, you're not in trouble," Kendra replied quickly. "Not at all."

"Of course not." Lynch added, "You've been honest with us, right?"

"I *have* been." Babs shook her head. "This was all Tricia's idea. I thought I was doing her a favor. The next thing I knew, I had all these FBI agents crawling up my ass."

Kendra smiled. "Disturbing visual aside, no one's trying to get you into trouble. We just want to find her. May we come in?"

Babs opened the door wide. "Sure."

Kendra and Lynch stepped inside. It was slightly larger than most dorm rooms she'd seen, but the layout was similar: beds, desks, small window.

Kendra pointed to a tightly made-up bed on the right side of the room. Over the headboard, a single brass hook held over a dozen award medals. "Tricia's bed?"

"Yep. I sure don't have that many medals," Babs said. "And she's got about twenty more in her desk drawer."

Kendra nodded. "I believe it. Tell me, did she give you any idea where she was going?"

"No. I didn't even know she *was* going anywhere. I thought she just wanted to get away from all the media. Ever since people started talking her up as the next big thing, life has been crazy for her. And it really got intense after *Sports Illustrated* did that profile. I was happy to play decoy for her while she slipped out of the aquatic center. I didn't think it was a big deal."

Kendra looked at the books and papers on Tricia's desk. "Does she keep a datebook?"

Babs snorted. "How old do you think she is? Uh, no. I'm sure she just uses the calendar app in her phone like everyone else I know."

Kendra winced. "I guess I deserved that. How about a change of clothes? Did she take anything with her?"

"Actually, yes. I checked after I got back here. She took her suitcase. It's usually under her bed. She must have packed it up and loaded it into her car while I was out last night."

Kendra lifted the bedspread and looked underneath, where there were several small open boxes and packing materials strewn about. She was about to put the bedspread down when something caught her eye. She pulled out one of the boxes, which featured a graphic of a claw-shaped knife.

Lynch took the box from her. "This is a karambit."

"A what?"

"A knife used in Indonesian martial arts. What is she doing with this?"

Kendra pulled out the other open boxes, and Lynch let out a low whistle. "Butterfly knives, ring blades…Does Tricia know how to use these things?"

"She thinks she does. She studied martial arts after that creep almost killed her a few years ago." Kendra looked up at Babs. "Have you ever seen her use these things?"

"Never," Babs said positively. "I don't think they're

even allowed on campus. I guess she's always just kept them there under her bed."

"Well, only the boxes are here now." She glanced at Lynch. "She appears to be serious about trying to face off against Milo." She moistened her lips as she added, "Alone."

Lynch sighed. "Which is why we need to find her first."

Kendra stood and turned back toward Babs. "This is important. Can you give us any idea where she might have gone?"

"No." She frowned. "Except..."

"Yes?"

"It has to be someplace she has access to a pool. No matter what, she's going to keep training. She's not going to throw it all away now."

Lynch shook his head. "I'm afraid that doesn't narrow things down too much."

"It's all I got." She shrugged. "Sorry."

"It's okay. Thank you." Lynch handed her a card. "Call if you think of anything else, okay?"

"Sure." Babs turned back to Kendra. "You know, she really liked you. She wouldn't have tried to hide anything from you if she could have seen her way clear."

Kendra's gaze was drawn back to the darkness under Tricia's bed, where the girl had kept those wicked blades to protect herself. She shivered. Then she forced herself to smile. "Well, it seems she couldn't see her way clear this time. But thank you for telling me. If you run into her, let her know that we're only trying to help her." She kept her gaze away from those boxes as she headed for the door. "Let's go, Lynch."

———◆———

They got back to Kendra's condo at a little after midnight.

Lynch closed the front door but didn't turn on the lights. "You haven't said a word since we left the dorm." He gently cradled her face in his hands. "Are you going to tell me why?"

"Maybe I can't forget all those exotic weapons we pulled out from under Tricia's bed," she whispered. "She's an athlete. She's young and brilliant and yet life twisted her until she felt it necessary to gather all those terrible weapons to keep herself alive. Sometimes life can be shit."

"Not as long as she has someone like you to untwist her." He kissed her gently. "It's all a question of balance. We had a tough day, but we made some discoveries; tomorrow we'll make a few more. Maybe one of them will show us the way to get Tricia to sit down and listen to us. She told you that she'd call you. Give her a chance." He kissed her again. "Are you going to send me home? I promise all I want to do is hold you and make you forget those damn weapons." He chuckled. "Well, maybe that's not all, but we can discuss that later. May I stay?"

She could feel the vibrant *aliveness* of him in the darkness. Whenever anything went wrong Lynch was always there to strike that balance. Lord, she needed that tonight.

She slid her arms around his neck. "I think that would be a very good idea," she said huskily. "I want very much to have you hold me tonight, Lynch…"

———

The call came at three forty in the morning.

"Hello, Kendra," Milo said mockingly. "I hate to

disturb your rest, but I felt I had to touch base with you. You must be feeling very upset, and I wanted you to know I'm always here to reach out to you. I understand you've lost our swimmer. How sad for you."

She fought the shock, shaking her head to clear it. "How kind, Milo." Then when she felt Lynch stiffen against her, she pressed the SPEAKER button. "But I don't need anything from you. If you're talking about Tricia, you're the one who lost her all those years ago. Was she your only failure? I was wondering why you were so determined to bring her back."

"She wasn't my failure," he bit out. "If I'd been doing the kill instead of Barrett, I would never have lost her. I was always the master and he the pupil. Now I have to go to the bother of cleaning up his mess."

"I thought you did that at Pine Valley," she said caustically. "That was also a disaster."

"No, it wasn't. If you hadn't stepped in, I wouldn't have had a problem. But I don't regret it, you've been very exciting. That's why I called you tonight. I want to make certain you know that right after I take care of Tricia, you'll be next. She won't be alone for long."

"You're bluffing," she said scornfully. "You don't even know where she is."

"I don't have to. She'll tell me. Do you believe I'd spend all these years learning to be the perfect Alpha and not be able to read one young girl? She thinks she's so intelligent that she can bring me down. It won't happen. I'll watch and wait and then I'll pounce." He chuckled. "And then it will be your turn. Good night, Kendra. I'll see you very soon…"

He ended the call.

She took a deep breath and then sat up in bed.

Lynch muttered a curse and then watched her as

she slipped on her robe. "Come back to bed. He just wanted to disturb you."

"Well, he succeeded. But you know...I think it's more than that."

"What do you mean?"

"He was fishing. Fishing for information about Tricia. As much as he was trying to pretend he knew exactly what was going on, he was trying to see if we knew where she was."

"I heard your end of the conversation. You didn't give him anything."

"I have precious little to give."

"He didn't get what he wanted."

"I'll be back soon. I'm going out on the veranda and get some air."

She wasn't out on the veranda for more than a minute before she heard him behind her. His arms slipped around her waist from behind. "You let him have the last word. You should never let an asshole have the last word."

"I'll remember that next time." She leaned back against him. "I was occupied with trying to decide if he did know where Tricia was."

"Like you said, bluffing."

"Or trying to lead me totally down the wrong path. It's hard to tell with a devil like him."

"Yes, it is."

"Well, I refuse to worry about it. As far as I'm concerned, he's nothing but a liar. He only called me to get what information he could. But if he thinks we're trying to find Tricia, we need to make sure that our phones, our texts, and all of our communications are locked down tight. We can't let him know anything we're finding out to track her down."

"I agree. I have a scanner in my car. I'll sweep everything for listening devices to make sure we don't give him any leads."

"Good. And we'll find Tricia and keep her safe from him."

"Fine resolutions. Any others you'd like to share?"

"Yes." She turned in his arms and held him close. "I'd like to go back to bed and have you hold me again. Will you do that?"

"Absolutely. Any particular reason?"

"He tried to ruin what you gave me tonight. I won't let him do it. Someone told me you never let an asshole have the last word."

"He must have been very wise."

"Every now and then he comes up with a gem." She nestled her cheek against his chest and then turned and led him toward the veranda doors. "Let's see if this is one of them."

———◆———

Milo twisted the disposable flip phone in his hands and broke it in half.

Kendra Michaels didn't know where Tricia was, he was certain. He could hear the worry in her voice, as much as she tried to hide it.

It didn't matter; Tricia couldn't stay hidden for long. The Tricias of the world needed to be center stage, basking in the limelight. In that way, she was like all his other targets.

How sad.

For years, he'd worked with his recruits for their singular mission: to target those pathetic souls who thought they were God's gift to humanity, just like the arrogant and entitled people he'd grown up with. Over the years, he'd coordinated the killings of young, rising-star politicians, athletes, scientists, and countless others. In all that time, the FBI had failed to identify a pattern because there was always more to the murders than met the eye; without anyone realizing it, he was stealing the world's future.

Milo smiled. As soon as he was finished with Tricia Walton, he was ready with a new slate of victims. And he'd chosen his next recruit to carry out the tasks.

Exciting times.

———◆———

The call Kendra had been waiting for didn't come until the next afternoon.

"Hello, Kendra. Did you miss me?"

It was Tricia!

Kendra inhaled sharply. "You could say that. When I didn't want to break your neck."

"You'd have to stand in line," Tricia said. "And I don't believe you'd be willing to let Milo get ahead of you. I know I wouldn't. But then that's what this is all about, isn't it?" She paused. "Never letting Milo get ahead of anyone again. How angry are you with me?"

"I'm not angry. I'm just worried and sad and thinking that this could be an incredibly bad mistake."

"And you could be right," she said quietly. "But it's one I've spent years preparing myself for. I suppose I always knew it would come down to this."

"You alone? You couldn't know," she said between set teeth. "Because it's stupid and you're not stupid. You just got discouraged and scared for all of us. But you should have realized that was what Milo wanted. He feeds on fear."

"I do know it," she said. "Because he's tried to do that to me since the day I got away from him. But I'm not afraid any longer." She was silent a moment. "I think you taught me that, Kendra. I've watched you and Olivia and Lynch. No matter what happened you just accepted it and then went on the attack."

"You didn't need to be taught," Kendra said. "I knew that from the moment I met you. I just want you to let us help. Can't you do that?"

"I'm afraid not." There was genuine regret in her voice. "I've never had a friend like you. I don't believe I could bear to lose you. I'll just have to go along with the plan. I'm sorry that I can't give you what you want."

"So am I." Kendra's voice was suddenly hard. "Because it just means I'll have to take it. I don't give a damn about your plan. I'm certain it's as clever as you are. But I'm not going to let Milo get within a yard of you. We haven't stopped making plans of our own just because you decided to opt out. For instance, I'm going to text you a few photos of Milo so that you'll recognize him when you see him." She pressed the button. "He's not bad looking but he has a...tightness that I don't like. We're having problems with Griffin, so don't count on him. But you can count on the rest of us. We're going to be on your trail every minute." She paused. "And on Milo's. Like it or not I won't leave you alone. Because I don't believe I could bear to lose you, either. If you decide to come to your senses, give me a call and we'll do it together."

Tricia was laughing. "Just what I said."

"What?"

"You accept whatever comes and then go on the attack."

"Only when I'm not left a choice. Did you get the photos?"

"Yes, all three. It may be helpful."

"That was the aim. That's all I want."

"I know." Tricia's voice was gentle. "It's all you've ever wanted. I hope you get what you want. But I doubt it, Kendra. Not if my plan works. Goodbye, my friend."

She cut the connection.

Kendra's fists clenched. "Son of a bitch."

Accept and go on the attack.

Kendra called Lynch and filled him in on her conversation with Tricia.

After she finished, he paused before speaking. "Obviously, when she gets something in her head, she can't be easily talked out of it. Reminds me of someone else I know."

"This isn't a time for jokes."

"Who's joking?"

"I'm worried about her. I wish we knew where she was."

"Well, when you were talking to her, she was about fifty miles north of San Diego. She was on the I-5 freeway."

Kendra wasn't sure she'd heard him correctly. "What are you talking about?"

"I reached out to one of my sources. I've arranged for them to send me a text whenever her mobile phone pings a cell tower. It just came in. Her phone hit three towers during the conversation you just had with her."

"You know that already? I've been part of

investigations where it's taken hours to get that kind of information."

"I guess I have better sources than the police departments you were working with."

She sighed. "Of course you do."

"Unfortunately, that means she's still on the move. We'll have to wait for her to make another call to home in on her position."

"It's strange, but I just told her that we'd never give up and we'd do everything to find her. I had no idea that you were already zeroing in on her."

"Things are moving a little fast. We would have discussed it soon. I wasn't trying to keep you out of it."

But things always moved fast with Lynch, Kendra thought dryly. With all his contacts and tech assistance he was able to function at lightning speed. "I'll accept that for the moment. Let's just have the discussions a little quicker."

"Correction noted and accepted. It won't happen again."

But Kendra was already moving on. "I don't know how Tricia thinks she's going to find Milo when all the resources of the FBI haven't been able to do it." Then she had a sudden thought. "Unless…Tricia has a plan for him to find *her*."

"Interesting. A dangerous plan."

She shuddered. "You got that right."

Lynch was receiving a text. He raised his phone and stared at it.

She asked curiously, "Another message from your source?"

"Your source, too. A text from Griffin. Check your inbox. It looks like Tricia Walton has resurfaced somewhere else."

"What?" Kendra gasped and she leaned over to look at his phone. "Where?"

"In the sports section of the *San Diego Union-Tribune*. She gave an interview to their columnist. It just went live in the last five minutes." Lynch skimmed the story. "You'll want to read this. Tricia's quit her swim team and pulled out of the next several solo events. She says she's leaving town to train on her own."

Kendra picked up her phone and found the link in Griffin's text. She was dashing through Tricia's interview. "She also says she doesn't know when or if she's coming back...She wants to simplify her life and get back to her roots. She wants to be by herself and get back to a time and place of her life that's been lost to her for years now, when and where she first fell in love with swimming. Back when she was a high school sophomore..."

"That was the year she was attacked," Lynch said grimly.

"Exactly." Kendra looked up as the realization hit her. "Oh, no. Shit. Tricia's going to the summer house."

"Her family's lake house?"

"Yes." She put down her phone. "And what's more, she wants Milo to know it. That's what this interview is all about. She wants to draw him out."

"Are you sure?"

"No, how could I be? But I'm betting I'm right about it. That's where everything changed for her." Kendra paced across the room. "Remember? Tricia told us so herself. After she was attacked out there, her family boarded up the cabin and they never went back. That part of her life came to an end. She wants to take it back, and part of that is ending Milo once and for all."

He cursed softly. "I think you may be right."

"Then we have to go out there. *Now*."

"Do you know where it is?"

Kendra reached for her tablet computer. "It'll be in the police crime report when she was attacked. I have it right here."

CHAPTER

19

Tricia sat on the picnic bench at the water's edge, staring at the rippling waves. Lake Spindle was one of thousands of lakes in California's High Sierra, but this one had always been special. To her family, this had always been *their* lake, ever since her great-great-grand-parents had purchased all of the livable surrounding land over a hundred years before. Even in drought years, the small lake received a generous supply of water from the Sierra snowpack, providing a spectacular focal point for family gatherings and summer recreational activities. The property's lakefront cabin, dubbed Endless Summer, had hosted generations of good times and cherished memories.

Until the day *he* arrived and destroyed everything.

No one in her family had visited there since the hor-rible day she'd been attacked, and the years were not kind to the boarded-up cabin. The paint was chipped and weathered, and wild brush had overtaken the surrounding area. The utilities had been turned off long ago, and rodents had overrun the place.

It didn't matter. She wouldn't stay for long. She'd spent the afternoon sweeping and preparing the cabin, and she was ready.

She pulled her jacket closer as the sun set behind the mountain in front of her. How strange it was to be back. She'd wondered what it would be like to return to this place after so long. For much of her life, this cabin and lake felt more like home than anyplace on earth.

Now, strangely, it felt that way again. She'd spent years preparing herself to punish the son of a bitch who'd taken so much from her, only to have all that effort come to naught when she thought he'd been captured.

Now, miraculously, she had a second chance. This is who she really was, who she had worked so hard to become. Not the *Sports Illustrated* golden girl, but an avenging angel who might bring some balance to her and her family's world.

She checked her watch. It had been over four hours since her *San Diego Union-Tribune* interview had been posted online. Surely Milo would take the bait.

She looked up at the ridge and two-lane road that extended for miles. It was the only way to reach the cabin, originally constructed to serve a now mined-out quarry in the next valley. From her vantage point, she could spot any approaching cars long before they'd see her.

She'd chosen the perfect place for her rematch with a monster.

Two hours later, he still hadn't arrived.

Patience.

If not tonight, then tomorrow. Or the day after.

She'd waited all these years, she could wait a little while longer.

She stood and looked up at the full moon, which bathed the lake and surrounding area in a beautiful blue glow. Any other night, she'd be going for a swim.

But this wasn't just any night.

She glanced back at the cabin, where a pair of burning oil lanterns were visible through the open door. It was the only opening in the boarded up structure, meant as a signal to Milo that she was in residence. She'd parked her car in easy view from the mountain road, but now that night had fallen, she hoped that the flickering cabin lanterns would be enough to confirm that he'd find her there.

She'd be there, all right.

But not inside. Outside, just a few yards away, hidden in the brush just a few yards from the cabin. She'd wrap herself in a thermal blanket and wait all night if that's what it took.

She picked up her binoculars and scanned the road. She hadn't seen a vehicle for hours, and even then, it was just a Parks and Recreation jeep from the nearby town of Bishop. She swept her binoculars across the tall pines, knowing their deep shadows could easily hide any number of threats, both animal and human.

It didn't matter. She was prepared. She felt her jacket pocket for the .38 automatic that the boyfriend of one of her teammates had loaned her. The gun was there along with two ammo cartridges. She hadn't the time to practice with this particular weapon, but she'd trained with others like it.

She continued the sweep with her binoculars,

tracing the road on its journey along the edge of the valley. She'd have to pay special attention there; if someone approached on foot, it might be difficult to see them in the shadowy area just above the cabin.

A chill went through her. What in the hell was she doing out here?

Only what needed to be done. No time for self-doubt.

She lowered the binoculars and listened. She'd forgotten how still and quiet it was out there, and it seemed even more so after having grown accustomed to the din of the city.

She walked back toward her car.

Craaack!

She froze. What was that?

She heard it again.

Just a rustling in the tree branches, she decided. Probably a bird or a squirrel.

She opened her car trunk and pulled out a blanket and a camping stool. Then she took out the Indonesian thumb blades she'd taken from her dorm room and carefully slipped them on her thumbs, avoiding the razor-sharp edges. They were low-key but effective if you knew what you were doing with the blades. She'd made certain she knew what she was doing and had taught herself not to make a mistake. Together with the gun and other weapons in the trunk she felt well equipped to face Milo. Then she took out a large thermos of coffee from the trunk. She shook the thermos. Only half full. That should be enough to—

"Hello, Tricia."

A belt snapped around her neck!

She struggled to breathe. Her attacker leaned close and whispered in her ear, "It's been a while."

It was Milo! He had come for her.

She swung the thermos around, but he slapped it from her hand. "Play nice," he whispered. "I've waited a long time for this."

She tried to speak, but only gagging noises came out.

"You can't be surprised," he said. "You practically gave me an engraved invitation. You think I can't smell a trap?"

He loosened the belt around her neck, and she coughed before speaking. "Not...a trap."

"Sure it was. The only question was how many of you were out here waiting for me. I've been watching you for hours. I had to walk miles so you wouldn't see me. Imagine my surprise when I realized it was only you out here. Do you have a death wish, Tricia?"

She bared her teeth. "You know...better. I've survived both you...and...Barrett..."

"Until now." He reached down and took the gun from her jacket pocket.

She looked down. Dammit. He'd caught her by surprise. But there had to be some way to salvage her plan. "Wanted...to do...it myself..."

He pulled her away from her car. "You should have known better. I'm disappointed, Tricia. I respected you. You're a fighter. You alone managed to get away from us. But maybe it was just dumb luck."

"It...wasn't."

He chuckled. "Now you're talking like the champion I thought you were. But I'm afraid I'm still not going to make this quick or easy for you. I've had much too much time to think about what I would do once I caught you."

She glanced around, still trying to find a Plan B.

He jerked the belt to the left, pulling her away from the cabin. He was leading her toward the water.

"You've been living on borrowed time, Tricia. As long as everyone believed Barrett tried to kill you, who was I to rock the boat? But once he was dead, it was open season. Unfortunately for you."

"Unfortunately for *you*."

He chuckled again. "That's the spirit. This is going to be fun." He pushed her down to her knees next to the lake. "You always liked the water, Tricia. Did they tell you how I gave the Spalman boy that statue of a naiad, a water sprite? That was in your honor, because she was able to drown her victims. I thought that would please you. But I'm not sure you're going to like *this*."

He struck her back with his knee and forced her face-first into the water! He tightened the belt around her neck while digging his knee farther against her back. Her submerged face pressed hard into the algae-covered lake bottom.

Her first instinct was to thrash around, but instead she let her body go limp. Her lungs were already starting to ache, but she had to play it smart and conserve her energy.

Because she had to prepare herself. She flexed her fingers.

Get ready... Get set...

Now!

She swung her arms back and dug her thumb blades deep into his thighs near his penis.

Even underwater, she could hear his screams.

Yes.

She arched her back and lifted her head, just breaking the water with her nose and mouth. She sucked in a lungful of air just before being pushed back under.

She swung her arms back and stabbed his legs again with the thumb blades.

He screamed again.

This time she rolled and thrashed with every ounce of her energy, pulling herself free of his grip. She stood and staggered toward the cabin.

She could hear him running after her.

Good. Follow me, bastard.

She knew she'd have a better chance of losing him if she ran for the trees, but losing him wasn't the plan.

Not this time.

She picked up speed and slid through the cabin's open doorway. He was a heartbeat behind. He pulled open the door, knocking aside the small tree branch she'd used to prop it open.

He barreled inside. The door closed and locked behind him, pulled by the spring door closer she had installed only hours before.

She retreated to the farthest point of the cabin's main room, illuminated in a golden glow by the two glass oil lanterns.

He moved toward her and smiled. "I'm afraid you've made a grave error in judgment."

She grabbed one of the oil lanterns and held it up. He hadn't seen the bolts, hinges, and empty containers of odorless paint thinner scattered on the floor next to the door. "Have I?"

He nodded. "But I've changed my mind. I'll make it quick. You won't suffer, Tricia."

She stared him in the eye as she raised the lantern. His circle-square neck tattoo almost seemed to dance in the flickering light. "No, but *you* will suffer."

She hurled the glass lantern to the floor in front of him, and it exploded in a fireball!

Tricia turned and bolted through the rear door-way. She swung down a two-by-four over the pair of iron barricade brackets she'd bolted to the exterior doorframe.

She could hear him pounding on the door over the sound of the roaring flames.

She backed away. She had drenched the floor and walls with the flammable paint thinner. It wouldn't take long.

Milo was now trying the boarded-up windows. He pounded and screamed, but the boards didn't budge.

She picked up the tire iron she'd placed outside the cabin just in case he'd manage to break free. Then she backed even farther away from the burning, crackling cabin as the flames consumed it from within.

Milo's pounding and screaming stopped. Surely nothing could be alive in there.

"Bitch!"

Milo had broken through one of the windows and was coming after her again! His shirt was on fire and his face was twisted and pain-racked as he tore after her.

She braced herself and swung the tire iron and struck him in the shoulder. He acted as if he didn't even feel it. Maybe he didn't, she thought frantically. His expression looked crazed as he moved toward her again.

She swung the tire iron again and this time hit his cheekbone. Oh, he felt that, she thought fiercely. He screamed and then lunged forward, his hands outstretched.

"Get down, Tricia. Now!"

It was Kendra's voice, Tricia thought dazedly.

"Tricia, drop to the ground! Do it!" Though she

couldn't see her, Tricia instinctively obeyed the order and dropped onto her stomach.

And from there she saw Lynch close in on Milo. His arm was around Milo's neck, and he was jerking it back. The fire had been extinguished from Milo's shirt, but flames had spread down to his pants as he tried to wriggle free.

Milo looked down at Tricia. In that moment, his agonized look was replaced with one of eerie calm. Even as the flames spread past his knees, Milo reached into his charred jacket and pulled out a handgun. He raised it toward Tricia's head.

Crack.

Lynch had given Milo's neck a savage twist, and it snapped. He released his hold, and Milo fell to the ground as flames continued to consume his body.

Then Kendra was kneeling beside Tricia. "You look half drowned. Are you okay?"

Tricia nodded, her gaze on Milo. "Is he dead? He kept coming at me, but I had the tire iron. Though I thought the fire would do it."

"He's dead," Lynch said as he got to his feet. "And by the look of him, you must have given him a really rough time one way or the other."

"It had to end. It couldn't go on."

Kendra looked back at Milo's burning body. "I wasn't sure we'd make it in time."

"I didn't expect you to," Tricia said wearily. "It had to be me. I had to be the one." She rubbed her temple. "But thank you anyway." Her gaze went back to Milo. "I wonder what it will feel like to be free of him."

"Good," Kendra said. "Because he never really held you. He just thought he did. You were always in charge."

Tricia smiled at her. "Yeah, that's right. It's good to have you around to remind me." She lifted her head. "I hear a siren, that must be the volunteer fire department. I made sure they were on duty. I didn't want to risk having any wildfires because I was planning on getting rid of that scumbag."

"Yes, I can see you'd want us all to be environmentally correct," Lynch said. "But we may be having a couple more visitors soon. The official police reports were somewhat vague about how to get out here, but one call to Trey Suber was all we needed. His personal serial killer database is more thorough than almost any in the world. We'd already notified Griffin that he should probably come by and see if Milo might be around. He and Suber will both probably be here." Lynch paused. "And when he arrives, I'm going to take total credit for ridding the world of Milo. It might tarnish your reputation as America's Olympic Sweetheart, so we'll leave you out of it." He grinned. "And I assure you, it will only enhance my rep."

"I can see that," she said quietly. "But anytime you change your mind and want me to tell the full truth, I'll do it. I knew there might be ramifications."

"But you went full steam ahead anyway." Kendra made a face. "And damn the torpedoes." She stood up and held out her hand to pull Tricia to her feet. "Okay, let's go meet your volunteer fire department and see what we can do about salvaging the situation, and make sure you get a chance to go for those medals."

Four hours later, the embers of the cabin were still smoldering when the medical examiner removed what was left of Milo. Griffin and Suber stood on the outskirts of the scene consulting with the local police.

Tricia sat on her camping chair with the thermal blanket wrapped around her. She looked up at Kendra. "Am I in trouble?"

Kendra shook her head. "You're a hero."

"I don't feel very heroic." She turned toward Lynch. "You picked up the barricade brackets."

"They're in my car trunk. That will keep investigators from having to ask questions they'd rather not."

Griffin and Suber walked toward them.

"How are you holding up?" Griffin asked Tricia. "Is there someone we can call for you?"

She shook her head. "I've already called my mom and dad. They're on their way from Seattle." She nodded toward the pile of ash where the cabin had been. "Though I'm not sure what they'll think of my remodeling job."

"I'm sure they're just glad you're okay," Kendra said.

"They are. They've been talking about tearing down this place and rebuilding. I guess I forced the issue."

"Milo did that," Suber said. "You did the world a favor, Tricia."

"But what's next for you?" Kendra asked Tricia.

Tricia thought for a moment. "I need to get even more serious about training. There's a great coach in Phoenix who wants to work with me."

"I imagine they'll be standing in line," Kendra said. "Particularly after your performance at Long Beach. Are you sure you're ready for that? You've been through a lot."

"Yes." Tricia shed her blanket and sat up straighter. She lifted her chin as she gazed out at the horizon. "You bet I'm ready!"

EPILOGUE

G et down here," Olivia ordered when Kendra answered her phone. "Tricia just blew into my condo and she's running around trying to wrap three days' work up in one day. I'm trying to give her lunch, but she keeps asking me questions about my computer preferences for next year's podcasts. I need someone to run interference."

"You never have trouble with scheduling. You're the boss, tell her to adjust and give you the days you need."

"Won't work. She only has one day. Get down here." She ended the conversation.

One day? What the hell was happening?

Kendra was still wondering that when Olivia opened the front door of her condo five minutes later.

"Not too bad." Olivia tapped her watch. "You must have dropped everything to get here that soon. I do like it when you let me control a situation."

"Be real. You always control the situations." She patted Harley as she entered the foyer. "Where is she?"

"Here!" Tricia lifted her head from under Olivia's desk. "I just had to make an electronic adjustment. Hi, Kendra. Glad you could make it. I'm having a problem with Olivia. She doesn't recognize there's a time constraint."

"How unusual. I wonder how she managed when you weren't around. Am I supposed to be referee?"

Tricia shook her head. "I think you were brought down to keep me out of her hair so that she could finish making lunch. But you'll be a magnificent distraction."

"My thought exactly," Olivia said as she snapped a leash on Harley's collar. "But it will take time to settle her down so I'm going to take Harley for a walk. Otherwise, she'll just transfer her attention to dog training instead of that computer. I'll see you both in about forty-five minutes." Then she and Harley were out the door.

"Done." Tricia was pouring coffee in Kendra's cup. "Now you can sit down and have coffee and then relax. Okay?"

"It works for me," Kendra said. "I'm just here to do my duty to Olivia and keep you from driving her crazy. I was just about to leave to meet with my clients."

"Olivia told me that you planned on doing that." She poured herself a coffee and sat down across from her. "She said that you sometimes needed time away from all the bad stuff to cleanse the palate. This one left a very bad taste in your mouth?"

"Exceptionally bad."

"Me too." She suddenly knelt in front of her and took Kendra's hands in her own. "Doesn't Lynch help?"

"Sometimes. But he has his own battles to fight. We all do. I wouldn't have it any other way. Why should I burden him with mine?"

"You wouldn't be a burden to me." She was looking down at Kendra's hands. "Not ever. So don't ever think that you would. I'll tell him so, if you like."

"I don't think that will be necessary." Kendra was smiling at her. "Lynch does kind of like me."

"I know," Tricia said. "Who wouldn't? But you need more than that. I think we should be best buds."

"We *are* best buds," Kendra said. "Haven't you noticed?"

Tricia nodded. "But I want to be like you and Olivia. My parents are having a fit about me going to Phoenix and working under that special swimming coach. They got scared and I promised I'd leave tomorrow." She said coaxingly, "How about it? I'll give you one of my first medals I win at the Olympics."

"I'd be honored, but our relationship can't be like anyone else's because each relationship is different and special." Kendra squeezed Tricia's hand. "And always will be."

"I guess I knew that." Tricia made a face. "But you know me. I wanted it all. Maybe next time?"

"It wouldn't surprise me." Kendra chuckled. "I know how determined you can be."

"What's next?"

"We go forward and see what we can find around the next corner." She tapped her temple thoughtfully. "I'm sure it can be just as exciting."

"Will you come to watch me when I go for the

medals?" Her face was suddenly luminous. "Now, that would be exciting."

Kendra should have realized Tricia would immediately dive into the deep end. "I'm sure there are rules about who gets to go on jaunts that prestigious," she said warily. "Suppose we discuss it when you get closer to the games."

Tricia shook her head. "I think that we should make plans now. You're right, it might be difficult." She snapped her fingers. "But Lynch would probably be able to swing it. Why not? He does all kinds of stuff like that, doesn't he? Diamond mines, getting rid of dictators, dangerous extractions, and—"

"Hold it." Kendra held up her hand. "I'm not about to involve Lynch in a complicated situation like that. It's not as if anything world shaking is going to be decided by—"

"It would be world shaking to all those athletes," Tricia interrupted soberly. "It might be world shaking to those countries who sent them." She made a dismissive gesture. "But you're right, you shouldn't be involved in this."

However, Tricia hadn't mentioned who should be involved in her planning, Kendra noticed. Not a good sign. "And I'm not saying I don't want to be involved in your career. It's very important to me. Suppose I go to Phoenix and visit you after I get done with my therapy sessions?"

"That would be great." Still no commitment.

Kendra would definitely have to mention something to Lynch. She jumped to her feet. "In the meantime, let's go ahead with getting the duties you promised Olivia out of the way. I'm not great with computers, but I know enough about dog training from you and Olivia to get a couple lessons in today."

"I thought you were going to class?"

"I was, but it was just a fill-in until I could take over my regular schedules down the road." She smiled as she added lightly, "And that was before I knew one of my best buds was going to take off for Arizona. My kids would agree that we couldn't afford to shake the world of those athletes who are trying to do a little world shaking of their own…"

———

TWO DAYS LATER
PINE VALLEY MEMORIAL SERVICE
PINE VALLEY, CALIFORNIA

"It's terrific, isn't it? The Bureau did a pretty good job setting it up. You'd never dream all the pain and agony that took place here."

Kendra turned in shock to see Metcalf staring at the names of the victims on the flower-trimmed list posted at the arched doorway that led to the outdoor seating area.

"Yes, you would." She took a step closer to him. "All you'd have to do is go down the hill and see the crater and it would all come back to you. What are you doing here, Metcalf? I wouldn't think you'd ever want to come back here."

"I don't, but I lost friends here. I had to say good-bye. I didn't get a chance that day. I turned away for an instant and they were gone." His lips twisted with pain. "And I didn't realize until Lynch showed up at my front door how much I needed to do that."

"Lynch?" She instinctively looked around the area. "Lynch brought you? Where is he?"

"He's waiting in his car in the grove. He tends to attract attention whenever he shows up at a Bureau function. He didn't want to take the spotlight away from the victims or families. He said this was for me." He looked at Kendra. "He told me I should never waste the opportunity to tell someone goodbye if I got the chance. They might not know it, or remember it, but I would. It kind of made sense."

"Yes, it does." She blinked hard to stop her eyes from stinging. "And he should know. There have been a lot of goodbyes for Lynch."

"I guess there have." Metcalf straightened his shoulders. "And I've got a few to say now myself, so I'd better get to it. Have you already been in?"

She nodded. "I'm an outsider, remember? I just came to pay my respects to Cynthia Strode's family. She was the only one I really knew."

"I knew all of them," Metcalf said thickly. "I liked Cynthia a lot." He turned and walked toward the arch. Then he suddenly turned back to look at her. "And you're not an outsider. Neither you nor Lynch could ever be an outsider. For God's sake, the two of you helped bring that monster down." Then he was walking under the flower-bedecked arch and down the aisle toward the visitor seating.

She watched him for a moment and then turned and walked toward the pine grove. Lynch saw her coming and got out of the Lamborghini to meet her.

"You ran into Metcalf?"

"Yes, I should have offered him a lift myself. I never thought he'd want to come."

"It was no bother. You were busily getting yourself ready to draw yourself into your cocoon, and I thought you might need the time to yourself."

"Into my cocoon?" She looked at him inquiringly. "What are you talking about?"

"After you go through one of these particularly violent episodes, you need to go dormant for a while. The healing process strikes different people in different ways. You withdraw and go back to your music therapy clients, where you won't have to confront violence." He smiled. "Usually, it means I'm jettisoned out of your life for a while because I remind you too much of things that go bump in the night."

"Really?" She raised her brows. "How immature you must think me."

"No, I just realize we all have different coping mechanisms," he said quietly. "I respect yours more than you believe."

"And what are your coping mechanisms?"

"I'll let you discover them for yourself. I like the idea of you leaning on me when you need someone to be there for you."

"Not fair, Lynch."

"Not much is, Kendra." He grinned. "But I do try."

Yes, he did, she thought, more than any other man she had ever met. He'd walked with her through so many situations and always been with her at the end of the path. "But you still think I'm going to jettison you because you remind me of the part of my life I want to forget."

"Good possibility."

"But if I did that, it would mean I just paddle along and never change or grow at all."

His eyes were suddenly narrowed on her face. "Where are we going with this, Kendra?"

"I believe that depends on both of us. You're telling me how predictable I am, and I'm just going along for the ride."

"Bad mistake?"

"You've made worse." She was walking toward him. "But not lately. It's true that I've been puzzling about our relationship and how to resolve it. But I've always known that it's me who has to do it. Always my choice."

She was close to him now and she could see his intensity, those piercing blue eyes, the way he always looked at her. "But I want to be more generous. I want to include you in the decision."

He reached out and his forefinger gently touched the hollow of her throat. "Did I ever tell you how much I love the feel of this hollow? No, don't move. I'm listening…"

"Then pay attention. You offered to take me away after this nightmare was over. You were rather insistent about it."

"And you didn't think it was a good idea."

"I didn't have time to think about it. I was too busy thinking about you. I'll probably always be thinking about you unless you really do something weird and turn me off."

"I promise I'll do my best not to," he said solemnly.

"Then here's what I'm saying." She reached up and kissed him on the lips. "I like you. I love sex with you. I even respect you. We don't know where we're going from here, but I refuse to be terrified every minute because you might not be around tomorrow. I really don't want you to go out and get yourself killed, but if you do, I guess I could take it. I'm not going to be scared about what might be. If I get too upset, I'll just go after you and make certain that it doesn't happen." She took a step back away from him. "Now I'm going to drive home and pack a bag and hope you haven't changed your mind about that trip. I think we should go to Spain. I've heard it has beaches and atmosphere and wonderful music."

"What about your clients?"

"If you'd asked me, instead of assuming you knew what I'd do, I'd have told you that I've already arranged to take a few weeks off from my therapy sessions. I spent the last few days interviewing a substitute."

"You could have told me," he said mildly.

"You were too busy making the final report on the Johannesburg situation to the Justice Department. Besides, you were evidently having such a good time analyzing my every action, maybe I thought you might object to my displaying a thought of my own."

"Ouch."

"Does that mean you won't take me to Spain?"

"It means you don't have a chance of escaping. I obviously have to revamp my entire way of thinking where you're concerned. I believe Marbella, Spain, might be just the place to do the research."

"Good." She smiled at him. "Then take Metcalf home and I'll see you back at the condo." She looked back over her shoulder. "Oh, and if you get a call from Tricia, don't take it until I can talk to you."

"Don't worry, we're not taking her to Spain," he said as he got back into his car. "She talked me into the Olympics, but enough is enough."

Oh, shit. Too late, Kendra realized. Tricia had already gotten to Lynch, and it seemed they were all going to be best buds at the Olympics. Well, why not? Tricia could be fun, and she might need someone to watch over her.

"Something wrong?" Lynch was looking at her face.

"No, nothing is wrong." She smiled at him. The Olympics seemed a long time away right now. In the meantime, they had Spain, and she had Lynch, and who knew what other adventures might pop up? "Hurry. I can't wait!"

ABOUT THE AUTHORS

IRIS JOHANSEN is the #1 *New York Times* bestselling author of more than fifty consecutive bestsellers. Her series featuring forensic sculptor Eve Duncan has sold over twenty million copies and counting and was the subject of the celebrated Lifetime movie *The Killing Game*. Johansen lives near Atlanta, Georgia.

ROY JOHANSEN is an Edgar Award–winning author and the son of Iris Johansen. He has written many acclaimed mysteries including *Deadly Visions*, *Beyond Belief*, and *The Answer Man*.

Iris Johansen and Roy Johansen have written ten stories in the Kendra Michaels series.

DON'T MISS KENDRA MICHAELS IN HER NEXT THRILLING ADVENTURE!

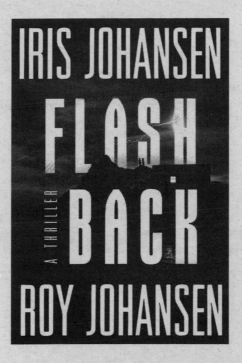

COMING SUMMER 2024

For a complete list of books by

IRIS JOHANSEN

VISIT
IrisJohansen.com

 Follow Iris Johansen on Facebook
Facebook.com/OfficialIrisJohansen

 Follow Iris Johansen on X
@Iris_Johansen

For a complete list of books by

ROY JOHANSEN

VISIT
RoyJohansen.com

 Follow Roy Johansen on Facebook
Facebook.com/RoyJohansen.Author

 Follow Roy Johansen on X
@RoyJohansen